Chronicles
of the
SPANISH CIVIL WAR

A Shadow of Treason

A NOVEL

TRICIA GOYER

deleted

MOODY PUBLISHERS
CHICAGO

Cover Design: Chris Gilbert, Studiogearbox
Cover Image: Taylor S Kennedy/National Geographic, Stockbyte and
             Bettmann/CORBIS
Interior Design: Ragont Design
Editor: LB Norton

Library of Congress Cataloging-in-Publication Data

Goyer, Tricia.
  A shadow of treason / Tricia Goyer.
    p. cm. — (Chronicles of the Spanish Civil War)
  ISBN 978-0-8024-6768-3
  1. Spain--History—Civil War, 1936-1939—Fiction. 2. Americans—Spain—
Fiction. I. Title.

PS3607.O94S53 2007
813'.6--dc22

2007020266

ISBN: 0-8024-6768-7
ISBN-13: 978-0-8024-6768-3

We hope you enjoy this book from Moody Publishers. Our goal is to provide high-quality, thought-provoking books and products that connect truth to your real needs and challenges. For more information on other books and products written and produced from a biblical perspective, go to www.moodypublishers.com or write to:

Moody Publishers
820 N. LaSalle Boulevard
Chicago, IL 60610

1 3 5 7 9 10 8 6 4 2

Printed in the United States of America

$\mathcal{D}$ear Reader,

A few years ago when I was researching for my fourth World War II novel, I came across a unique autobiography. One B-17 crewmember I read about claimed to have made it out of German-occupied Belgium after a plane crash due, in part, to the skills he picked up as a veteran of the Spanish Civil War. Reading that bit of information, I had to scratch my head. First of all, I had never heard of the war. And second, what was an American doing fighting in Spain in the late 1930s? Before I knew it, I uncovered a fascinating time in history—one that I soon discovered many people know little about. This is what I learned:

Nazi tanks rolled across the hillsides and German bombers roared overhead, dropping bombs on helpless citizens. Italian troops fought alongside the Germans, and their opponents attempted to stand strong—Americans, British, Irishmen, and others—in unison with other volunteers from many countries. And their battleground? The beautiful Spanish countryside.

From July 17, 1936–April 1, 1939, well before America was involved in World War II, another battle was fought on the hillsides of Spain. On one side were Spanish Republicans, joined by the Soviet Union and the *International Brigade*—men and women from all over the world who volunteered to fight Fascism. Opposing them were Franco and his Fascist military leaders, supported with troops, machinery, and weapons from Hitler and Mussolini. The Spanish Civil War, considered the "training ground" for the war to come, boasted of thousands of American volunteers who joined to fight on the Republican side, half of whom never returned home.

Unlike World War II, there was no clear line between right and wrong, good and evil. Both sides committed atrocities. Both sides had deep convictions they felt were worth fighting and dying for.

So on one side we have: the new democratic Spanish government, Communists, Socialists, the "Popular Front," anarchists; free thinkers, artists, musicians; peasants, workers, unions; the Republicans, the International Brigade, Thaelmann Battalion (German Communists), *La Marsellaise* (French-British battalion), "the people," the Basques of northern Spain, Basque president Aguirre, "the Reds," Fernando Valera, Steve Nelson. The Soviet Union backed the Republicans. A number of volunteers made their way to Spain to fight under the Republican banner, including the English-speaking Abraham Lincoln Brigade from the United States.

On the other: General Franco, General Mola, the Nationalist Rebels, Fascists, Hitler's Nazi forces, Mussolini's Italian troops, the Spanish military, Moroccan cavalry, the established Catholic Church, the monarchy, "right-wingers," wealthy landowners and businessmen. Fascist Germany and Italy supported Franco.

During the Spanish Civil War, terror tactics against civilians were common. And while history books discuss the estimated one million people who lost their lives during the conflict, we must not forget that each of those who fought, who died, had their own tales. From visitors to Spain who found themselves caught in the conflict, to the communist supporters. Basque priests, and Nazi airmen . . . each saw this war in a different light. These are their stories.

Tricia Goyer

Characters

Sophie Grace, twenty-five, American, aspiring artist, in Spain to join her fiancé

Eleanor Winslow, (deceased) American author of letters given to Sophie

Michael, her fiancé

Hector, a matador and friend of Michael's in Bilbao

Paulo, their friend from Madrid

Cesar, a bodyguard

Maria Donita, young Spanish woman whom Sophie feels is a threat to her relationship with Michael

Emilio, now her husband

Benita Sanchez, friend of Michael

Luis, Benita's husband (mentioned)

Walt Block, newspaper correspondent from New York who befriends Sophie and helps her get into Spain, aka James

Kimmel, a pro-Franco reporter

Lester McGovern, a British agent

Derrick Wilson, a co-conspirator

José Guezureya, friend of Michael

Ramona, José's wife

Juan, José's father

Pepito, fellow ranch hand

Ritter Agler, pilot in German air force
Isanna, woman he desired, who married another
Hermann Göring, German general
Monica Schull, American, "assistant spy"

Philip Stanford, American, soldier in volunteer Abraham Lincoln
    Brigade
Attis Brody, Philip's best friend, deceased
Charles, an American trench mate

Deion Clay, African-American, also in Abraham Lincoln Brigade

Father Manuel Garcia, a priest in Guernica
Sister Josefina, from the convent in Guernica
Armando, childhood friend of Manuel's
Nerea, Armando's wife
Berto, young Spanish man in Paris

Petra Larios, daughter of wealthy family of La Mancha, left with-
    out family
Ruy and Rafael, her cousins
Edelberto, boy she met on holiday; cousin of Michael

José Antonio Aguirre, first Basque president
Steve Nelson, Croatian-born leader of communist party in U.S.

Show the wonder of your great love,
you who save by your right hand
those who take refuge in you from their foes.
Keep me as the apple of your eye;
hide me in the shadow of your wings
from the wicked who assail me,
from my mortal enemies who surround me.

Psalm 17:7–9 (NIV)

Chapter One

*N*o one told the rescuers not to talk, yet instinctively they sifted through the bits of brick and shards of glass as quietly as possible, alert for the slightest sound of human life beneath the rubble of the tailor shop.

Deion Clay paused for a minute and wiped his brow with a soot-blackened handkerchief. He refused to look at the other buildings surrounding him, reduced to heaps. The sight caused a deep ache in his gut. All he knew was underneath this pile a few families had taken refuge in the basement.

Deion had been walking through the streets sometime in the night, offering help to the injured, when he heard the cries for help. And although they had fallen silent for the past few hours, he clung to the faintest hope. It was all he had.

Though hundreds of rescuers had swarmed the area last night, fighting the flames, most citizens from Guernica had since bundled up every meager possession they could scrounge and headed out of town with oxcarts carrying the children and old women. Perhaps twenty still worked alongside Deion, their skin made even blacker by soot than his natural color. They continued to dig, refusing to give up hope for the missing wife, son, or brother.

The attack had been devastating. Bombers had filled the skies in two waves that lasted nearly an hour each. Smoke continued to sting his eyes, and he again wiped away the tears. What the bombs hadn't destroyed, the fire had. Yet Deion understood why the handful of workers stayed, and he vowed to stay with them. How could one walk away from his whole existence without knowing that every last stone was overturned? He knew they'd give their all in hope of one more person being pulled from the rubble alive.

As Deion sifted through the debris, he sifted his motives as well. To find life under the wreckage meant he'd come for a purpose. To save a life would prove Spain hadn't been a mistake after all.

He sucked in a deep breath of recommitment and surveyed the rubble for the line of least resistance. So far they had excavated several feet of a narrow hallway leading to the basement. They were on the right track. They had to be.

"Here, *amigo.*" An older Spanish man handed him a shovel.

Digging in, Deion worked to dislodge the powdered plaster and brick. He scooped a pile and dumped it into a dented pail on the ground behind him. Without a word, the Spanish man passed it back down the line, where another man dumped it into the street.

The men around him scurried around as one, not needing words. The ragged line moved like the black ants Deion had watched as a boy. Working in unison under the intense Mississippi sun, they had quietly moved mounds of dirt thousands of times their own weight. These men seemed to be doing the same. Their wide eyes showed their emotions fluctuating between fear, disbelief, and weariness. Just yesterday, before the German planes swept over the small Spanish town, they'd been bankers, farmers, and schoolteachers. Now that world no longer existed.

Just as America no longer seemed to exist to Deion. The land of freedom, of opportunity. The land where men walked the street without ears pricked for the slightest sound of enemy bombers. Such peace seemed like something from a child's storybook.

Sure, things had been tough back home, with the recent economic depression and all, but it was nothing like this. And, he hoped, it never would be. Deion shook his head, unable to imagine New York City or Chicago under attack with bankers and businessmen sifting rubble caused by enemy bombs. If he did his job well—if all the volunteers for liberty did—America would stay safe.

Deion turned to see some men coming toward him carrying wooden beams, broken and splintered. One man worked the beams into place between the ground and the top of ceiling to support the slow advance of those digging.

The tension in the pit of his stomach tightened with each strike of the shovel's tip. One wrong move could cause the whole thing to collapse onto the people still trapped underneath, crumbling like a tower of playing cards.

One man's soft moan grabbed Deion's attention. He reached under a brick near Deion's feet and pulled out a soggy brown paper package. With trembling fingers he untied the blackened string, revealing a gray suit coat. He said something in Spanish that Deion didn't understand. Had the coat belonged to a brother, a friend?

A choking sob issued from the man's throat. With a louder sob, he pressed his face into the lapel of the jacket as his trembling, clawlike fingers gripped the fabric.

The gray suit coat reminded Deion of one his friend Jeb had often worn while collecting money for Spain in the subways of New York. Some gave to the Communist cause, nickels and dimes mostly. But they wasted much more playing craps or buying drinks at the corner bar. And what difference would it have made if all those who talked of Spain had actually come? Would fifty, a hundred, five hundred more men have made the difference? Could scenes like this have been prevented?

A moaning wind rocked the branches of a scarred tree next to the shop and swept down into the rubble, caressing Deion's sweat-covered face. He pushed his shovel in deeper, then paused. He held up a hand, stilling the others.

A voice blended with the wind's moaning. It cried again for help. Yes, it was a woman's voice, joined by a baby's cry.

The man next to Deion called to her. Even though Deion couldn't understand all the words, he assumed the man was telling her to save her energy. No doubt they all realized it was possible the limited air supply could be used up before those trapped were reached. The baby's cries continued. A few minutes later they finally stilled, and Deion hoped the mother had comforted the infant in her arms. He refused to consider the alternative.

They pressed on to what Deion assumed was the door to the basement. Though it was still in its frame, it was twisted and crushed. Cautiously he pushed against it, gaining mere fractions of an inch with each groaning effort. When he could finally see past it, four faces peered up at him. Two women, a young girl, and a baby blinked at him, as if trying to focus. Deion didn't know if their wrinkled brows were due to the sunlight or the color of his skin. They'd most likely never expected a colored man to rescue them, especially after hearing the horrible tales of the Moors from Africa who fought with the Nationalists.

The woman studied Deion's face for a moment, then slowly blinked her eyes and handed him the baby. He snuggled the child to his chest, and a warmth surged through his frame. He'd never felt more alive.

But before he had a chance to hand the baby over, a loud rumbling in the distance filled his ears. Enemy ground forces. They could advance into the town by tomorrow. Or maybe sooner.

"Come." Deion reached his hand toward the woman, and though she didn't understand his English words, she reached for his hand and climbed out. The other woman and child followed—out of the darkness and into the light.

Chapter Two

Sophie Grace lifted the thick blackout curtain, made from cloth once bought for nuns' habits, and allowed the red-tinted sunlight into the supply room. A recurring image filled her mind—the picture of the small child lying limp in her mother's arms. But it wasn't a nightmare. It was yesterday's memory, and one she couldn't shake.

Even from her grade-school days, Sophie had dreamt of being a mother. In her neighborhood she had called together the younger children and organized their play. Patiently, she'd read to them from her storybooks under the shade of the oak tree in front of her brick home in Boston. But the events of the last few days caused her to reconsider her dream.

Raising children wasn't only about showering love and attention, but about facing the hard things of this world. She'd seen parents trying to protect their little ones during bombing raids in Madrid. She witnessed the poverty of the Spanish countryside, where no one was protected from lack of food and supplies. And then there were the mothers and fathers weeping over babies lost in yesterday's bombing. She could see the shocked face of a young woman holding her dead child, crying his name over and over. Wouldn't it be better never to have known and loved a child than to lose one? Lose one in a war such as this?

With thoughts of motherhood came unwanted memories of Maria Donita. Sophie refused to let one thought linger on the beautiful young Spanish woman who carried Michael's child. Michael, the man she herself would have married by now. The child she should carry.

Even though she had new hope in a relationship with Philip, the pain of betrayal stung. Somehow it was easier to remember the Spanish mother's tormented expression than to think of those estranged images—the faces of Michael and Maria. The thought of them together.

Sophie wiped her eyes that brimmed with tears. Her gut ached, and she knew if she hurt this much for a child she didn't even know, she'd never survive the hardship and tragedy Spanish mothers faced daily.

It was something she was learning about herself—she didn't handle loss well. First she'd lost Michael to a sniper's bullet; then even her memories of their love were destroyed by the knowledge of his betrayal. Then her friend José was injured when they took a wrong turn and found themselves on the front lines. A brave American had rescued them and transported José to a hospital, never to be seen by her again. She'd heard he had recovered and traveled to Guernica, where he married his fiancée, Ramona. But now Sophie was here as well, and when she asked around, no one seemed to know him.

Throughout the war, Sophie discovered she was stronger in some ways but weaker in others than she had thought. Losing those she cared about always punched a gaping chasm in her soul.

In less hectic days she'd dealt with horrifying images, such as the mother and child, by taking up her sketchbook and pencil, or easel and paints. The only way to wash them from her memory and work them through her emotions was to commit them to paper.

Now the war had robbed her of an abundance of time to paint, to process. The convent overflowed with injured people, and the wounded continued to stagger in, due to the continued efforts of the few dozen rescuers who remained in town.

Flies covered the faces of the crying, injured children. They'd screamed for parents lost, but at least they lived. And thinking of them and their future made Sophie more determined to use her art to tell the story of the people's fight. If her paintings could make even the slightest difference . . .

She realized the importance of getting her photographs and paintings of the bombing of Guernica to the press. The sooner the world knew the truth, the sooner others would fight for the cause of the Spanish people. But Sophie knew she would have to wait her turn. Survivors fought to get out—by cart, by vehicle, by rail.

Yet she wasn't really eager to leave, for two reasons. First, because every extra set of hands was needed to care for the sick and injured. Second, her time with Philip was short. Before long he'd return to the front lines, and who knew when she'd see him again? Yet another impending loss . . .

The children had been some of the first to be evacuated by train to Bilbao, a coastal city just a few hours' drive west of Guernica, and hundreds more of the injured who were lucky enough followed them. Behind the "Iron Ring," a vast fortification of bunkers and trenches, they hoped to find safety.

Hospital workers struggled to care for those who remained, with no water, little light, few medications, and too few staff. Sophie mindlessly carried soiled bandages to a back room where a team of nuns worked diligently warming water on a woodstove. With solemn faces they scrubbed the bandages clean. Sophie handed them to Sister Josefina and was rewarded by a weary smile.

Like the nuns, Sophie had worked day and night with hardly any rest. And like them, Sophie had a clear view of the destruction from the convent's second-story window—the heaps of debris, people lying on mattresses outside the hospital, and others walking through the torn-up streets looking for missing family members.

Yet that was not the only view that troubled those who worked in the convent. Anyone who walked to the other side of the building and looked out the window could gaze upon the green slopes of Guernica leading to Lumo. The wealthy lived in that area. Their fine white homes still dotted the hills. And their churches and convents remained untouched.

Sophie had heard that the Astra-Unceta pistol, machine gun, and bomb factory remained untouched, as well as the stone bridge over the Mundaka and the two army barracks. Either the German bombers had completely missed their targets, or there was another reason they'd hit the center of this town—a reason that didn't make sense.

As yesterday was the customary market day, the town had been full of people. And when the church bell announced approaching planes, even those who found refuge in basements and dugouts were not safe.

First the bombs shattered the buildings. Then the firebombs burned them. Then came the fighter planes that machine-gunned those who ran from the fire.

She'd heard from one of the nurses that, in addition to the buildings, houses, and market, the small hospital in town had also been hit. All forty-two wounded militiamen who were being cared for there were killed. And on the outskirts of town, victims lined the fields waiting for burial. They had been killed in a variety of ways, mostly by fire. Though firefighters had battled the edges of the blaze that dominated the town, it had been impossible to penetrate farther inside the city center where the majority of people were taking shelter.

Yet the finest areas of the town and the richest among them had missed destruction. Why?

Sophie returned to the supply room, and with gloved hands removed the surgical instruments from the sterilizer and laid them on a tray. From the open window she saw a cold, thin rain falling straight from the dismal sky. The gray clouds looked like she felt.

Suddenly a pleading cry interrupted her thoughts, and she hurried toward the surgical room, wondering if she could help.

A young man's face was turned away, staring at a wall, refusing to look at the nurse. "Please, no, it will hurt!" he cried again.

"Try to relax. I am just going to look at it." The nurse's voice was calm but firm.

The young man winced as gloved hands probed his arm. Sophie could tell from his pale face that he was fighting nausea as his face faded to a pasty white.

A young girl—a sister or friend perhaps—sat on the hard wooden chair next to his bed, shivering.

Sophie hurried to their side and placed a hand on the girl's shoulder. Then she reached for the boy's free hand. "You're doing beautifully. It is almost over. Just a minute more. Oh, you have pretty hair, *amiga*. So curly."

The girl turned her attention away from the nurse and the blood on the boy's injured arm. She lifted a hand to her hair. "It's like my mother's hair."

The boy winced, and Sophie wasn't sure if it was because of the nurse's probing fingers or the mention of their mother.

"Do you have someplace to go after this?" Sophie asked. "Are you leaving town?"

The boy refused to meet Sophie's gaze. "Our home—it was not hit," he mumbled. "We were just in the market—that is how we were injured."

"Everyone else in our family is fine." The girl shrugged gracefully. "We are lucky, I suppose." She seemed embarrassed.

And even though Sophie didn't mean to, she looked at the two differently, wondering if their parents were pro-Franco. Is that why the homes of the wealthy were not hit? She was struggling for something to say when she heard footsteps behind her. She felt a hand on her shoulder and turned, looking into Philip's face and light blue eyes.

"You haven't gotten much sleep, Sophie," he said. "I think you should rest. I've asked one of the sisters to make up a room in the back."

"And what about you?" Sophie rose and squeezed his hand. "You've been as busy as I have." She gave one parting glance back to the boy and girl and blew out a sigh of relief, thankful for the distraction.

"There is a group of soldiers in the garden. I'm staying with them." Philip's tone made it clear he wanted no special treatment.

Sophie didn't argue, but instead stood and allowed him to lead her to a far room. His warm hand touched the small of her back. In the room, a nun sat on a single cot. She held a small book in her hands.

"Oh, I'm sorry. I didn't mean to interrupt." Sophie paused in the doorway.

"Interrupt, no. I was waiting for you." The nun patted the spot on the cot beside her.

"Really?"

"I heard from some of the other sisters that we had an American woman helping here. I wanted to meet you."

Sophie sat beside her.

"I'll leave you two." Philip offered Sophie a small wave and a smile, causing a sweet peace to touch her soul. "See you in a couple of hours . . . at minimum. You get some sleep, you hear?"

"Of course."

He shut the door behind him, and Sophie turned to the nun.

"He is a man in love."

"Really?" Sophie couldn't hide her hint of a smile. "How can you tell?"

The nun smiled in return. "I may be a nun, but I'm still a woman. He loves you, that one does." She patted Sophie's hand. "But that is not what I wanted to talk to you about. I have a gift for you." She handed Sophie a Bible. An English Bible.

"Where—where did you find this?"

"I did not find it; it was given to me." The nun's accent was thick. "My grandmother, she was from America. She met my grandfather in Paris and then moved to Spain. This was back in the day when most young women didn't move halfway across the world for such things."

Sophie nodded, understanding too well.

"I kept this Bible all these years," the nun continued. "I can speak some English, but I cannot read it. I kept it until I found a special person to give it to. There are also some letters tucked in the pages. I do not know why they were never mailed. I'm not even sure who they were written to. And since I cannot read the words, they are a mystery even to me. I have prayed for years that God would show me the right person to give this Bible to."

"Really? And I'm the one?"

"Do you think a nun would lie?"

"No, I did not mean any such thing. I am so sorry." Sophie saw the twinkle in the nun's eyes.

"*Sí*, I want you to have it. But I cannot stay long. They need me in the surgery."

"But I have so many questions. I would love to know more about your grandmother and her trip to Spain. How did she do it? What was it like for her to make the change? Did she ever see her family again?"

The nun rose. "I think you will find the answers in these letters."

"I don't know what to say. Thank you."

"Just tell me that you will read them, and someday—when the war is over, when our town is rebuilt—you will return and tell me the story."

"Yes, of course."

The nun rose and offered Sophie a quick hug; then she left, shutting the door behind her.

Sophie touched the name embossed in the front cover. *Eleanor Marie Winslow*. And just as the nun had said, there were letters tucked within the pages. Sophie's interested was piqued, but her eyes burned. Her eyelids grew heavy.

Laying her head on the small pillow, she pressed the Bible to her chest and closed her eyes. As she drifted off, she thought of all the gifts that the pain of war had brought her . . . her art . . . friendships with Walt and José and with Deion, who faithfully drove her around . . . and now this Bible. And . . . Philip. Of course.

Chapter Three

*F*ather Manuel stared in disbelief at the second oak of Guernica. Though most of the buildings around it had crumbled to the ground, the tree—over one hundred years old—still stood, as did the council building where the Lords of Biscay had pledged their allegiance to the freedom of the Basque nation. The first oak had lived four hundred years, and many songs and poems had been written in its honor. Like the first, this second oak symbolized the traditional freedoms of the Biscayan people, and somehow—perhaps by the hand of God covering its limbs— the oak still stood.

The shade beneath the tree had provided rest for thousands of citizens over the years. The cool, fragrant dimness shaded any who took time to rest there for an afternoon siesta.

If only trees told their stories, there would be grand ones of victory at this spot. Perhaps someday it would tell of a victory over yesterday's destruction. Father Manuel prayed it would be so.

A cough tore through his raw throat, and tears sprang to his eyes. He covered his mouth as he expelled the smoky mucus that filled his lungs. The acrid taste of ashes coated his tongue. It was the taste of hell's fiery lake, and that alone would be enough to shun perdition.

He hadn't slept since the German planes descended on Guernica. And no matter how often Armando urged him to rest, Father Manuel's mind wouldn't stop replaying the events. His church had burned to the ground, and much of his parish, too. The lines of mutilated bodies waiting to be buried overwhelmed him.

How many of them had been ready to stand before the judge of the universe? The injured constantly filled his mind, even in the silence of the tree's shade. He had no idea how many prayers he'd uttered over the last twenty-four hours, how many last rites. Now his constant, desperate prayers for help failed to awaken his soul. Father Manuel felt like a failure.

Was it his fault? Perhaps he hadn't prayed often enough or said the right words. If he had known the Scriptures better, or walked more closely with his Lord, perhaps that would have made the difference. He had been assigned as the people's spiritual leader, after all.

He knew that even his closest friend, Armando, would chide him for such thinking. After all, it made no sense that the town's destruction should rest on the shoulders of one man. But logic could not displace his ruthless emotions.

He somehow felt that prayer was not enough. God was not responding to his silent cries. His heart was with his people. He knew that priests weren't expected to roll up their sleeves and provide manual labor, but that is what he longed to be doing— helping in more tangible ways. He wanted to be working *and* praying. Even now Armando helped to load injured men and women into trucks that would take them to safety; and he, the man of God, was supposed to be seeking the Father's favor.

So he'd come here, to the oak. Perhaps the tree reminded him of the cross of his Savior's sacrifice. And for some reason, the reality that this tree—a symbol of freedom and liberty—still stood helped him believe that God's hope could still be found amid the destruction. Though the sky was overcast and the air was putrid and dark, the sturdy oak's branches stretched toward the heavens with new green leaves trembling slightly in the afternoon breeze. He knelt before the large oak, grasped the silver cross that hung around his neck, and began to pray.

He caught movement from the corner of his eye and assumed it was Armando coming to talk to him, to urge him once more to rest. He lowered his head, trying to think of an argument that would justify his visit to the tree. And so Father Manuel was surprised when he heard a man's American-accented voice.

"Padre, do you have a moment?" The voice conveyed a sense of strength and importance despite the man's thin frame.

"Yes?" Father Manuel attempted to rise, but his knees buckled slightly as weariness gripped his limbs.

The man apparently sensed his struggle and placed a hand under the priest's elbow, helping him to his feet.

Father Manuel turned to look at him directly and saw a kind-looking man with a black hat.

"I only need a few minutes of your time. It's been a difficult few days, I know."

"*Sí.*" Father Manuel saw a heaviness in the speaker's eyes; a weariness even deeper than the destruction of Guernica weighed on this man's heart. A burden of a thousand thoughts within his head, each vying for expression.

The man motioned toward the steps of the council building, and they walked toward it. He turned and sat easily, while Father Manuel slowly lowered himself, feeling twice as old as his thirty years. Then the man pulled out two apples from his jacket pocket and handed one to the priest.

Father Manuel took the offering as his stomach rumbled. Without hesitation he silently mouthed a prayer of thanks and took a large bite, the sweet moistness filling his mouth. He wiped away the juice that escaped down his chin.

"I know you've been asked to go to Bilbao to speak on a radio broadcast there."

Father Manuel's mind was too tired to wonder how this man knew such a thing. "*Sí*, the bishop has asked me to come."

"I know it is a big request, but I need to ask you to change your plans. In my work through the newspapers I have heard that your life is in danger there. Instead, you must travel to Paris as quickly as possible. Travel to Bilbao as normal; then take the next late train out of the country. You will arrive in Paris early on Thursday. From there go directly to the Gate de Lyon. A newspaperman will be waiting, eager to hear the truth of who destroyed the town."

"The truth?" Father Manuel shook his head. "I do not understand."

"No, you may not now, but you will soon. If your testimony is not given to the right sources, lies will surround the destruction of Guernica. The lives of your people will be used as pawns by the Nationalist government. At this very moment news is going over the airwaves, stating that the Reds destroyed the town from the ground."

The man reached out and firmly clasped his hand. When he withdrew it, Father Manuel looked down to see a few crisp bills there—more money than his country parish saw in two months.

"What is this?" Father Manuel sputtered.

"Sorry, Padre, but you cannot travel to Paris on your good looks and fine character alone. And when you get there, you might be led to stay awhile. A few days, maybe more. It may not be safe to return; one never knows."

"But how can I do such things? How can I leave my country, my people? How can I follow the directions of a foreign man whose name I don't even know?"

"My name is Walt Block, and though there are many enemies who roam your country, I am a friend of the people and your cause." Walt waved his hand toward the center of town where the rubble still smoked. "What you once knew, Padre, is no more. Your people are shattered, yet your next mission could help bring salvation for your country. But don't take my word for it. Take it before God in prayer. Ask Him to give you peace about your path. . . . I have a feeling my request sits well with Him."

Father Manuel studied the man's face as he spoke, and he saw truth there. He knew the man had knowledge of a realm of influence that a poor country priest couldn't possibly understand. Also, with a stirring in his chest, he realized he'd be leaving his country to save the people. A foreigner in a strange place—like his beloved Lord. The thought both encouraged and frightened him as he humbly rejected the comparison.

With a heavy hand, he reached for Walt's, hoping to gain an ounce of the strength and confidence he witnessed in the man's gaze.

Ritter Agler walked from the debriefing room with a nagging ache that wouldn't let go. According to all accounts, the concentrated bombing attack of Guernica had been a great success. He would go down in history; he had no doubt. Yet one image wouldn't leave his mind.

The image of the woman and her Negro driver on the hillside. Sophie, who had saved him, cared for him. The one he'd once pretended to befriend. The one who haunted his dreams.

He couldn't make himself forget that truck on the hillside. He knew from the way she stood, the way she moved, who it was. How many days had he lain in that hospital bed, watching her paint the horror she'd observed. Watching her every move. Yes, it had certainly been Sophie on that hillside, and he'd almost fired his machine guns when he spotted her. He should have fired. Should have killed her. Then, perhaps, his memories of her would also die.

But he hadn't, and now, against his wishes, he agonized over whether she still lived. Had someone else taken them down? Or had they somehow managed to survive?

And why had she been in Guernica in the first place?

Mixed with his concern was his rage. For if Sophie had survived, she would no doubt paint what she saw. And her paintings would go around the world. And then all would know the truth that Germany worked so hard to hide—that they had a hand in Franco's schemes. That their force caused destruction for any in their path.

The pilots had been unable to fly today because of cloud cover and drizzle everywhere. And falling just as steadily were the lies that it was the Basco-Soviets who savaged Guernica.

Ritter walked to his room and turned on the radio, wondering and worrying if the truth of the destruction had been discovered. Instead, the airwaves carried Radio National in Salamanca, speaking on behalf of the government of General Franco. The announcer's voice filled his room.

"Aguirre lies! The Basque president lies basely. In the first place, there is no German or foreign air force in national Spain. There is a Spanish air force, a noble, heroic Spanish air force, which constantly fights against Red planes, Russian and French, piloted by foreigners. In the second place, we did not burn Guernica. Franco's Spain does not set fires. The incendiary torch is the monopoly of the arsonists of Irún, of those who set fire to Eibar, of those who tried to burn alive the defenders of the Alcázar of Toledo."

The announcer's voice paused. A few minutes later it started again.

". . . In these moments, news arrives from the Biscayan front that shows the falseness of Aguirre's speech. Because of bad weather, our planes have not been able to fly today and consequently could hardly have bombed Guernica."

At first Ritter felt a slight sense of relief that they hadn't been discovered. Their commander wished for their deeds to remain secret, and that wish was granted. But then he felt anger at the realization that, though they were following orders and had done their job well, there would be no recognition. Not now, not ever.

As soon as they'd been dismissed from their debriefing, a party had raged. German patriotic songs had spilled out the doors of the hotel's lounge. Ritter didn't join them. He knew even alcohol wouldn't help him forget his conflicted feelings toward Sophie, or being disrespected by his country as a man or as a pilot.

He'd come to Spain because Isanna wanted a war hero, yet she married another. And even though his deeds were heroic, did it really matter, if no one knew? So in the end, what was he risking his life for? He didn't care about Spain. Their fight mattered little to him, and the people even less. He couldn't forget that today didn't end the bombings, the destruction, the war. He'd get more assignments, each reinforcing that he flew without honor. And that others died without the appreciation or respect they deserved.

Tomorrow was another day. There would be more missions. Another day in which he might die for a cause he cared nothing about.

Yet to leave now and request a new assignment would label him a coward. And in the end, Ritter decided, he'd rather die with the honor he received from the few who knew about his missions than live with their disrespect.

Still, this decision did nothing to help him forget Isanna. He flipped off the radio and walked outside. After a five-minute walk, he strolled among the aircraft, walking to the piles of bombs. Hundreds had been used in yesterday's effort, each one causing untold destruction.

Thousands more remained.

Chapter Four

The few hours of sleep should have revived Sophie, but instead, when she awoke, she felt more drained than ever. Maybe it was the perpetual, tortured wail of injured men and women in the vestibule. She stood and glanced at the Bible on the small stand in the room. She tucked it into her satchel, then glanced into the hallway just outside the door.

Nothing had changed. Stretchers were continually brought in with torn, charred human beings, and rooms that once cloistered nuns had become morgues.

Or maybe her weariness was due to knowing that Philip would leave for the front lines—the killing fields—at the end of the day. So, after she changed clothes and freshened up, she stole a few minutes to talk with him.

They sat on the stairs of a church just down the street from the convent that was now being used as a hospital. Though the smaller one in town had taken a direct hit, this larger one still stood white against the clouded sky.

"So much has happened since we met." She sought out Philip's eyes and saw his caring gaze. "I don't know where to start. It's just too much. I mean, to come upon your foxhole when

I needed you most, and then have you by my side all those months as I painted. I didn't realize how much strength I got from having you at my side until you were gone."

He rested a hand on her shoulder, and she felt the caring in his touch. The warmth of his fingers near her neck spread to her chest.

"You've been through a lot, and . . ." His gentle voice paused. "Though I wasn't at your side over the last few months, you've never left my thoughts."

"Yes . . . I too feel this . . . special connection between us."

"You've made me so proud of you, Sophie. I mean, you never thought any of this would happen when you first came to Spain, did you? It must be exciting and scary and overwhelming." He took her hand. "And yet there is still a little hope inside you . . . isn't there?"

His understanding animated her tired soul. "That's what I mean," she said. "You really know me. You believe in me, in a way no one has before."

"And why wouldn't I? You amaze me, Sophie. Everything about you."

She watched him, trying to find her answer in the motion of his fingers entwined around hers. She had thought Michael was the only person she could ever love. He had taken so much from her—taken her heart. But being with Philip was different. She knew where she stood. Philip communicated with her, and he listened as she talked. She saw no secrets in his eyes. She had no reason to question his love. He didn't require her to give him everything. Instead, he freely offered her his thoughts, his care . . . his very being.

He glanced away, released her hands, and stood. He paced back and forth in front of the steps as if searching for the right words, then stopped to search her face. "Sophie, I—I'm returning to the front lines. I promised my commander. I told him that I just needed to find you, see if you were okay."

"I'm not naïve. I know what may happen out there, but I have to believe we'll be together again soon." She reached out and took his rough soldier's hand in hers. "And I am fine. Or at least I will be once I get to paint. They love my paintings, remember? They say they're making a difference. And you won't always be on the front lines, right?" she added. "I'll find you. I'll make sure they assign me wherever you are. There are breaks in the fighting, and we can see each other then."

He allowed her to pull him back down beside her, and she softly slugged his shoulder. "Just don't frown so much; you'll get me depressed. If these are our last moments for a while, I want to hear more about you. Not Philip, the soldier. Not about your time as a prisoner. But the real you."

"Is there a distinction anymore? It seems like Spain is all I know." He gave a humorless chuckle. "But I'm sorry. You're right. I don't want to waste our time together on this war."

He turned slightly to face her and opened his hands to her, taking her small hands in his large ones. "When I look into your eyes, Sophie, I see the same emotions I feel. They were there that day we headed to the battlefield, or at least a hint of them. But now, well, I guess the old saying is true. Absence does make the heart grow fonder."

The sound of footsteps interrupted them, and Sophie turned to see a nun coming her direction.

"Sofía, come quickly. You will not believe what is on the radio."

Sophie and Philip rose and hurried inside. For the first time since the bombing, most of the doctors and nurses were taking a break from their duties; they stood huddled around the large radio.

"It was Radio Bilbao," a doctor commented as they approached. "You just missed it. President Aguirre told the world of the bombing. He spoke in Spanish, not Euskera . . . which means his message was for the world, not only the Basque people. He said the Germans are denying responsibility. They claim the Red terrorists are the ones who set the town on fire."

"The Communists? But I have my photographs and paintings to prove otherwise."

"No offense, *señorita*," the doctor replied, "but your paintings will make little impression. Anyone can paint something from the imagination. But the photos, they are a different matter. Are they in a safe place?"

Sophie thought of the small room where her things were stored. She had never for a minute thought of this convent as anything but safe.

"Yes, of course. And I'll be leaving soon . . . to make sure the press gets them. I was just doing what I could to help here first. There are so many injured."

She turned to Philip, who nodded his agreement. Yet she could see in his eyes that he knew as well as she did that they both stayed for a deeper, more personal reason as well.

"And with your photos you must tell them what it was like to witness this event," the doctor commented, pushing his small glasses up the bridge of his nose. "For centuries, Guernica has been a shrine to the Basque spirit of freedom and independence. Here, at the foot of a venerable oak tree, Spain's monarchs once pledged to respect the rights of the local citizens." He sighed. "What has come of it? Now the town will be known more for how it was destroyed than how it lived."

"They're denying their actions. I cannot believe the Germans are denying their actions," Sophie commented.

"They have sought to wound us in the most sensitive of our patriotic sentiments . . . they made a statement against our liberty and democracy." The doctor wiped his hands on his stained surgical shirt. "And because of that, the blood of the people cries from the streets." He placed a hand on her arm. "It is up to you to make sure they did not die in vain, *señorita*. I appreciate your help here, but it is more important that you go to Bilbao. You must show the photos and prove our case."

Sophie felt Philip's hand on the small of her back, and she nodded. She thought of the words he spoke to her on the church steps and how he understood her ambivalence so well. The thought that she could make a difference in this foreign war caused her heart to pound.

That was not all, though, for the pit of her stomach filled with dread as she realized that, while her hands could only care for one person at a time, her art could reach so many more with the truth. And she knew that every moment she stayed kept the truth from being revealed.

She had to leave soon, even if it meant leaving Philip behind.

❖ ❖ ❖

José awoke to the sound of footsteps approaching and wondered if he was still dreaming. Yet if it were a dream, it would be more of a nightmare. The kind that chilled you to the core and hung around even after you'd awakened.

He'd had the mind of a poet since he was a child. His mother had told him so, but coming from her it was a kind way to say that he allowed his imagination to improve reality. The beauty and soul he discovered taming words were the same he experienced every day living and working with the finest horses in the world.

He'd taken a break from that for a time. He had to travel south, to the center of Spain. He had work to do in Madrid—work only he could accomplish. But now that he'd returned to the Basque countryside, every day it had been harder and harder to stay away from God's beautiful creatures.

At first, leaving the hospital in Guernica had been out of the question. And when he gained his strength, he began his new life with Ramona. He'd enjoyed all married life had to offer and told himself he'd have time to return to riding once the war turned in their favor.

But now, after the bombing by the German planes, all his thoughts were with those horses, and he knew he couldn't stay away. He had to know if they were safe. If they were being cared for as they should be.

He also thought of his father.

He was raised understanding that his father needed his help. His assistance with the horses, of course. And then, after José's mother's death, the old man needed so much more—including the smile on his son's face that reminded him of his beloved wife.

It had been hard for José to travel to Madrid, knowing the pain his absence caused at home. Yet he did so in hopes of more than just saving something priceless. His goal had been to save Spain itself. What foolish thinking. In the end it had almost cost him his life, and Sophie's life. He wondered again where she was and questioned when, not if, Walt would approach him again, pulling him back into the web of deception.

Not that any of it had made a difference.

José's senses were alert as he considered what the world had become over the last twenty-four hours. The stench, the piles of rubble, the cries of mourning in the distance. Beads of sweat rose at his hairline as he thought about what had happened to their town.

And Ramona—how many nights had he dreamt of their being together? But now José knew the best thing would be for them to part. At first when he'd found her, he only thought of love. That had been a foolish thing to do. He blamed the injury—the loss of blood from the neck wound and concussion—for knocking the sense out of him. If he had thought about it, he would have realized that, if he truly loved her, he would have stayed away.

There were too many people who wanted him dead. Who wanted him to keep silent about all that he knew. He knew they had found him on the road out of Madrid. Though others assumed it had been a Nationalist on the battlefield who'd shot him, José knew otherwise. He'd run from them, but he could not hide. They had assumed he was dead, and like a fool he'd used his momentary freedom to find Ramona.

José's determination rose like the smoke from the ashes of Guernica. He had a job to do before they discovered he'd cheated death. If Michael was still out there, that is.

But first, another task called to him. One he couldn't ignore. He couldn't be this close and not at least check on the horses. And though his wife believed he was packing his things for Bilbao, he instead prepared for the short trip to his home in the seaside village of Portugalete, where the creatures that had consumed him until the day he realized there was more to life than riding still lived. And where he'd first met Michael. The place where it all had started. Only ten kilometers distant, but worlds apart.

Still, José's chest ached at the thought of leaving Ramona. He could hear her in the kitchen, sweeping the floors and washing their breakfast dishes. It didn't matter that once they left, there was no doubt that the Nationalists would invade their town and their home. It didn't matter that there were still more injured people to care for. Ramona would not leave until the kitchen was clean.

More than anything, José wanted to go into the kitchen and sweep her into his arms. To nestle his face in the warmth of her neck and run his fingers through her long dark hair—yet he knew if he did, he would not want to leave.

Instead, he rose and stuffed only the most necessary of things into a small cardboard suitcase. He glanced at the wedding photo that sat on the small side table by their bed. It was one of the things he'd been taught, to disconnect himself from what he loved most in order to protect them—if only he'd clung to that.

He knew once he left, Ramona would be safe. She was traveling to Bilbao with the injured. She'd be protected there behind the Iron Ring. She'd also be safe from the men who assumed he was dead . . . and who would hunt him until they made sure he was.

When they were young, Michael had taught him to play chess. In chess they say sacrifice is what makes a champion—one must give up minor losses to achieve a major victory. But when would the losses end? When did they not become minor anymore? When would all his strategizing not turn into a loss?

José folded a riding jacket and slid it into the suitcase before strapping it shut. Then he stood, spreading his legs wide and folding his arms across his chest. He considered the woman he loved. Her face, her smile. He thought of the nights they'd spent together and the brightness in her eyes when she awoke in his arms. He'd do anything to protect her . . . even if it meant separating from her for a while.

He sucked in a deep breath and reminded himself he *was* doing the right thing.

Chapter Five

$\mathcal{R}$amona clung to the wooden sideboard of the canvas-covered truck as it chugged along the hilly road toward Bilbao, transporting injured soldiers to safety. The vehicle lurched to avoid a pothole, and she clung tighter, noticing that even though her hands looked red and raw from constantly scrubbing up for surgeries, her gold wedding band still sparkled in the light shining through the open back canvas.

She'd been the happiest woman in the world as José placed the ring on her finger with a vow of devotion. It had been a small ceremony, a simple one. Her parents had traveled to Madrid at the beginning of the conflict and hadn't been able to attend, yet the other nurses—now as close as sisters—had been there, rejoicing that true love conquered even war. But now Ramona wasn't so sure.

When José first showed up injured in Guernica, Ramona believed he'd clung on to life for her. After his long recovery, he was sensitive about the jagged scar on his neck and the smaller one on his forehead, yet Ramona had seen them as beautiful reminders of God's merciful hand in bringing him back to her.

But as she rode along, tears welled in her eyes and blurred

the ring's sparkle. Ramona was sure of one thing . . . from the look in José's eyes, she knew she wouldn't be seeing him anytime soon in Bilbao. When she asked about it, he told her he was called away to continue his work for the American, but she was not fooled. From the determination in his gaze, and his anxiety at leaving, she knew where he was truly headed. And though she often tried to tell herself it wasn't so, Ramona sometimes thought that José loved his horses more than her.

Now she was sure of it. She'd seen his apology in his eyes. He was abandoning her to try to save *them*. She could tell from the things he packed, the riding jacket, the boots, the breeches he always wore when riding. And secretly she hoped the horses would already be dead when he arrived. If not, she had no doubt José would risk everything to save them. Even his life.

The injured man who lay on the stretcher in front of Ramona moaned, and she stirred back to reality. With a soft shushing whisper, she took his hand in hers and hummed a Spanish lullaby, hoping to calm him. Ramona had talked the nun into allowing him to be transported to Bilbao even though the surgeon in Guernica had refused to operate. He'd said it was a worthless cause, but Ramona had known only one thing—there was no case too difficult for God.

As she held the man's hand, she prayed for a surgeon in Bilbao. It was up to the Creator of the universe to save this man. And she knew that somehow God asked her to take part in the miracle by voicing her prayers.

"You are stronger than you think," Ramona whispered, wondering if the words were for the man or for herself. "The pain is proof you are healing." She stroked the back of his hand with her thumb. "Without pain you are dead, so what is a little ache here and there, *si?*"

Heavy artillery sounded over the hills like far-off thunder. Despite the fear in the eyes of the other passengers, who included three other patients and a priest, Ramona found it hard to keep her own eyes open. By nine o'clock last night, the surgical teams had already performed a record number of operations, yet still more injured patients had lined the halls of the Carmelite convent.

Around midnight she'd hurriedly eaten a slice of dark bread

and sipped at scalding coffee. Now, twelve hours later, her stomach cramped in hunger, yet Ramona knew she wouldn't be able to eat even if she had a fine feast before her. The memories of what she'd seen turned her stomach. The injuries of the man they carried with them to Bilbao, with blood seeping through soiled bandages, did the same. And, as if reading her thoughts, another of the men lifted his bandaged arm slightly to inspect it and let out a moan.

But even more painful was the thought that José lied to her and didn't love her as much as she loved him.

The man moaned again, and the solemn priest sitting in the back of the ambulance reached over and patted his shoulder. Though his mouth moved in prayer, no words emerged. He lifted his eyes, and Ramona saw that they were bloodshot and weary.

"You should try to close your eyes. Have you slept at all, Padre?" she asked. Though she attended Santa Maria's church, she recognized Father Manuel from around town.

Father Manuel shrugged. "I'm not sure. I don't think so. Maybe that's not a bad idea." Still, he did not move or attempt to lie down.

She wanted to ask him about his parishioners but, from the look of him, she decided not to. Not only was his black robe filthy and torn, but he had the same scratchy cough, the same glazed look in his eyes as the others who'd seen what no human should.

"Three hundred bodies were found the first night. Then they doubled that. Of course, the journalists now arriving in town have quadrupled that number," Father Manuel mumbled, as if reading her questions in her gaze.

"*Pajaitos. Anglice*—the birdies. I heard the children. . . ." Ramona sighed. "That's what the children called the bombing planes: birdies. They brought such destruction, such fear. Let us hope that those birdies have migrated back to Germany. . . ." Her voice faded as the memory caused a tightening of her chest.

Father Manuel's eyes widened. "Then you saw them, the markings on the airplanes?"

"*Sí*. I was taking Sister Josefina lunch on the roof. She saw them in the distance and gave me a peek through her glasses—

what are they called?"

"The field glasses?"

"Yes. I looked through the field glasses."

He seemed flushed and slightly excited. "Then I need you to help me. To tell the press. The more eyewitnesses . . ."

"I don't understand. I heard you speaking with that man; you said you would share your story. Who would doubt a priest?"

His brow wrinkled, and Ramona bit her lip, remembering. Many had done more than doubt priests, far more. In the southern part of Spain, the people had killed them. She opened her mouth to speak, but closed it again, uncertain of what to say.

"Many will not believe." Father Manuel spoke with urgency. "Especially with reports that it was the Reds who burned the city down."

"And people believe that?"

The injured man before her moaned, and Ramona gently patted his hand again.

"People believe what they want to hear. Unless . . . unless many voices rise together to declare the truth." The Padre ran his hand down his jaw. "So will you join me, when we get to Bilbao?"

Ramona nodded her head to respond, then paused. She thought again of José and their last moments together. She remembered his firm embrace and the words he'd whispered in her ears. *Do your work, my love, and keep to yourself. Do not trust anyone—even the person you would usually trust the most. There are many with false motives, and one cannot look into the heart. And whatever you do, do not draw attention to yourself. It is the only way you can be sure to be safe until I come to you again.*

"I will . . . think about it," she told the priest. Ramona yawned, pretending her entire soul was not in conflict over this conversation. "Caring for the people is my first responsibility, of course—as I am sure, Padre, you know so well."

The bells of Santa Maria rang out, helping Sophie for the briefest moment to forget the acrid odor of burnt flesh that permeated the air.

She had felt brave with Philip by her side. They'd talked through the afternoon, and he had shared more of his story of being locked up in a damp prison cell because of a simple misunderstanding. He also talked about the peaceful knowledge of believing that, even from thousands of miles away, his father—or rather his father's faith—had most likely saved his life.

Sophie shared her experiences of the journey to Guernica, about getting knocked unconscious when their truck was hit by artillery, about the bombing. Yet neither of them spoke of the one thing that hung in the air between them like an invisible curtain—Michael.

When Philip was called away to help with the rescue efforts in town, Sophie knew she had to find Walt and get the truth about Michael out of him—no matter how much the truth hurt. She couldn't count on finding José now, and she couldn't live one more day without knowing whether her fiancé was dead or alive.

She found Walt in the convent gardens, helping to dig graves for the hundreds lost. Upon seeing her, he placed his shovel on the ground and motioned to a quiet spot near the stone wall.

"There's something I need to talk to you about," she said. "Or rather, someone."

She didn't have to prod. Walt opened his mouth and shared what she'd been waiting, and fearing, to hear.

"Michael is many men, Sophie. You, my dear, just happened to fall in love with one of them. It's been my job over the past two years to get to know his other sides. You'd better sit down."

She leaned against the rock wall. "I'm fine."

"Really, Sophie. You should sit." He led her to a small bench, then gently turned her jaw to face him.

"For two years?" She let that thought filter through her brain. Two years ago Michael was with her, in Boston.

"I have one objective in this war," Walt continued. "To keep track of Michael. To watch his every move and report it. He is too cautious to foster many close friendships, so I took the position of fellow reporter. Then I would not arouse suspicion. Reporters tend to move in packs as they follow a story. I have just cause to travel where he travels."

"You say *keep track*." She studied Walt's eyes. She saw care there, concern. And something else. She saw mystery and control, as if Walt had a thousand secrets and was carefully choosing which ones to share with her. "What do you mean by keep track? Walt, are you a spy? And if you are, why in the world would you devote so much time to one man?"

Instead of answering her, Walt stood and plucked a green leaf from an oak tree, twirling the stem between his fingers.

"Did you ever wonder, Sophie, where Michael's mother's sympathies lie?"

"His mother?"

She thought about the graceful Spanish woman. Carmen may have lived in a wealthy part of Boston, but in her kitchen one felt transported to the heart of Spain. The family's home was always filled with music—Spanish music that played from the gramophone. And the scents that had greeted Sophie every time she entered the home made her mouth water—even now. It seemed there was always something simmering on the stove.

"Did you simply assume she felt as you do—caring for the social cause? She was a dancer, yes, but she came from one of the wealthiest families in the country."

"I just assumed . . ." Sophie's mind began to jumble, as if Walt had uprooted every previous belief she'd held about Michael and his parents. It was true that many of Spain's landowners and businessmen supported Franco's Nationalists . . . which meant, Michael . . . ?

Suddenly all the conversations she'd had with her fiancé made sense. How many times had he chided her for not understanding the politics of Spain?

"But I don't understand. Michael's friends. They sided with the Republicans. Did they know? Or did he pull the wool over their eyes too?"

Benita, Luis, José—whose side were they really on? She wondered, but was afraid to ask. Still, she had to know.

"What about José? Where does he fit? Isn't it true they've been friends for years?"

"Yes, they are old friends. José worked on the estate of Michael's family as a stable boy. Every summer when Michael visited Spain, they spent time together."

"A stable boy! José seemed much more cultured than that. He told me he was a poet. . . ."

"Well, not a stable boy as you imagine one. More like a trainer of horses. José and Michael became friends as young children and have been so ever since—despite the fact that sometimes they believe differently. And that is why José is part of my network."

"Network?" Sophie wrapped her arms more tightly around herself.

Surely Walt was teasing her. In a few minutes he would crack a smile and tell her that it was all a big joke, that he was just trying to make her *think* he was a spy. She searched his face, wishing, hoping that Walt was a newspaper correspondent and nothing more, but the look on his face told her that he had a purpose for disclosing all of this. That he had brought her to Guernica for another reason.

"A network . . . of informants." Walt spoke bluntly, tilting his head back and scanning the sky as if watching for a sign from the heavens that telling her was the right decision. "I needed a network of men I could trust to feed me the information I need."

"You're scaring me—even more than the bombs falling on the city blocks."

"And why is that?"

"Because I know if you were truly a spy you wouldn't be telling me these things. Unless . . ."

"Unless?" Walt tilted his head, waiting for her response.

"Unless you're asking me to join your network," she blurted out. "Unless Michael is alive. Unless you want me to get involved with him again."

"You're a bright young lady. I knew you would be a good choice."

Sophie didn't need to ask again if Michael were indeed alive. And she didn't need to ask what Walt wanted from her. He wanted the unthinkable.

"What if I say no?"

"You won't."

A gruff laugh erupted from her lips. "Why not?" she nearly shouted. "Why shouldn't I refuse? He is dead to me. *He died before my very eyes*. How could someone do that? How could he pull it off? Besides . . . I've found someone else. . . ." She glanced toward the gate that Philip had exited no more than an hour earlier.

Had it only been an hour? Only an hour ago when she thought for sure she'd be able to bury the past, just as they buried the dead from around the destroyed city? Sophie was ready to start over. She'd accepted the fact she had come to Spain for two reasons—to paint for the people and to meet Philip. Had it only been an hour since she had concluded that she could begin a new life with someone who had become dear to her heart?

"You'll help because this thing is bigger than you, Sophie. It's bigger than all the numerous volunteer organizations that are giving everything for this cause. Bigger than painting canvases for the war effort. It's a matter of national security. The war could be lost or won according to what I'm asking of you."

Sophie laughed, certain now that Walt was joking. She was a mere girl, a painter pulled into a great big mess. What did she have to do with national security?

She was glad Walt had insisted she sit. Her knees trembled so violently she believed they wouldn't support her if she tried to stand.

Walt's eyes narrowed as he focused on her gaze. "This war is as good as lost if you don't help. Your paintings assisted the effort some, but this—"

"If you don't need me to paint, what do you need me to do?" A slight breeze stirred around her, and she brushed her hair back from her face. "Not that I've agreed to anything," she quickly added.

Walt sighed; then he took both of her hands in his. "I need you to get close to Michael. To get some information about a very important shipment."

"I can't do that. What about Philip?" She pulled her hands back, placed them on the bench for support, stood on shaking legs, and stepped away, trying to put space between herself and Walt's impossible request.

She couldn't even comprehend *seeing* Michael again, because the face of another filled her thoughts. "I really care for Philip. What would he think?"

"I know your feelings, Sophie. I could tell from the first

moment you spoke of him. That's why I brought him here. I brought him for you to say good-bye."

"Good-bye?" Again she turned to see if Walt was kidding with her—but his face was set with resolve.

"I'm sorry, Sophie." Walt removed his hat, turned it over in his hands. "There's no other way."

Chapter Six

$\mathcal{T}$elling her that his message was for her ears only, Walt directed Sophie to a small chapel in one corner of the convent. Sophie's gut told her to walk away. Yet for the rest of her life she would wonder what had been so important—if she could indeed have been a bigger help in the war.

In the end it wasn't Walt's coaxing, but the sight of an aged Spaniard that persuaded her to follow Walt into the chapel. Choking back sobs and leaning heavily on his cane, the old man was shuffling down the road toward a refugee transport truck. He dabbed his tears with the fringes of a woman's tattered shawl hung over his arm. Seeing him, Sophie realized that she could not refuse the task Walt asked of her if it would save even one person from such pain and loss.

Besides, it was too late to walk away. She'd been involved from the moment Walt had first approached her at the train station in France. He'd roped her in like a rodeo cowboy at a county fair. Now, the uncounted people whom this war had herded and destroyed simply to fulfill the grand dreams of little men prodded Sophie to play out her part.

She sat on the chapel's back pew and glanced up at the crucifix on the wall, whispering a silent prayer for strength to hear what would follow. Before sitting down next to her, Walt checked the side rooms and even the confessional to ensure they were completely alone.

Sophie inched away from him, distancing herself from the bad news she felt was coming.

He began with a heavy sigh. "Over the last fifteen or so years, Russia's presence in Spain has increased. In September, just a few months into the war, Madrid turned to Russia for help. Spain asked for arms above all else."

"That's not news. I've seen the Russian commanders and arms at the front lines. But are all the weapons from Russia?"

"Mostly. They immediately committed a hundred T-26 tanks and fifty fighter planes—no small number. Yet most are of poor quality. I wouldn't be surprised if some of the field guns came from the days of Catherine the Great."

"Still, that's better than nothing, isn't it?" Sophie brushed a strand of hair from her face, tucking it behind her ear. She could see in his gaze that Walt didn't agree.

"I'm not sure it is. The Reds place very strict conditions on their generous assistance. Some Spanish regimental commanders have been refused ammunition and medical supplies unless they join the Communist Party. And when it comes to the air war, the Soviets have control. They don't even consult with Spanish advisors. They have a very definite plan when it comes to Spain— mainly ensuring that their party is the next one in control."

Sophie tried to hide her frown, again thinking of Michael's chiding. How many times had he shown his disapproval when she had so quickly chosen sides without understanding the politics behind the war? The more she found out, the more complicated it became. She'd liked it much better when it was simply a fight between good and evil without any gray areas.

Walt cleared his throat and continued, running his hand across the smooth wood of the pew in front of them. "Spain paid for the Soviet aid with the gold reserves of Banco de Espana. A few months ago, Spain had the fourth largest gold reserves in the world, mainly due to the commercial boom during the Great War."

"Had?"

"I doubt if you've heard the name before, but the Russian economist Stashevsky suggested that the Spanish government 'keep a current account in gold' in Moscow. The Republicans listened to him, mainly because they were worried that Franco's troops would occupy Madrid and capture the gold."

"So they shipped it to Russia for safekeeping?" Sophie folded her hands on her lap, listening intently.

"Safekeeping isn't the word I would choose. They moved it to protect it from the Army of Africa—the hired Moors—that threatened Madrid, but they also used the gold to help buy arms and raw materials."

"So these weapons that you mentioned, these planes and tanks, they were not given freely?"

Walt smirked. "Nothing, my dear, is free in this world. Everything has a price tag, including the generosity of those who have a vested interest in Spain. And although I do not like the way the Communists are handling the matter, we need their help."

"The gold was supposed to be converted into foreign exchange through Eurobank in Paris," Walt continued. "In July the first dispatch of gold went to Paris, to pay for armament purchases in France. But 178 tons of gold were sent . . . and only 174 tons arrived."

"The rest was stolen?"

"Yes, except no one knows where or by whom. The government is calling the whole thing a clerical error, but personally, I think they're hiding something."

"But why hasn't any of this been in the newspapers? Surely the people have a right to know what is happening with their own gold reserves."

"Think about it, Sophie." Walt spoke with an intensity she hadn't heard before. "What do you think would happen if word leaked out that four tons of gold were stolen and hidden somewhere between Madrid and Paris?"

"The people would stop fighting and start searching," she whispered.

"That is exactly why word of this cannot get out. The people will put down their arms for false hope of riches, and in the end, all they love about Spain will be lost. In the end, their cause will be abandoned." Walt cleared his throat. "Besides, only higher officials even know about the reserves and the purchases from Russia . . . the people have more important things to think about. Like surviving until tomorrow."

"And if the gold is found . . . then what?"

"Then the shipment will be sent to Russia, as planned. Russia has already limited their amount of aid because of the theft. More gold means more help. And more help . . . well, that can make the difference in a war lost or won for the people of Spain."

Sophie replayed the words in her mind. *The people of Spain.* When she'd first arrived, they were a curiosity to her—she enjoyed learning about their customs and way of life. But the more time she spent with them, the more she understood their hearts. She thought of José and his friendship, and Benita and Luis, who welcomed her into their home. She thought about those who used to walk by the side street window, and their simple lives. They were a passionate people, a caring people. They lived each day to the fullest, yet generously offered a hand to those in need. In the months she'd been here, she realized it was the people who had captured her heart.

Sophie stood and walked to the stained glass window. Her finger traced the lead that secured the multicolored pieces. The shape and color of each piece made no sense on its own, but together they formed an exquisite picture. So too were the events of her time in Spain. Piece by piece, the story's colors and shapes came together. She discovered that, amazingly, the mysterious stranger she'd met on the French border, the one who had seemed to be of no consequence, was actually the lead binding all the individual pieces of her experience in Spain together into one image—an image she honestly wished she didn't have to see.

She thought about Philip. He was putting his life on the line to give the people what they desired most—a chance to govern themselves and rise above their lowly station. If she could tell him, what would he say? Would he urge her to help in any way she could, just as he was doing?

Sophie took a deep breath. "But I don't understand. What about me? What about Michael? How does he fit into this whole mess?"

"Before I tell you that, Sophie, I need to warn you. The observer's eye is useless unless it can tell what it sees. Many have already lost their lives—not in getting the information, but in getting it back to us. I have only shared the basics. Nothing you know now is of any consequence. If you wish, I can put you on the next train to Paris, and you can walk away from all this mess."

"And from people who need my help and from the man I love."

"Yes, I am afraid so." Walt briskly rubbed his forehead and looked at her with mournful eyes, as if apologizing without words.

"Then I have no choice. It seems I'm here for a purpose, that some grand schemer brought me here."

Walt blew out a heavy sigh and folded his hands on his lap. "Exactly, Sophie. That's exactly right."

For the next half hour, Walt carefully explained the story of the Spanish gold.

"In September the council of ministers agreed to transfer the gold and silver from the Banco de Espana to Moscow. Ten thousand crates traveled through various ports, watched over by the Soviet secret police and guarded by a detachment of *carabineros*. It's estimated the 510 tons were worth at least 518 million. But all the gold did not arrive as planned."

"Five hundred and eighteen million dollars?" It was a number Sophie couldn't even comprehend.

"That's just the worth based on its weight. The shipment was filled with ancient artifacts, such as Aztec gold and rare coins. In truth, the shipments are valued even more."

"So first the gold is sold for much less than its value, and then some of it is lost as well?"

"That's right," Walt said. "The amazing thing is that someone took an interest in the gold long before the civil war even broke out. And, though a foreigner, he just happened to be in town when the shipment was made. Not only that, he disappeared around the same time the gold did."

"Michael," Sophie said flatly, thinking of all those days he was in Madrid. She faced bombings and helped care for refugee children, while he stole the very funds sent to help their cause? Not only that. Could it be possible he faked his death so that no one would raise questions when he disappeared the same time as the gold?

Anger stirred within her, and she thought again of Maria Donita, wondering what part *she* played in all this.

"How could he do such a thing?" she blurted out. "How could he take the funds that could help so many?"

"That's not the only trouble for the Spanish people," Walt continued. "As soon as news of the gold reserves leaked, the value of the Republican *peseta* collapsed on the foreign exchanges, falling by half, which means that there is no other country willing to help—because they have no way of ensuring they will receive payment for any troops or arms provided."

Sophie felt the impact of this news like a heavy burden weighing on her shoulders.

"I know what this means. You want me to return to Michael and see what information I can discover. But what about Philip? I told him just yesterday how much I care."

"Yes, I know, but consider this. Now that Philip realizes how you feel, he can return to the front lines with renewed energy and desire to fight the battle he came for. What did you think? That he would be able to follow you around as you move from battle scene to battle scene painting for the cause? That you would continue your romance in the midst of a war? I promised Philip's commander that I'd return him within a week's time."

"So you think that I can do this without telling him?"

"Yes. Once you get the information—which will take a month at most—you can continue on with Philip as if nothing ever happened. And because of your help, the people will have the arms and men to win their fight."

"And Michael? Just where is he now?"

"He's in Bilbao, but . . . well, I've arranged for your meeting."

"I was already planning on traveling there, with the priest. He asked me to go with him."

"The priest is already gone."

Sophie cocked her head and gazed at Walt. She didn't even want to ask how he knew that, or how he was involved with the priest. She didn't need any more to think about than what he'd already told her.

"When Michael sees you, he will try to make things right. He will confess his love and ask for your forgiveness. And you are to do what he asks."

"Forgive him?" Just saying those words caused a heaviness to weigh on her chest.

"Yes. I can see that look in your eyes; you don't think you can pull it off. But you *can* do this, Sophie. You must, to be sure your side wins. And remember, Philip will not need to know. I just need your help for a few weeks, a month at the most. No one else can get close enough to Michael. You are our only hope."

"This cannot be happening." She lowered her face into her hands. "I came here because I met this wonderful guy and wanted to get married. I didn't get that, but I found something more. I found my heart through these paintings. I found Philip. More than that, I found God here. I've discovered that He is real."

"Well, if that is the case, what if God has something more for you?" Walt gazed at her with intensity in his eyes. "I know a bit about the Bible, too. What if you have arrived 'for such a time as this'? Maybe God brought you here knowing your one life could bring hope to so many."

"That's easy to say—but not so easy to do. I don't think I can pull it off. I can't imagine seeing Michael again." She grew light-headed just imagining seeing him face-to-face. The image of his dead body invaded her thoughts, and she felt both sorrow and anger realizing what he had put her through for . . . for wealth. "What if I can't convince him of my sincerity?"

"You have to pull it off—or at least try. I wouldn't ask if there weren't so much at stake. We're talking about lives. Thousands and thousands of lives. Just walk out these doors. Look around at the destruction. What you see outside is a minor thing compared to what could happen next if these people can't get the arms and support they so desperately need. The lost gold can be used to obtain it."

Sophie walked to the open door and scanned the flattened city. She knew that if she had had the power, she'd have sacrificed anything to prevent the bombing. To save the lives of these people. And it could happen again . . . unless she stepped in.

"I'll do it." She folded her arms over her chest. "What must happen first?"

"I have two assignments for you. First, destroy the paintings . . . and then give me the film with the photographs of the bombing. I will develop them for you. I'll leave some with you, but I'll take the best ones and have them published . . . under a different name." He pulled a small knife and a sheaf out of his pocket. "To gain Michael's confidence, you cannot be involved with those photographs at all. If Michael found out, you would lose all his trust."

"And second?"

"And second, say good-bye to Philip."

"How long do I have?"

"Half an hour. But whatever you do, don't mention me or anything of this assignment. As far as Philip is concerned, you're traveling to Bilbao for safety, and you'll keep in touch through letters. Tell him nothing else."

"I demand an hour. And you have to give it to me." She lifted her eyebrows and met his gaze. "After all, you need me."

Walt's eyes sparkled. "You never cease to amaze me, Miss Grace. You are right, but you also need me. There are a few more things you'll need to know, and I'll talk quickly, for your one hour is ticking down, starting now."

Walt then told her exactly what type of information she needed to keep her ears open for, concerning the gold and the people Michael was involved with.

"And what do you want me to do after I get the information?"

Walt's beady eyes focused on hers. "After you get it, I need you to leave the country. It's not safe—any of this. In fact, that is why I'm assigning someone to shadow you."

She cocked one eyebrow. "Maybe you? You're the one who got me into this mess, after all."

"I cannot do it; it would be too obvious. And Philip must return to his regiment."

"What about Deion? He's injured, and surely if he wasn't with me, he'd be sent back to the States."

"That's out of the question. A black man in Spain will bring more attention than you need. The person I'm thinking about will be invisible, even to you."

"You mean I'll be going alone?"

"I mean it will *seem* like you're going alone, but don't worry. Someone will be watching over you."

"Like a guardian angel?"

"Exactly."

Sophie crossed her arms over her chest. "I'd rather have someone I can see . . . and talk to." The two aches, of facing Michael and of leaving Philip, joined as one large pain in her heart.

"Yes, but isn't that what faith is all about? Trusting in what you cannot see?"

"*Sí*, I suppose it is."

"And unfortunately, faith requires us to take giant leaps into the unknown. . . ." And with that, Walt led her out of the chapel door into the new life that waited outside.

Chapter Seven

Tears wet Sophie's cheeks, and she hugged her legs to her chest and let her forehead fall to her knees. She'd told Walt she needed a few minutes to compose herself, but that was an understatement. She needed a lifetime.

Michael had lied to her—planned his own death, knowing the pain it would cause. Or did he truly know? How could he understand the pain of having her heart ripped from her chest? How could he comprehend her fear of being left alone in a war-torn country?

She doubted now if he had ever loved her. Had pursuing her just been a distraction—something to add some excitement to his time in Boston? Sure, he'd proposed, but obviously he'd never counted on following through . . . or on her following him.

From the moment she entered Spain, she'd experienced hurt upon hurt. Death, destruction, loss. A sob caught in her throat. Sophie had never felt so out of control. She lived each day at the mercy of others. To feed her, care for her, keep her safe—tell her where to go. There'd been those who did their best to help her in Spain, and yet they couldn't meet all her needs—no one could.

Oh, God . . . The emotion of her helplessness choked her.

I am so lost and confused. I try to follow my heart, and it keeps get-
ting broken again and again. I try to be strong, but my own longings
pull me down. I can't do this alone.

And as she sat there on the small cot, with the scent of ashes saturating her skin, she realized just doing her part wasn't enough. She loved with all her heart, but that in no way guaranteed love's return. With good intentions she helped those in need, only to be misused and lied to. Only one love was guaranteed to be returned. Only by offering to God her talents, her energy—herself—would she get out of this mess with her soul intact.

She thought of Philip. Sweet, gentle Philip. Even he could never love her perfectly. Yet she was okay with that. She knew he'd try to give her all the love he possessed. And she wanted to try in return. But now . . . Sophie pressed her face into the pillow once again and let the tears flow.

Minutes were ticking by, and Sophie knew she didn't have time to wallow in her sadness. Every minute spent vacillating between dogged certainty and tears of regret were minutes she wasn't spending with Philip.

She rose from her bed and took the knife from her pants pocket. She had created the paintings at Deion's urging as soon as the city was bombed. He told her that these captured images would matter. That she would be able to tell the world what really happened. She had already given Walt the film . . . he said he'd find a way to get it to the press at the right time without there being any connection to her. But she still had two other assignments from him that she'd promised to finish within the hour.

Sophie approached the two canvases leaning against the wall. She raised the knife and paused. For the briefest moment she questioned if she should follow through. What if Walt wasn't telling the truth? Could it simply be a ploy to get her to destroy evidence of the German bombings?

She stood there for a full minute replaying everything he'd told her, and she knew it was all or nothing. Either she believed him fully . . . or, well, if he wasn't trustworthy, then she had bigger things to worry about. Besides, deep in her gut she had a feeling Walt told the truth. He'd brought her Philip, after all. He didn't have to do that. And he'd told her the truth about Michael. If he trusted her with so much, how could she not trust him?

So with long swipes, she slashed the knife into the first canvas and tugged it downward until it sliced through the images of the airplanes bombing Guernica. She slashed at the planes as if she could knock them out of the sky with her knife. Over and over again, she took out her anger over Michael on the pigmented forms she had painted with her own hand. She then did the same to the second canvas.

When she'd finished, Sophie left everything just as it lay. The nuns would think someone else had caused the damage—either that, or they'd all be evacuated before they even had a chance to see the mess. With a sigh she put the knife back into its sheath and tucked it into her satchel.

She ran her fingers through her hair and took a deep, resigned breath. One mission accomplished—the easy one. Now to find Philip.

Sophie did her best to wash her face and tidy up. Still, her eyes carried the evidence of her crying. Nearly an hour had already passed, but she didn't care. What would Walt do if she took a couple more minutes? It's not as if he would call the whole thing off.

She found Philip waiting for her outside the convent, his packed duffel bag on the ground by his booted feet. She paused at the top of the steps. Philip also hesitated, then opened his arms to her. Sophie ran into his embrace. She wrapped her arms around his shoulders and pressed her face into his neck, breathing in his scent and attempting to hold back the sobs.

"Oh, dear Sophie." He stroked the back of her hair. "Please don't be sad. We'll see each other again. God will protect me and keep me for you. Believe that, okay?"

Sophie nodded, but she knew she'd break down the minute she gazed into his eyes. Eventually she forced herself to step back and look into his face, her pounding heart once again betraying how much she cared for him. Could she pull this off without Philip finding out? She couldn't bear the thought of his doubting her love for even one minute.

She tried to act as casual as possible. "Be safe, Philip. I mean—just watch out. Don't try to be too brave."

"You either. No running through enemy territory with a blanket wrapped around your shoulders." He gave her a small grin. "Do you promise to write?"

"Of course, as often as I can. Although I have to admit I'm much better with a paintbrush." She dug her hands deep into her pants pocket. "Do you think they'll send you back to Madrid?"

"Probably. Most of the Internationals are around the outskirts trying to protect the city."

"Are they still bombing heavily?" She winced, imagining Philip once again huddling in a bloody ditch, bombs exploding mere feet away.

"I suppose they are. Pray the Nationalists run out of fuel or bombs. . . ."

"One can only hope."

"So will you think about me?" He cocked his head, meeting her eyes, then frowned as if he saw through her brave front to what Sophie was trying so hard to hide—uncertainty, sadness, her betrayal.

Sophie evaded his gaze. "All the time." As she whispered the words, she felt a deep ache in her chest.

"Me too. Every day. Every minute," he whispered, taking her hand.

"I'll look you up as soon as I can. . . ." She squeezed his hand, wishing she could hold it forever. "And I'll be in touch as often as possible. Please don't worry if you don't hear from me." She wiped at her eyes, willing herself to stay strong.

"I thought you said you'd write." Philip gently extended a finger to wipe away a tear from her cheek. "Why wouldn't I hear from you?"

"Oh, I don't know . . . but just don't worry if you don't." She glanced back at the convent. "You know how crazy war makes things."

Sophie's fingernails dug into the palms of her balled-up fists with each lie.

"Miss Sophie?" Another voice interrupted her thoughts, and she turned to see Deion's smiling face.

"Sorry to interrupt, but I'm leaving too. They said I'm well enough—I can go back to the front."

She turned and offered Deion a hug. She noticed satisfaction in his gaze—pleasure that he'd be able to fulfill the work he'd come for.

"That's wonderful, but what did I tell you about that 'Miss' business?" She stepped back and took in his smile. "You take care of yourself, too, you hear? Oh, yes, and there is something I heard about you, Mister."

Deion scratched his head. "What was that?"

"That you helped dig out some women and children from underneath a collapsed tailor's shop. Everyone is talking about the dark hero who came to town."

"Ah, it wasn't anything more than any other soldier would have done."

"Are you kidding?" Philip butted in. "You shouldn't take it so lightly. Those people you saved sure are thankful." He winked at Sophie. "You can be sure you'll be hearing more stories about this guy."

"We'll keep in touch, right?" Deion gave her one more quick hug; then he moved to the cab of the truck. "I'll leave you two to your good-byes."

"Not good-bye," Sophie murmured. "Just see you later."

Philip placed a slow, tender kiss on her forehead. "See you later," he whispered. Then, with another kiss on her cheek, he turned and climbed into the cab of the truck. But before he shut the door, he paused. He lifted his hand and curved his finger, motioning her toward him.

Sophie folded her arms over her chest and approached.

Philip cocked his head, his gentle blue eyes trying to penetrate her soul. "Sophie, is everything okay?"

"Of course not. You're leaving, and I don't know when I'll see you again." She brushed away her tears, then wiped at her dripping nose.

"There's something . . . in your eyes. Like something's wrong." Philip shrugged. "Or maybe it's just me, reflecting the ache I feel in my heart."

He gave her one last hug, and she soaked in the feeling of his arms.

"Are you sure everything's okay?"

Sophie slowly nodded and sucked in a deep breath.

"It will all work out, you'll see." He stroked her cheek with his finger. "I just have a feeling it will all work out."

Without another word, Sophie stepped back and waved.

The truck started, then drove out of town. The canvas-covered bed was filled with injured soldiers on stretchers, again moving to what they hoped would be a safe place.

"They have to leave before the Nationalists arrive." It was Walt's voice. "This area has pretty much been abandoned; they've given up trying to hold it."

Sophie refused to turn and meet his gaze. "Okay," she said flatly, steel in her voice. "My first two assignments are done. What's next?"

"Come . . . we need to find another quiet place. There is more I need to tell you. Things for your eyes and ears only."

They found a garden, most likely tended by the nuns, and Sophie sat on a tree stump. Her gut ached, and weariness washed over her. More than anything she wished she could find a blanket, spread it out, and drift away to sleep where she didn't have to face the reality of what Walt was asking.

"Sophie, you need to know this first." He spoke with a gentle tone. "Wars are fought on three fronts. The men in the battlefield are evidence of the first. These men give their lives, but two other battlefields are equally important—if not more so. The second is the foreign chancelleries where diplomats consider how much help they can give, and to whom—with their own best interests in mind, of course. And the third is the bankers, from the little clerk to the ministers of finance. Where the money flows, there is power. Your Michael is involved in the third."

"He's not my Michael," she said wearily. "From the day he died, he's been dead to me."

"You say that with your mouth, but I see something different in your eyes. Once a piece of your heart is given away, it's not so easy to reclaim—even if you indeed have found someone more worthy to give it to."

Sophie sighed and poked a finger into the neatly raked dirt at her feet. Below the ground, Sophie knew that small seeds had been planted in hope of a future harvest. The only problem was that the nuns wouldn't be around to see it. If anyone benefited, it would be the Fascists.

"Walt, while I appreciate your commentary on love," she said, sifting the dirt with her fingers, "I'm more interested in the economic factors right now, if you don't mind."

Walt cleared his throat, and she could tell by his stance he would play her game. If she wanted all business, he'd give her just that.

"The Republican side had two advantages—control of Spain's gold reserves and control of the major cities."

"And the Nationalist side?"

"Agriculture. We all know that without food, even the strongest force will weaken."

"Which means both sides have to look outside Spain for help."

"You're a quick study." Walt removed a cigarette from his shirt pocket, lit it, and took a long draw. "There is no question the war would be over now if Franco had taken over Madrid from the start. The gold reserves were the salvation of the Republicans, but now I question if even that is enough. You see, some believe the Republicans' actions have simply prolonged the war and contributed to the suffering of the Spanish people."

"Yet if Russia sends more help . . . well, that's sure to make a difference, isn't it? Then maybe others will get involved too?"

"Stalin isn't concerned about a world revolution. He simply wants his say in what's happening here." Walt took the cigarette out of his mouth and flipped the butt into the soft dirt.

Sophie watched it smolder.

And as she watched it, she realized that she feared one thing most—that the long tentacles of Michael's influence would seize her, gripping until she'd not be able to shake them. He'd so easily pulled her in before . . . would she be strong enough to resist this time?

Walt looked past her, waving at someone on the roof above. Sophie turned and lifted her gaze, noting a nun with field glasses on the roof of the convent. After she waved back, she returned to studying the sky.

"When you're with Michael, I need you to listen for a specific name, Lester McGovern—though that is merely a nom de guerre. He is a British agent, as English as the queen. Last we heard, he was on assignment with Michael, and he told us he was on to something big. He hoped to send a full report in a few days' time. It's been two weeks since we've heard from him."

Walt leaned down and used the end of a stick to sketch a map of the Basque region of Spain in the dirt. Sophie watched intently, burning the image in her mind.

"We assume that Michael will stay in this region." Walt pointed to the area along the northern coastline. "This is behind what the Basques are calling the Ring of Iron. They feel they're protected there, but they don't know who walks among them."

He tossed the stick to the ground. "Yet, even if they leave this area, do not worry. Go with them, and we will go with you. You won't see us, but know we will be there."

He spent the next few minutes talking over various procedures, such as things to do to tell if she was being followed, or how to know if her items were searched when she wasn't around.

Sophie's mind swelled with information, but she knew she wouldn't forget a single word—her hope of seeing Philip again depended on it.

"Okay, I understand," she said with a sigh.

With a swipe of Walt's shoe, all evidence of their conversation was wiped out.

"Remember that your efforts are for the good of the people. You are part of a noble line of work." Walt dared crack a smile.

Sophie lifted one eyebrow. "Oh, really. And how's that?"

"Moses employed spies before taking Canaan. Julius Caesar before landing in England. And just think, someday your efforts for the Spanish people can be viewed on an equally grand scale."

Sophie stood and brushed off her pants. "Well . . . if that's it, I'd like to get this over with."

"There's one more thing." Walt pulled out something from his shirt pocket. It looked like a tiny piece of rice paper. "This telephone number is for urgent communications. It also contains a code and several cover addresses outside Spain. Keep this on you at all times in case you need it. And don't be afraid to flee the country if you ever feel your life is at stake and you can't contact us."

She took it from his hand, noting it wasn't much larger than a postage stamp. "And if I'm caught with this?"

Walt's gaze narrowed. "That is not an option. If you think they're on to you, distract them, crunch, and swallow. It will be gone."

Sophie looked at the paper once more and slid it into her pocket. "Yes, well, let's just hope it never comes to that, agreed? I want this whole thing to be over and be on my way to the front lines to find Philip in a month's time."

Chapter Eight

Petra Larios bolted upright, her heart pounding as her eyes opened. The high-low peals of the church bells echoed through the destroyed town of Guernica. She had drifted off again, perhaps because most of the night hours she'd lain awake, staring out the window for any sign of the enemy at their doors. Not those who had destroyed the town, but the town's survivors, who were lashing out against the wealthy—ransacking the homes that the nearly universal carnage had somehow missed.

The sun's rays filtered through the large windows into the elegant yet unfamiliar room where she had slept, once again reminding Petra that she was alone in the world, and her life would never be the same. Like the films that had played at the cinema back home, the events of the last nine months ran through her mind unabated.

When her father was killed in their home in La Mancha, she had been forced to flee to Guernica. She had found refuge for a time in this quaint, historic town, but no longer. Petra wondered if there was any safe place in Spain.

Before her father's death, Petra was alerted that something was wrong when *Señora* Rossi approached their door in La

Mancha weeping, blurting out a mix of cries and prayers. The landowners from the neighboring towns were disappearing, she had reported, along with everybody else who had money and status.

That night, as she considered *Señora* Rossi's warnings, Petra's ears had heard the uncharacteristic sound of large trucks rumbling through the village. Gunshots followed, and she didn't discover until days later that sometime in that hour, one of those shots had taken her father's life. Not wishing to wake his family, he'd waited for his executioners with the front door open. And although Petra had not heard him leave, she'd heard him die. Just one shot out of hundreds crumbled Petra's whole life.

While her mother and brothers had wailed at his loss, Petra fought to accept it was true. As a parade of visitors stopped by to offer their condolences, she sat in the parlor perfectly still, her hands folded on her lap. Only the day before his death, Petra's father had chided her for not being ladylike. Now he was gone, and she had no heart to run and chase her brothers as she had for the first seventeen years of her life. She wanted to be a lady now. She wanted to make her father happy. If only she had done so before! How much trouble had she brought him instead?

"Petra from the fields of La Mancha." She spat at her image in the mirror, still that of a child despite her seventeen years.

Mancha meant stain. In La Mancha country, the arid earth was orange-red and as close to the color of bloodstains as soil can get. In La Mancha country, the earth was soaked with her father's blood, staining her soul. For the first time, Petra felt the name fit.

She thought again of the olive groves sloping upward to gentle ridges with rows of enormous windmills turning in searing hot winds. They were only memories now.

Two days after her father's death, she witnessed the same fate overtake her brothers. Petra knew then it was only time before she herself faced the guns. Her mother must have realized it too and intervened in an attempt to save Petra's life. She had sent Petra to Guernica, but for what? To be killed by enemy bombers? Or would her countrymen kill her simply because they felt her family's status and wealth made her the enemy?

Petra from the fields of La Mancha—that's what the men and women who worked her father's land had called her. They said she was from the fields because, on days when there was no school, she only returned inside their fine home when the sun set, or when her stomach rumbled for dinner. Why sit in the dim coolness and quiet when she could run through the hills with the hot breeze whipping her dark hair around her face? But that was then. She didn't know who she was anymore. Or where she belonged.

Petra rose from the bed and pressed her hands against the wrinkles in her white blouse and blue pleated skirt. She ignored the view of Guernica from her window as she moved to the vanity and grasped the ivory-handled hairbrush, yanking it through her tangled, waist-long auburn hair. Meeting resistance, she tugged harder against the strands, hurting her scalp. Tears filled her eyes, not from the pain, but from the realization that she'd never be the elegant beauty her father had desired. She slammed the hairbrush onto the vanity, quickly twisted her hair, and pinned it on top of her head. She could dress up, but she'd never be a lady. She could think back to all the days before July—before her world ended—but that didn't change the fact that she was alone. No one cared about her here. And she was no longer safe.

The bombers had flown over the town just a day ago, northeast to southwest. That was one thing Petra was good at—maps, directions, locations. It was as if she were born with an internal compass that could point her in the correct direction at any time. Her skill had helped her driver more than once as he had brought her to Guernica.

When she had finally arrived at her aunt's house, Petra quickly remembered why it was not her favorite place to visit. Shunned by her cousins and mistreated by her difficult step-uncle, she found every possible excuse to avoid the family. So when her aunt and step-uncle had gone into town for lunch, she said she was too tired to join them. A short time later, she heard the insectlike buzzing of many airplanes, and then the bombs began to fall.

Petra had fully expected to die under the constant bombardment, so what good would it do to run? Instead she sadly, calmly sat among her relatives' beautiful furnishings and waited for the inevitable. The midday twilight of Guernica's rising smoke engulfed the house, but she lit no lamps. The bombs fell for hours, but none landed near the house.

After the last bomb had fallen, Petra dared to leave her aunt's house for a few minutes. What she saw defied comprehension. Less than a mile away, on the other side of Calle Allende Salazar, the town was a heap of flaming rubble. Yet returning to the house, nothing was out of place. The polished floors shone, reflecting the setting sun through the widows. The family photographs of her grandparents, aunt, step-uncle, and cousins hung straight. Every last china teacup remained in its place in the hutch.

One hour passed. Then three. Then five. By the next morning, when no word had arrived, she knew for certain her aunt and uncle were dead. Yet not even one tear fell. They were strangers to her, distant relatives who knew little about her until she showed up at their doorstep. And Petra's cousins didn't give her the time of day. She had no idea where to go next.

Her stomach growled in hunger, and she realized she hadn't eaten since the bombing. She rose and padded barefoot toward the kitchen when she heard her cousins' voices on the other side of the closed kitchen door.

"In town they're saying the rich were protected from the bombs because of their leanings. You've seen the town. Father and Mother are dead for sure. And what of us? I've heard some of the wealthy people have already been rounded up. Maybe they were killed. They will come for us too, I know." Ruy cursed under his breath. "They will drag us into the streets and get their revenge. We must leave, hide ourselves."

"How can the townspeople believe we had anything to do with it? Just because we are wealthy doesn't mean we welcomed the bombers. We loved our town as much as anyone else," Rafael answered.

Petra could hear the fear in his voice.

"*Sí*, but they do not know this. Father's friends—some were rounded up months ago. Imprisoned. Most likely dead by now. They were considered Fascists."

"What about the girl? Where will she go?" Rafael asked.

"Petra?" Ruy spat her name. "She is no concern to us."

"Yes, but if the Moors come, as it has been rumored . . . well, you've heard what they do to women."

"Pst. Rumors. I doubt the Moors are this far north. I expect their main concern is Madrid. Besides, if we take her, she'll just slow us down. . . . "

Petra didn't need to hear any more. She didn't need them. She'd lost her parents, her life. If she could live without her family, she could live without Ruy and Rafael.

Forgetting about food, she hurried back toward her room. On the way, she noticed a door ajar to one of the maids' small rooms. All the help had fled last night, after the bombing, returning to their families in the countryside. Remembering that, Petra knew what she must do.

Entering the room, she took a quick account of all she'd need. She rummaged through a trunk at the end of the bed. Grabbing a worn satchel from under the bed, she packed some things; then she quickly changed her clothes, leaving her fine dress in a pool of fabric on the floor—leaving behind the carefree girl she had once been.

Petra blew out a breath and left the room, wondering where to turn next. She remembered a boy she once knew and wondered if he'd remember her. They'd met when both their families had been vacationing in Madrid. He lived in the north—not too far away. They could escape. Maybe they'd even cross to France and start a new life together.

Walt paced the small room in which Sophie had rested just a few hours earlier. He took three strides from wall to wall, then turned to do it again, rethinking his conversations with the young woman and worrying he'd told her too much. Information was power. Or it was death. Above all else, the most dangerous part of his work was relaying the right amount of information to the right person at the exact moment it was needed.

He glanced toward the closed door and listened for footsteps outside. Then he knelt beside the cot, lifted it to the side, and worked the loose boards free. He pulled out the small suitcase, laid it on the floor, opened it, and pushed aside the prints he'd just developed. Sophie's photos of enemy bombers. Ones that could never bear her name, for risk of her life. And more than anything, he needed her alive. She was the only one who could get close enough to Michael, Walt knew.

Walt carefully folded his suit coat and felt hat, placed them inside, and snapped the case shut. He had less than an hour to wait before the other journalists arrived. He, more than anyone, knew the importance the press played in this war's tide of events. He also knew that the reporters who waited for events to happen, then chased after them, missed most of the story. Walt's duties behind the scenes as a spy helped his work on the front page in ways he hadn't anticipated.

Since he'd arrived before the others, he already had written two reports. One he'd transmitted to the London *Times* under another name—James Kimmel, a pro-Franco reporter and his most well-known alias. The second he had to wait to submit until the other pro-Republican journalists arrived. Walt needed them so they could tour the town and submit their reports together.

He hated the fact that his work sometimes benefited the Fascist cause, yet he knew it was important for his cover. James Kimmel's story of Guernica's fate—its being destroyed by Reds—was already circulating through newspapers and over the radio. Walt's true story of the German bombing raid would be printed in smaller publications that would be of little consequence. Yet both reports accomplished one thing—they proved to his superiors that he was doing his work and hunting down the war's important stories. The slanted news reports proved his loyalties . . . or so they thought. In truth, his main goal all along had been to work with the Communists to keep track of the gold reserves of Madrid.

But one could not track the gold without also following the tide of the war. Or following the man who had also been tracking the gold long before the first gunshot ever sounded in Spain. Yes, Walt had gotten to know Michael well. He'd watched his every move in Boston and in Spain. And now he would get closer than ever through Sophie.

The bonus of his inside position also afforded Walt the opportunity to pass on key information to his Soviet friends. In his reporting, generalizations of battles did not interest him; he wanted the unit names, numbers, and strength of formations. And within the limits of security and censorship, he also appeared keen to pry out information about reinforcements and the direction of the next push forward. What made the papers wasn't nearly as important as the classified information he was able to pass on.

But today Walt's concerns had changed dramatically. They centered on the one person Michael trusted without question. Walt hoped she could pull it off—hoped Sophie's anger and feelings of betrayal wouldn't override her smarts.

He knew Michael—more than anyone, perhaps. He knew Michael didn't worry about attracting hounds. Michael, no doubt, knew others tracked the gold. And the best way to deal with a hound was to get *him* off track.

He thought of Sophie again.

Or in this case, get *her* off track.

Chapter Nine

The train had arrived to carry away refugees from Guernica. Sophie had no intention of leaving with them. Instead, she waited under a haze-dimmed sun for the next group of correspondents to arrive.

Her shoulders trembled, and she felt her resolve weakening. Walt had likely had months, maybe years, to train as a spy. She had only a few hours to get used to the idea of reuniting with Michael, not to mention learning and processing all the information on how to send emergency messages to Walt or other "contacts."

The train's whistle pierced the air. Sophie once again slid her hand into her slacks pocket to reassure herself that the small piece of rice paper was there. Though only the size of a postage stamp, it held all the information she would need. If only she had more to cling to—something substantial to strengthen and guide her.

She thought of the Bible in her satchel. She hadn't had time to read it, or even open it, since she'd received it, and she thought it unlikely that she would anytime soon. As it was, it took all her concentration just to remember all the information from Walt. Her stomach knotted as she thought about meeting up with Michael and leaving town with him.

"The Nationalists will be here Thursday morning," Walt had stated matter-of-factly. "Italian and Moroccan troops are joining the Spanish. You must leave town by then. You cannot wait. Make sure Michael joins you. We need his information, and he can't be put in danger. To lose him is to lose everything we know about those gold shipments."

Sophie didn't ask how Walt knew these things. How he knew which train would bring Michael. Or how he knew the movements of Nationalist troops and men.

"What can I possibly say to make sure he will leave with me?" she'd asked.

Walt had offered an encouraging squeeze on her shoulder. "You're a bright girl, Sophie. You'll think of something."

"Wonderful. Thank you for putting the weight of saving the world on my shoulders."

Walt leaned forward and bumped her chin with his knuckle. "It's not the whole world you must save. I wouldn't do that to you." He sighed. "It's just Spain you must worry about."

Sophie pressed her fingertips to her temples and sighed. "That makes me feel so much better."

The whistle of the locomotive sounded again as it arrived at the platform, and Sophie searched the windows for Michael's face. She saw someone in the second car who looked like him.

Her mind flashed to the memory of the body on the sidewalk, and the pool of blood. How many nights had she cried herself to sleep thinking of his death and his betrayal?

She tried to look closer as the train slowed to a stop, but the hazy air denied her a clear view. The man's face was turned slightly as he spoke to someone seated in front of him.

Sophie held her breath as she waited for him to exit the train. Then, like something from a dream, Michael appeared at the coach's door. Wearing a gray cotton jacket, he stepped down lightly to the platform. His camera case—identical to the one she had "inherited" after his death—was slung over his shoulder, hitting his side as he quickly moved. Then he turned toward her, and his eyes widened into a look of disbelief. He took two hesitant steps, and his jaw dropped as his gaze shifted to the heaps of wreckage beyond her. He paused in midstep, and his eyes widened even more.

Finally their eyes met, and Sophie bit her lip. And it was only then that she believed he was alive. She pressed the newspaper tight to her chest, and more than anything she wanted to stride up to him and slap him. She wanted to yell at him, to curse him for putting her through this. But instead she took a deep breath, forcing her fury deep inside, and met his gaze, willing herself not to cry.

His green eyes softened, and his mouth parted as if he wished to speak, but no sound escaped.

Sophie made the next move. Slowly, cautiously, she walked toward him.

"Michael." She forced an evenness into her voice, remembering Walt's assignment and the fact that she didn't have much time to get Michael back on that train and out of town. She unfolded the paper to one of the photographs taken by "Arnold Benedict." She couldn't stop her hands from trembling.

"Michael, I . . . I knew these pictures were yours. Everyone told me I was crazy. But I just knew. Even though I saw you—" She paused, unable to say the word. Her chin quivered. "Even though I saw your—" Her voice caught in her throat, and Sophie realized she didn't have to worry about trying to act believable. "Oh, Michael . . ." She gulped down a sob and placed her face in her hands.

With a few steps he reached her, yet he hesitated. Instead of pulling her into an embrace, he gently grasped her arms.

"Oh, *Divina.* I'm so sorry. Your life—I was so worried about your safety. I knew from . . . from the bombings, the troops— you would die if I didn't take such drastic measures." He paused and lifted her chin, forcing her eyes to meet his soft green gaze. "I'm so sorry, Sofía."

She didn't argue. Not because she didn't want to, but because she had a part to play. Thousands, millions of lives depended on her. She remembered again the additional help they could receive from that gold.

He took one more cautious step toward her, then pulled her into his embrace. "The plan—my death—it wasn't my idea. It's just that we were all so worried. I knew you wouldn't leave me," he repeated, pressing her face to his chest. "I knew you'd never leave as long as I was alive."

Sophie nodded, but another face filled her mind. She thought of the beautiful young woman with the long black hair who had never tried to hide her infatuation with Michael. More than anything, Sophie wanted to ask him about Maria, but instead she stood frozen in his arms.

"I know you only thought of me," she finally managed to say. "I understand."

Sophie wiped her face and looked around, noticing soldiers and refugees climbing onto the train that waited to depart. According to the schedule, the next one wouldn't be leaving for hours. Then she remembered Walt's prompting. According to him, the next one wouldn't leave at all.

This train was her last chance.

"Somehow I knew you were still alive," she continued, speaking louder to be heard above the movement and voices of the others on the platform. "I would have known—as close as we were. My soul would have told me if you were dead."

Sophie thought back to that day she'd spotted his coffin. Bombers had threatened to bear down on their city as they did every afternoon, but she had no longer cared if she lived or died. She hadn't known how she would continue without him.

Yet, instead of Sophie spilling tears over the wooden box, Maria had stepped into the role of grieving girlfriend. Sophie thought also of the child Maria claimed to carry. Walt had told her that nothing had happened between Michael and Maria, that it was all lies, but she wasn't sure whom or what to believe. After all, from the moment she'd been approached by Walt at the border, it seemed truth was handed out only when deemed "necessary," and not before.

"The train. This was the last one I could wait for." She lifted her hand to his face, running her fingers down his jaw. "I have to go to Bilbao. I wish you would come with me."

"But I just—"

"I know you just got here, Michael, but it's dangerous. I've heard that the Nationalists will be here by morning. It's not safe for me to stay—for you either, for that matter. And besides." She lifted the camera in the satchel. "I already have photos of the town burning—better ones than any of these men will get. And I'm an eyewitness report. I was here during the bombing. I saw it all."

She blew out a long breath and fanned her face. "This is like a dream. I really don't know what to say. I have so many questions . . . but if you'd rather meet later in Bilbao . . ." She stepped back from his touch, lifting her satchel from the place she'd set it at her feet.

"No!" Michael blurted out. "I . . . we need to talk. I can't let you leave without explaining. I'm sure seeing my body—" He shook his head. "And I still don't understand. Why are you still in Spain? How did you get here?"

"It's a long story. So much has happened. . . ." Sophie didn't need to fake her emotions. Michael no doubt saw the truth of her pain in her eyes. She glanced back over her shoulder to the hillsides, where heavy artillery continued in a constant pounding. "It's been a long few months, and it hasn't gotten any easier. I'm scared to stay . . . and just as scared to leave here alone."

Michael glanced at his watch; then he ran his fingers through his dark hair. "Then don't worry about staying. Photos of this town don't matter to me as much as you do, *Divina*. We can get back on this train."

Sophie eyed him suspiciously. It was almost like having the old Michael back—the one she'd met in Boston. Looking into his handsome face, she saw that man again.

But as Michael led her to the train, a thousand memories reminded her that looks could deceive. He had much to explain; that was for sure. But what she truly needed to know she couldn't ask.

Chapter Ten

A cow bellowing outside his window woke Ritter. He'd had very little sleep, thanks to a recurring nightmare. In it, he had lost his will to kill. He'd crashed again behind enemy lines and lay injured in bed, watching Sophie paint. As she painted the rows of He.51s lined up outside the window, he confessed his questions about involvement in this war. He admitted following orders for a cause he didn't really believe in.

Now, opening his eyes to the new dawn, Ritter wondered if this dream foretold the future or reflected his subconscious thoughts. Either way, thoughts like those could affect his reactions and get him killed in air combat. He'd better get his head screwed on right, as he had early patrol in a few hours.

He rolled out of his bunk and sought composure in the early morning light. He looked out the window to see his morning bugler. Large, sad cow eyes stared right at him. And rather than purging the memory of Sophie, those eyes brought the dream back with even greater vividness.

Sophie's gaze, those caring, penetrating eyes, had forced unimaginable words to gush from his mouth. He'd tried to defend his involvement in Guernica's bombing, even though the memory of it haunted him. His words had poured forth, and even now in wakefulness he struggled against the nightmare's bonds of ugly truth. Yet the rumbling of engines starting around the base as they were serviced by the ground crews forced him to think only of the present. He forced the dream out of his mind, wiped sweat from his brow, and considered only today and his duty to his country.

With a flick of her tail, the cow lowered her head to the lush grass in the field adjacent to the barracks.

At least some creatures were at peace in this world.

He was due to take off in an hour, and he'd heard that enemy activity had picked up drastically after the Republicans received more Polikarpov fighters from Russia. Those little planes were fast, maneuverable, and heavily armed.

Ritter wasn't keen on meeting these new aircraft with only his obsolete, fixed-gear biplane fighter as a weapon. His He.51 was inferior, and the Russian pilots knew it. Ritter's advantage lay in his skill and experience as a seasoned combat pilot. He'd heard that all trained Russian pilots had returned to Russia as instructors, taking their combat skills with them, which meant he could anticipate sending the new, inexperienced enemy pilots to their last reward.

Ritter shook out his flying suit to evict any tiny tenants from their hideaway. Flying into combat with ants in one's pants was not the best way to start the day. Thirty minutes later, after a quick breakfast and stroll across the airfield, he found his crew chief in the plane's cockpit.

The grizzled sergeant nodded at Ritter as he approached, and Ritter knew he was running up the engine to make sure all twenty-four plugs fired and the propeller would change smoothly from low to high pitch. Ritter watched as the man checked both magnetos and pulled the mixture off until the engine stopped from lack of fuel. He then shut it down, climbed out, and saluted.

"Good news. The plane is ready and safe to fly." The sergeant then relayed Ritter's ammunition count.

"No squawks?" Ritter ran his hand down the body, noting that minor bullet holes from the last mission had been patched.

"Not a one," the sergeant answered. "This BMW engine will

get you home without a hitch—provided the pilot doesn't get lost."

The man laughed, but Ritter didn't join him. Instead he eyed the Spanish pilot who approached, striding up to the sergeant's side wearing the Nationalist Air Force's dark blue cap with bright green piping and tassel. Ritter could tell from their nods of acknowledgment that the two men knew each other. Yet the Spanish man's gait slowed as he noted Ritter's uniform.

Despite the man's own gold rank stars below a winged badge, the Spanish pilot's eyes widened at Ritter's presence, and Ritter almost felt as if he could read the man's mind.

A real Legionarie. A member of Jagdgruppe 88 Fighter group . . .

Ritter crossed his arms over his chest and cocked his chin slightly, taking pride in his own spotless breeches, riding boots, and leather flight jacket. Yet the truth was he wore the three silver stars of the Oberleutnant ranking with minimal pride. The uniform adopted was designed to allow the Germans to pass unnoticed. The color chosen matched the traditional olive- or khaki-brown of Spanish army uniforms. He knew only his light hair and black beret with the death's-head badge gave anyone reason for a second glance.

New pilots arrived daily—both German and Spanish. And since most tours rarely lasted more than six months, Ritter wondered when he'd leave. Not that he had anyone calling him home.

"They say you are one of best," the man said in halting German. "You are hero for outsmarting the enemy and living among them."

Ritter shrugged. "Not hard to do—outsmart them, that is."

"Do you mind if he watches your takeoff?" the crew chief asked.

"Why would I mind?"

A grin filled the Spanish pilot's face.

Ritter climbed into the cockpit, adjusted his leather helmet, and made sure his goggles were clear of dirt and oil. When he was strapped in to his satisfaction, he motioned his crew chief to pull the chocks so he could start his taxi to the dirt runway's takeoff end, forty meters away. As the plane approached the departure point, he checked the wind sock and saw it was limp.

He advanced the throttle a bit, put in some down elevator to raise the tail skid from the ground, hit the left brake, and spun the plane around on its main gear. When he had the nose lined up, he reduced power, and the tail settled to the ground. His was the first flight of the day, and he literally had the sky to himself—except for the circling hawks, that is. He knew to keep his eye out for them in the rapidly heating air.

Ritter advanced the throttle slowly and, as the plane gathered speed, he fed the down elevator to raise the tail to gain speed and improve his visibility over the cowling. Like most planes, the Heinkel had no tail wheel.

The needle in the airspeed indicator came alive and rapidly climbed. As he felt the plane lighten, he eased in some up elevator, and the Heinkel broke ground. When he cleared the tree line, he started a gentle climbing turn to the south, heading for his target. When he reached his cruising altitude, he reduced power, increased the prop's pitch for more speed, and tweaked his mixture for better fuel economy.

His assignment was to strafe the new railhead and put the switching yards out of action. He only had a few light bombs and knew the best way was to strafe railroad cars and buildings, then drop his light ordnance in the largest complex of train rails he could find. If he were lucky, the rail cars would catch fire and burn the ties and the buildings. The fire might even spread to other locations.

If he were really lucky, he might even hit an incoming train.

This train ride reminded Sophie of another. Only this time, instead of travelers attempting to get into Spain, the passengers were refugees eager to get out of Guernica—desperate to escape the destruction, though it seemed no place in Spain was safe.

Sophie followed Michael through the overcrowded passenger cars. Everywhere she looked, scared and injured men, women, and children sat on the hard, wooden benches, packed together like sardines and clinging to their meager possessions.

Michael slid his camera from its case and snapped some photos. His motions were familiar, yet foreign. And even though she took in his face and the movement of his hands as he worked his camera, she had a hard time believing it was really him.

She turned from Michael back to the people. They looked tired, hungry, scared. Still, they had not forgotten their common courtesies, and some scooted over to make a spot for Sophie on one bench.

Sophie sat next to an old woman who held a small puppy. The dog whimpered, but the woman paid it no mind. Sophie looked into the puppy's sad face and felt the same. Alone. Scared. Confused. She only wished she could whimper. She was tired of being strong and trying to hold everything in.

With no room to sit, Michael knelt before her. He returned his camera to his case and took her hand in his. "I'm so sorry, *mimo*. What can I say? It was a foolish plan, to lie in such a way. My hope was to get you out of the country, then to find you again."

Again Sophie bit her lip and forced herself not to mention Maria or the child. Walt had done a fine enough job explaining the motives for Michael's actions, but Sophie wanted to know his heart.

"I don't know what to say. And you're right; I would never have left if you had . . . lived. As it was, José and I didn't quite succeed when we tried to escape Spain." She glanced around at those sitting closest to them, eyeing the foreigners with curiosity, wondering if spies also sat among them here. "But we'll have time to talk . . . later."

Sophie looked more closely at his face, noticing for the first time that Michael looked thinner. She noted dark circles under his eyes and concern in his gaze. Concern for her, perhaps. Or maybe just concern that he'd been caught.

The train lurched, and she glanced out the window. Outside of town, the villages appeared untouched. An ancient church, a flour mill, a bridge. It looked like her first view of the Spanish countryside. Only the refugees and carts clogging the road were different, troubling.

Among the traffic on the narrow road was a truck similar to

the one that carried Deion and Philip away from Guernica. With everything in her, Sophie wished to turn her head and take a second look to see if they were in the cab. Yet she didn't dare. Until she discovered the information Walt needed—the information that would help the Spanish people—Sophie had to forget.

After gazing at the road himself, studying the refugees they passed, Michael squeezed her hand and looked up into Sophie's eyes. "How did you do it? How did you find me?"

"It was easy. Once I saw the photos in the newspaper, I knew you must be alive. But to actually find you . . ." She shrugged. "I only had to look where the most intense fighting was. I knew you'd be there."

His features softened, and he offered her a slight smile. It both pleased and frightened Sophie how easily she lied.

"Got any smokes?" the man next to Michael asked in Spanish.

Michael shook his head. Sophie looked at the man's soot-colored face, realizing how quiet everyone else had been, most likely curious about their English conversation. Now was not the time to ask more questions, to draw more attention. But she did have one thing she wanted to say.

"And to think I was going to promise you my heart forever. No matter what happened, my promise would have remained. I would have given everything for you, Michael. "

"And now?" he asked.

Sophie looked out the window, away from Michael's intense gaze. "And now I don't know." She answered honestly, realizing that anything but the truth would blow her cover for sure.

The tiny Heinkel was not a very efficient bomber, but it performed its ground support duties well enough. Ritter had over an hour of straight and level flying before he located the strike zone, so he moved his body into a comfortable position and tried to relax.

Suddenly, disturbed air rocked the plane. He glanced to his right but saw nothing. He racked the ailerons over. Sure enough, his top wing had been hiding another plane. He looked closer and saw a young, boyish-looking blond pilot almost flying formation with him. It wasn't his wingman, but a Russian pilot in a Polikarpov I-16—one of the open-cockpit versions.

The Russian pilot slowed his milk-bottle-shaped fighter and offered Ritter a smile and a salute. It was obviously a cocky good-bye gesture. Ritter immediately slewed his fighter sideways and pulled the engine power to idle. The much sleeker Russian Republican plane shot ahead of him. Ritter kicked the rudder pedal and went to full power, causing the 750 hp V-12 engine to surge his biplane directly in back of the Rata—an appropriate nickname for the rodentlike airplane.

Ritter placed the Russian plane in his gunsight, framed for a perfect kill shot. But for some reason, his fingers lost the power to engage the machine guns and send the boy pilot to his death. Ritter's heart pounded. He tried again, but his trigger finger wouldn't obey the nerve signals from his brain. He hesitated and forced his finger to fire, but now he had no target.

The Rata's pilot had pulled up into a loop and was already almost on Ritter's tail. Ritter cursed. His slow biplane fighter was simply no match for the retractable-geared monoplane that had been copied from the famous Gee-Bee racers. More than anything, he wished he flew a Bf.109B, a new plane Germany had sent to test. Unfortunately, too many flaws had been discovered, and they'd been sent back for modification.

Ritter glanced behind him and realized the plane was gone. He thought the Rata had headed for home until the distinct noise of machine guns erupted, and the sound of bullets riddling his left landing gear brought a rush of nausea. From his view in the cockpit, he watched as the wheel fairing flew off and the tire twisted off the rim. Ritter knew the Russian wanted to play. With a turn of his wheel, he obliged.

He rolled his Heinkel sideways with aileron and rudder; then he pushed full left rudder, holding the plane vertical. This gave the Rata pilot a very small target.

As expected, the much faster Rata shot by above him, preparing for his next run on the biplane. When the Heinkel had leveled off, Ritter dumped his load of 250-pound bombs. He didn't want a stray bullet hitting them and blowing him and his airplane to pieces. He counted them to make sure both had been ejected, and then continued his dive.

Ritter wiped his brow, then spotted the Ebro River below him. It wound its way between tight canyon walls back to his home base. With his heart pounding, he firewalled the BMW engine and entered a dive, hoping the biplane held together. He glanced around, looking for the Russian again and ignoring the climbing airspeed indicator that slipped past the redline.

Finally he passed under high cloud cover and glanced up just in time to see the Rata heading down directly at him. He knew he only had one attempt to make it between the protecting walls of the canyon. If he failed, the Russian pilot would paint another kill symbol on the side of his airplane.

The Rata still wasn't in range as Ritter banked the He.51 between the walls of the canyon. His shredded tire flopped in the slipstream. Then the whole aircraft vibrated as the tire flapped against the landing gear fairing.

Ritter dropped below the ridgeline and literally skimmed the fast-flowing water. Suddenly, a tall tree came into view. He hauled back on the elevator, barely missing the reaching branches. As he slewed his biplane around a curve, his heart stopped. A pair of transmission lines stretched across the canyon. If he climbed above them, he would give the trailing Rata the target he needed to send a burst into his crippled airplane. If he dove for the deck, he'd have to clear the water by two meters and go under the wires by about ten. If he miscalculated, it was all over, yet he had to take the low route.

Ritter slowed the plane to gain more reaction time and lowered the nose toward the rushing water, trees, and bushes along its side. He gripped the control stick and stared at the high-tension wires. They reminded him of a spiderweb stretched in anticipation of an incoming fly.

Ritter lowered the nose again until the damaged tire flapped just above the rocks. With a *zing*, the wires whisked over his top wing, and he knew he had made it.

The good news, when he reemerged from the canyon, was that he had the sky to himself. It appeared the pilot had decided against taking his fast-moving fighter down into the canyon. Instead, the Russian was probably headed back to his Republican base to tell his buddies how he had saluted his last victim and then forced him into the wall of a canyon. Who would ever check, or even care?

Yet Ritter was not home free. He still had to get his plane back on the ground with the shot-up tire. He doubted the landing gear's leg would hold. His mind's eye replayed the last time he'd seen a landing gear buckle under a plane. In an instant the plane had folded, then flipped onto its back. The pilot had been crushed before he knew what happened.

He slowed his Heinkel down to a little over stall speed and literally crawled through the sky back to what had become his home. This base was more of an airfield than an air base—no runways, just a mowed farm field that was rough, even for a plane with an intact landing gear. It still retained a washboard effect from years of growing crops in furrows. Seeing the air base in the distance, Ritter took a deep breath.

He gradually descended to an approaching altitude so he could make a circuit over his field. As he hoped, his crew chief, who waited for his return, noted the damaged gear. Ritter watched as he motioned to others, alerting them to a possible crash landing.

A plan started forming in his exhausted mind. His plane had a large tail skid and no tail wheel. So, he guessed, if he could place the one good wheel into a furrow and let the tail down into the soft ridge, the plane would slow rapidly and the tail might remain down. He knew of hidden furrows along the edge of the field that hadn't been flattened by the airport crew. It was worth a try.

He circled the field while slowing the plane. He made one very low-speed pass over his intended touchdown area to make sure there were no rocks or other obstacles that he could not see from higher up. When he decided now was the time, he lined up with the furrows on the south side of the field, pushed his prop into low pitch so he could have all the power available if he needed to go around, then eased the mixture control to full rich for the same reason.

With one eye on the airspeed indicator, he slowed the plane down to just above stalling speed and held it straight with the rudder, occasionally kicking rudder so he could see around the engine, which blocked his view straight ahead. His approach looked okay, so he tightened his seat belt, shut off the fuel, turned the master switch to off, and concentrated on getting the plane slowed. He hoped when it touched down there would be little speed to bleed off.

The plane had lowered to three meters when it started to shudder, causing a quiver to move through his limbs, a sure sign that a stall was fast approaching. He lowered the nose a bit and applied right aileron to keep the good wheel on the ground and the broken one in the air. When he heard and felt the tire rolling in the dirt, he applied full right aileron, which dropped the right wing even more, raising the damaged left tire away from the ground. He kept the plane going straight with the rudder. When the wings stopped lifting, he pulled the control stick back, slamming the tail skid into the soft dirt. The left gear leg broke off, but the tail skid dug in and slowed the plane almost to a stop. Then, as if moving in slow motion, the nose fell gently into the dirt and the plane came to an abrupt stop. Ritter let out a slow breath.

It was only then that he noticed the trickle of sweat running down his forehead. He grabbed his flying scarf to wipe it away. He pulled the scarf back only to notice it wasn't sweat, but blood. Without his realizing it, one bullet from the Rata had grazed his head.

A dark cloud cover descended over the field, and from somewhere Ritter heard voices calling to him, approaching. The sky darkened even more, and he wondered what blocked out the light. Ritter wiped his goggles as his world went to gray.

Then black.

Chapter Eleven

$\mathcal{P}$hilip stuck his head out the truck's window, thinking he would be sick. His head ached. His stomach too. His mind kept flipping through images of the previous days. The long rows of bodies waiting to be buried. Or parts of bodies. Men, women, children. The memories refused to leave his brain.

He knew that wasn't all that sickened him. The idea of leaving Sophie behind . . . again. Of not being there to watch over her. Of not being able to protect her in the days ahead. More than that, the look in her eyes had unnerved him. The pain she attempted to mask behind the smile. The words she didn't speak. The apology in her gaze.

An apology he didn't understand.

Petrol fumes from the engine refused to allow him fresh air, so Philip blew out his breath, drawing his head back inside the truck's cab.

The truck rumbled by a small village that appeared more like makeshift rows of shelters. So different from the high-rise buildings and fine cathedrals of Barcelona and Madrid.

Yet even in the midst of such poverty, a church rose from the center. The finest building in town, to be certain—the focal point of the people's world. Or at least it had been.

The truck jolted, and Philip held on to the door to avoid slamming into Deion next to him on the seat. His mind tried to put together the pieces of his nine months in Spain. He'd come with his best friend and fellow sprinter, Attis, in hopes of helping him win victory at the Workers' Games. Not only was the medal not won, the race hadn't even been run. Instead, Philip had chosen to stay in Spain to protect his friend, who insisted on volunteering in this foreign conflict. Attis had failed at that, too.

He'd joined the Internationals as a member of the Abraham Lincoln Brigade, yet even in the middle of the fighting he didn't fully agree with their ideals. Sometimes it seemed the Spanish people fought to replace one set of governing ideals with another. They would still follow the dictates of powerful men imposing views on them. Yet would changing their allegiance to socialism and communism improve their welfare? Philip was unsure. Yet this hope propelled him to fight.

After all, anything had to be better than fascism. Sure, Franco favored the Church—or rather used it to gain support—but from what Philip could see, his deeds mocked all that Christ stood for. Franco's fight for power and control of the Spanish people seemed to mock God. In fact, there were few places these days in which true Christianity was lived out.

The one place Philip witnessed true faith was in his father's letters. He wrote about the work he did in his community. How his parents helped take care of a family who had lost both father and mother in a house fire. How they formed relationships with some widows in town, bringing them together once a week for dinner and to study the Bible. The letters also always included his father's prayers. Prayers that came right from his heart and made him homesick to know this man—his father—better.

This kind of faith worked for a soon-to-be retired pastor from Washington State. But what about everyone else? Did his father's God care about Philip, too? About Spain? Could true Christianity be lived out here, in the midst of war?

He glanced back over his shoulder and watched as the church steeple grew smaller and smaller in the distance. Soon, only the utmost point of the steeple remained in view as the truck crested a rolling hill. It was easier to believe in God with Sophie around. To believe God somehow had a plan in bringing their lives together halfway around the world. But now he went one way and she another. He let out a sigh and looked at his hands, surprised to see his fingers clenched in anxiety.

I can't do it. I can't let go.

He thought of praying for the strength to release her, but he couldn't do that either. The fact was, he didn't want to release her. He focused his eyes on the road ahead, unseeing.

The air from the side window began to lose its smell of smoke and destruction, and he tried to come to a place where he could trust that God had a plan in the parting as much as the bringing together. Yet instead of peace filling his heart, his anxiety mounted with each mile.

God, I'll do anything for You if You just bring us back together again. If You can keep her safe. If You can make her mine . . . forever.

The driver didn't say a word as the daylight faded. He looked straight out the windshield and hummed a catchy jazz tune. On the seat next to him Deion slept, his head resting against the back of the seat and rolling from side to side with each bump. And at that moment, he was jealous of his friend— envious of his zeal for the communist cause. And for holding on to his heart.

Father Manuel was thankful for the clean clothes offered to him before his meeting. He dressed in a cassock that was just slightly too big and ran a brush through his dark hair. He had been called to give his story to the bishop in Bilbao, yet he could not forget the warning of the man with the dark hat. The thin man had told him to skip the meeting and instead tell his story in Paris. Yet Father Manuel shook his head in disbelief. Who was he? The stranger was no one of importance. How could a simple country priest's life be in danger?

More than anything, he wished that Armando were with him. But Armando had remained in Guernica, helping to bury the last of the bodies. Then he was off to find his wife, Nerea.

"You have an important meeting," Armando had urged. "I will find a spot on the next train out of town, I promise you."

Father Manuel glanced at the clock on the wall. He still had a few moments before his meeting, so he made his way down to the lobby of the small hotel to see if there was any more news about the war. In the center of the lobby, a small group of men and women huddled around a radio, listening to a news report and grumbling among themselves at an obviously new turn of events.

"What's going on?" Father Manuel asked the man closest to him.

"We heard on the radio, from the mouth of President Aguirre himself, that German aviators in the service of the Spanish rebels bombed Guernica. But now they are giving a new report. Listen. It is a man from Franco's headquarters who speaks."

Father Manuel scooted closer, focusing his full attention on the announcer's voice.

"We wish to tell the world loudly and clearly about the burning of Guernica. Guernica was destroyed by fire and gasoline. The Red hordes in the criminal service of Aguirre burned it to ruins. The fire took place yesterday, and Aguirre, since he is a common criminal, has uttered the infamous lie of attributing this atrocity to our noble and heroic air force."

The man beside Father Manuel cursed; then he turned. wide-eyed. "Sorry, Padre, but can you believe such things? And the Spanish church backs this story completely—you just missed their words. A professor of theology in Rome even declared there was not a single German in Spain, and that Franco needed only Spanish soldiers—who are second to none in the world—to fight for his cause. I pity anyone who tries to speak otherwise—standing against the Church itself!"

The words echoed in Father Manuel's thoughts as he remembered the warning from the man with the hat. He glanced to the clock in the foyer, knowing he had less than an hour to make it to the bishop's palace. Yet, if the Church backed Franco, what good would his testimony do? Why did they wish for him to come? Unless . . . unless their plan had been to silence him all along.

"There is proof to the contrary," Father Manuel said to the man with the pencil-thin moustache and large grayish-brown eyes. "There are some who witnessed the truth. They clearly saw the German markings on the planes."

The man shrugged. "*Sí*, that may be so, Padre, but who will believe a few voices in comparison to these official reports?" He waved his hand toward the radio.

"There are photographs, too," Father Manuel found himself saying. "A women correspondent from America was there, and she took photos herself. I am certain she is on her way as we speak, to share them with the world."

"Photographs?" The man's eyes widened even more. "Can this be true?"

"I was there. I saw her taking them."

"You were there?" The man took a step closer to Father Manuel and touched his arm. "You must tell me more."

Father Manuel felt a strange sensation wash over him, and he pressed his lips tight. There was something in the man's eyes. And though Father Manuel couldn't put his finger on it, he had a feeling he shouldn't say another word.

"Really, I would love to hear your story. You look hungry, Padre. Tired. Perhaps I can buy you some coffee at the café here. You are staying in this hotel, aren't you?"

More prickles shot up Father Manuel's arms, and he knew he had to get rid of this man at once.

"No, I am staying with friends close by. I just came here looking for a friend. And I wish I had time for coffee, but I must be going. I have a meeting in ten minutes." The three lies flowed out of Father Manuel's mouth in such quick succession, he didn't fully realize until all the words were out just what he had done. He felt heat rising to his cheeks.

He immediately thought of the woman, Sofía, and for the first time wondered if his words could place her in danger. In Guernica he knew most people in town, and he knew who was worthy of his trust and who was not. Yet here . . .

"Yes, I need to go," Father Manuel said again. "It was nice to meet you, *señor*." He nodded a farewell, then quickly hurried out of the lobby into the city packed with refugees who had come to find protection behind the Ring of Iron.

As he walked down the crowded street, Father Manuel

uttered a silent prayer that the woman would indeed get her photographs to the press soon.

He barely glanced at the people and buildings that he passed. Resolve filled him as he moved in a direction away from the bishop's palace. Yet the voice of his conscience continued to whisper that he was a fool and should go there. What would they tell him? Was it true the Church stood behind Franco's explanation of the bombing of Guernica?

While the Basque priest had little in common with those in the south, he was still under the leadership of Rome. A leadership that sided with Franco. This realization flooded Father Manuel with understanding of the burden of his testimony. His words would stand against the Church . . . if he were allowed to speak.

Nowhere does one find signs of bomb splatter, Father Manuel repeated in his mind, words he'd also heard the reporter say.

"The large craters were caused by exploding land mines. . . . As if they know anything. As if he were there," Father Manuel muttered to himself, swinging his arms as he walked faster. "I can understand them bombing Madrid. Or even Málaga or Barcelona. But why Guernica? Why now? And what is my duty . . . and to whom?" None of it made any sense.

Not knowing where to turn, Father Manuel returned to his hotel. On his way back, every few steps he was approached by sad little groups of refugees from Guernica who recognized him and wondered if he had news of their loved ones. Scattered among these people were armed soldiers on full alert, adding tension to the air.

Eager for some solitude and thankful that the man with the moustache was no longer in the lobby, Father Manuel entered his small room and settled on the bed, watching the clock and realizing, as the hands approached three o'clock, that he had disobeyed a direct order from the Church.

A knock on his door startled him, and Father Manuel opened it cautiously. "Armando!"

Father Manuel swept his smiling friend into his arms, feeling as if he were ten again. He felt as relieved as the time when he'd been freed from his teacher's reprimand by Armando's persuasive talk and charm.

Only this time Armando could do nothing to help. Father Manuel had defied a request by the Church, and he had made up his mind to head out of the country on his own. The lives of his people were at stake. As a man of God, he knew it was up to him to act, to tell the world the truth, despite his fears.

The door was barely shut when Armando studied Father Manuel's face. "You didn't go to the bishop's palace, did you?"

"No. I'm going to France instead. A reporter is waiting to hear my story—it is the only way to get the truth to the outside world."

"Then I will join you. I—"

"Absolutely not." Father Manuel puffed out his chest, feeling a rush of energy course through his limbs.

"Will you let me finish?" Armando ran his fingers through his dark hair. "You're always too quick to speak your mind. I've come to join you on your trip as far as the border. Then I must return and check to see that Nerea is fine. She's staying in the home of her cousin for now, and is safe—but as we know, the safety of a home, a town, can diminish from one moment to the next."

With his words, Father Manuel got another image of the planes sweeping, releasing their fury on those who in no way deserved it. And while he wanted to tell Armando that even a trip to the border was too much, he didn't argue. The fact was, his soul settled knowing his oldest, closest friend would be at his side up until that moment.

"You can do that? Come with me to the border?"

"Of course. I only wish it were all the way. When do we leave? In the morning, before dawn?"

"No. This evening. We must make the next train in two hours."

"I'll be ready. I will meet you at the station."

"And if you are not there?"

"If I'm not there, I am dead." Armando chuckled. "And in that case, I will not be joining you, no matter how much I wish to do so."

Chapter Twelve

*F*ather Manuel never dreamed he would leave Spain. He was a Spaniard, called by God to serve the people. As the train carried him to France, he pondered how God would use him now. Many of his congregation were dead, the rest scattered. And after defying the church leadership, would he ever have another congregation to shepherd? With the Nationalist troops bearing down, most of the townspeople had fled Guernica.

He and Armando joined the people in their flight, but theirs was for a different purpose. Father Manuel was running *to* something; he was running toward truth. But he was doing the bidding of a stranger. He didn't know what would be in store for him when he arrived.

"Comfortable?" Armando asked, adjusting a blanket over Manuel's lap.

Father Manuel noticed how Armando spoke lowly and gently; they acted more like father and son than two friends the same age. Yet Manuel didn't mind. He felt as if years had passed in the last week, not days. He felt like an old man.

"As comfortable as one could be, I expect," he mumbled, glancing at the small town passing outside the window without really seeing it. His mind was elsewhere, on the homes and buildings left behind—reduced to rubble. All he knew, destroyed and burned by German bombers.

Father Manuel stiffened as he recognized, a few rows ahead, the reporter who had spoken with him in Guernica. The man wore the same black fedora hat low over his brow.

Eventually he rose and shuffled over. He leaned down to Armando first. "Excuse me, *señor*, sorry to interrupt. May we switch seats for only a few minutes? I would like to talk to the priest, if you do not mind."

Armando eyed him cautiously and did not answer.

Manuel reached over and patted his friend's hand. "It's all right, Armando. This man is a reporter. A good man I have met before."

The man's eyes widened with appreciation. "Thank you. I only need a few minutes, I assure you."

Slowly Armando rose and moved to the seat the man had vacated. But he turned slightly to observe the man's every move.

"It is wonderful you have someone like that. Is he your brother, perhaps?"

"No, a friend," Father Manuel replied simply, "but close enough to be a brother. We have known each other since before we could talk, walk even. I believe our mothers were friends from the time we were carried in their wombs."

"Similar to John the Baptist and our Savior then?" The man gave a caring smile.

"Similar, maybe. But neither of us qualifies as holy." Father Manuel let out a low chuckle. "Though I serve God to the best of my ability, I am afraid it is often not enough." He patted the man's hand. "What was your name again?"

"My name is Walt." He settled back into the seat. "I watched you in Guernica. I saw the way you take care of your people. You are to be commended."

Father Manuel shook his head. "I just do what needs to be done. When I look around at the devastation and loss, I know it's not nearly enough."

"But would it ever be enough?" Walt cocked an eyebrow. "Can one ever get to the place where he has served all he can?"

Father Manuel recalled all the people of his small parish before the war. The widows, the orphans, the drunkards. Their needs had overwhelmed him. But now, after the bombing, all their needs had been multiplied tenfold. If he had to consider all the hurting men and women in Guernica, let alone Spain, he'd never be able to sleep or think of anything else. He folded his hands in his lap. "No." He sighed. "I suppose I never will."

"But you can do this one thing that will reach many, sharing the needs of your people. You are a wise man. I assume you did not go to the bishop's palace."

"No. I did not go. I did not even send an excuse, or tell them where I was headed instead. I am not sure I will remain a priest when I return, but . . . well, what you said made sense. And after I heard the news reports in the hotel, that the Church had sided with Franco's story, I could not take the chance of being told not to speak. Better not to know what the bishop was beckoning me for than to defy any order he might give me to keep silent about the truth."

"You have done very well, and I am sure you have sought the Lord's guidance." Walt cleared his throat and leaned close. "I did not want to tell you this before, but you might be in Paris for longer than you first thought. Do you still have the money? You did not give it away?"

Father Manuel could feel the small purse he'd tied to a string and hung around his neck. "Yes, I have it. But why would I need to stay longer? Is sharing my testimony with the reporter—the one I'm to meet at the Gate de Lyon—not enough?"

"It is a start. But there are so many more—hundreds, thousands, you can personally reach. I am sure you are aware that the World's Fair is coming to Paris. I have seen the construction of the Spanish pavilion myself. All the world will be there, everyone of importance. My news service requests that you come and tell your story to the reporters there also. And your friend—" He offered a slight wave to Armando. "Your friend is welcome also."

"The World's Fair? I am sorry, but that is out of the question." Father Manuel straightened in his seat and felt a flutter in his lower gut. He opened his mouth again, searching for the perfect excuse . . . yet could find none. It just seemed wrong. The mere idea of staying in Paris for weeks, maybe longer, caused heat to creep up the back of his neck. Leaving Guernica had been difficult enough. Leaving Spain, even worse.

"I see you are bothered by this." Walt rubbed his brow, then shrugged. "But I assure you that the greatest thing you can do for your people now is to get the world involved. Make them aware of the deaths, the destruction. You have seen things with your own eyes that the world does not believe has happened. And who better to testify than a priest? They may not believe others, but they will have no choice but to believe you—"

The voice of the train conductor cried out that Pasajes was just ahead, and from behind them a baby's wail interrupted his words. Father Manuel was thankful. He didn't need to hear more.

"I am sorry. I will meet with your reporter friend in Paris, but I cannot stay. After that, I will return and visit the bishop's palace." He sighed. "I'm sure the Nationalists will have a firm position in Guernica by then, so where else could I go? I am a servant of the Lord. I have not the freedom to make another decision. Sometimes I question if I am doing the right thing even now."

"*Sí*, I understand." Walt rose and tipped his hat. "I wish you the best, and perhaps we will meet again."

"If God so desires. But perhaps not." Father Manuel's words came out firmer than he'd intended. "God's blessings be upon you, my son," he said, waving the sign of the cross.

The man returned to his seat and Armando hurried back, plopping down next to Father Manuel just as the train pulled into the station.

"And what was that about? You seem flustered." Armando searched his face. He took the blanket from Manuel's lap and readjusted it.

"A request I am afraid I cannot grant. He asks me to stay in Paris longer and meet with reporters who will be attending the World's Fair, of all things." He watched as the train pulled to a stop, and Walt stood and exited the train.

Armando cocked an eyebrow but didn't say a word; then he looked past Father Manuel out the window. "I wish I could join you, but Nerea . . . I just cannot leave her for that long." A wistful look came into his eyes. "If she could come, that would be different, but every moment we're apart I long to see her again."

An unexpected ache filled Father Manuel's chest. He knew Armando would do anything for that woman, as he should.

Father Manuel had once loved the Church that much. He'd served with boundless energy. When had that changed? Perhaps it was when the people hadn't responded as he had hoped. Or maybe when they refused to love in return, and instead gave minimal care to their faith and even less to their God?

He rose from the train seat and took the opportunity to stretch, wondering how long before they reached the border.

Perhaps if he still had love in him as he once did, then he'd be willing to do anything for the Church—even stay in Paris.

Sophie tucked her satchel tight to her side as she passed through the crowds of people in Bilbao's main square. With quickened footsteps she followed Michael to a simple house not far from the city center. Before they even made it to the top of the front steps, a thin man bolted from the front door and opened his arms to them.

"Michael, you are back. This is a surprise, but you are welcome. I suppose you saw enough of the destruction and decided to return where it is safe." The man paused and turned to Sophie as if seeing her for the first time. "And who is this beautiful *señorita?* Please, let me take your luggage and welcome you into my home."

When she didn't hand over the bag, he reached for it himself, then took her by the elbow and led her inside. The man looked slightly familiar, but Sophie couldn't remember where she had seen him before.

"You must stay as long as you like, and do not refuse, *por favor*. Do you like my home, *sí?*"

She glanced behind her and saw Michael following with a wide grin.

"Your home is very beautiful," she hurriedly said, trying to get a word in. She spotted a beautiful cape hanging from one of the walls. "Oh, my, that is beautiful. Is that yours?"

Michael stepped forward before the man could answer. "Hector, this is my fiancée, Sofía. I believe I told you about her before." Michael turned to her. "And, Sophie, this is my friend Hector, one of our country's great matadors. Do you remember when we saw him that day in Madrid?" He nodded to her, and she knew she was supposed to agree.

"Oh, Hector, sí. I remember now. How could I forget?" She smiled at him. "You were like a dancer, your movements so graceful in the ring."

Michael nodded, and Sophie knew she'd said the right thing.

Hector smiled even more broadly, and his feet seemed to take on a lighter step as he walked to the cape. "Sí, I am privileged to be a matador, and the son of the greatest bullfighter in history." He bowed respectfully. "And this, señorita, is the traje de luece, suit of lights. My father wore it in Toledo when he got two ears. And I too have done the same."

The cape was beautiful, hand-embroidered blue satin. There was a photo near the cape that showed Hector in the complete outfit, including satin pants and a matching short jacket.

"Touch it. Touch the cape," Hector insisted.

"It's so beautiful. I don't want to dirty it."

"No, I insist." He took her hand and lifted it to the cape. "Feel how heavy it is? See those glittering stones? It takes as much energy to wear the outfit as to fight the bull!" Hector laughed.

They talked about bullfights and some of Hector's close calls, and Sophie still wasn't sure what the point of all this was.

Finally, after nearly an hour had passed, Michael broached the subject of their visit.

"I thank you for opening your home. My newspaper will no doubt be sending me off soon, and I just need a place for us until I can find a more permanent place for Sophie—a safe place. I am sure you can understand."

"You know my home is always yours. And for Sofía, too. She can stay as long as you need. After all, our families have been the closest of friends for years."

"Thank you, Hector, for your generosity," Sophie said with a smile, but inside her stomach felt sick. She took Michael's hand and squeezed it tightly. The whole point of returning to Michael was to stick by him and seek information about the gold. They'd only been back together for half a day, and he was already looking to find a "safe place" for her.

Hector showed her to a room. Then he gave her a fresh basin of warm water and a towel to freshen up. Sophie closed the door behind her, but she was almost afraid to take too long. She needed to stay in Michael's presence as much as possible, and she didn't know how soon he would leave again.

The same thing had happened in Madrid. Work often called him away, and they had spent more days apart than together. He was always finding someone to care for her, which is how she had met José. Or someone to stay with, which is how she met Luis and Benita. And while they were all wonderful people, this time Sophie refused to be brushed aside so easily.

Quickly changing into a clean skirt and blouse, Sophie brushed her hair so it fell over her shoulders the way Michael liked it. Then she gingerly laid out her belongings in a specific pattern, remembering the tips Walt had given her so she'd know whether someone had rifled through her things.

She laid the Bible the nun had given her on the side table and opened it to one of the pages that held a letter. She turned the letter so the stamped corner was on the inside, top section of the book. Then placing her satchel on the floor, she gingerly pulled a bit of string off the hem of the bedspread and laid it over the zipper. She scanned the room one more time and prayed a silent prayer before she headed for dinner.

Sophie's shoes clacked on the tile floor as she made her way to dinner. Her stomach rumbled at the scent of fresh bread and soup, and she realized how little she'd eaten over the last few days. She mentally prepared herself to talk about witnessing the bombing of Guernica, without mention of Deion or Philip or Walt, of course. She rehearsed in her mind what to do if anyone happened to mention any piece of information that she felt would help Walt.

Sophie rounded the corner and paused. In the dining room, Michael stood next to the elegantly set table. He was clean, shaven, and for the first time in a long while, he didn't have his camera case swung over his shoulder. He spread his arms outward toward her, and in his hand he held a single red carnation.

A lump formed in Sophie's throat, and her chest tightened. She knew he was simply trying to win back her favor. Trying to make her forget all the pain he'd caused. All the heartache over his death. All his lies.

The problem was, looking into the eyes of the man she'd loved for the past three years, anticipating his strong, protective arms opened to her and seeing his loving smile, she felt her heart begin to warm.

Chapter Thirteen

$\mathcal{D}$inner was nothing like Sophie had expected. While they ate a scrumptious meal prepared by Hector's cook, they talked about Spain, about the people, and touched on the fighting—but nothing too important, as if they were talking about an event happening overseas instead of here. They talked as if it were a distant war and not one that personally threatened their very lives.

Sophie mentioned the bombing of Guernica, but neither man asked any questions about what she had seen. As they lingered over wine, Michael told Hector how he and Sophie had met at the art museum three years earlier, and he knew it was love at first sight.

Michael glanced at her and winked. "I saw Sophie walking down the hall, and I had to catch my breath. I knew she was someone worth getting to know, but she never ceases to surprise me." His tone grew serious. "The last thing I ever wanted to do was hurt her. I thought that my sacrifice was the only way to ensure her safety, but every day since I hated myself for it. And I have missed her intensely."

Sophie felt her face redden. At her first opportunity, she excused herself for the night, telling them the long days and nights at Guernica had taken their toll, which was the truth.

After a good-night kiss on Michael's cheek, she hurried to her room. Sophie shut the bedroom door behind her and leaned against it, attempting to control her shaking. He did love her . . . or at least he claimed to.

She didn't know how in the world she would ever get the information Walt needed. She didn't feel at ease in Michael's presence. How could she when he had lied so completely to her? And how could she protect her heart with him talking like that? Her cheeks felt warm still.

What was she supposed to do now, sneak around the house and search for clues? The prospect was ridiculous—like something from a poorly made cinema.

Mostly, the realization that she was involved in some type of international espionage plot unnerved her. Who was she to be pulled into this? Especially if it was as big as Walt claimed. She was simply a silly girl who'd fallen for a boy. And now look at her—she needed to look for clues in a house where nothing seemed out of place.

The walls were brick, and the room had been scrubbed clean. On the bed to her left sat a feather mattress that looked recently filled, fluffed, and covered with two clean blankets. Her satchel was on the floor next to the bed. One small window gave her a view of the courtyard below.

At first glance, nothing in the room seemed different, and her satchel appeared just as she'd left it.

She slowly approached it, kneeling to look for the piece of thread she'd laid over the zipper. Her heart pounded as she noticed it was gone—brushed to the floor, where it lay under her bed.

She trembled, thinking of the next part of her assignment. Taking the hairbrush from her satchel, she stood in front of the window and brushed out her long hair, peering into the courtyard below.

Walt had told her someone would be watching. And he'd told her that brushing her hair in front of her bedroom window would be a sign to him that she was okay and still on task. Yet how did she truly know someone watched? What if Walt had just told her that to make her feel better?

She looked toward the small houses that surrounded this larger one and to the people milling through the streets. An inner peace stole over her, a sense that she wasn't alone. That Walt had indeed sent someone to watch over her, protect her, make sure she was okay—and was ready to remove her from any situation that threatened her life.

Suddenly a soft knock at the door startled her, and she turned. "Coming," she said, placing the brush in the window.

She opened the door to see Michael's smiling face.

"I'm sorry. I know I should let you sleep, but I just had to see you one more time. To believe you're really here and that . . . " He lowered his voice. "That you've found it in your heart to give me another chance."

"Oh, Michael." Sophie forced a smile. "I know you were thinking of my safety."

Sophie allowed him to pull her into his embrace, and relaxed her body so she could fold into his arms. She had a million questions—about faking his death, about the newspaper photos he submitted under the name Arnold Benedict, about Maria. Yet she knew she couldn't speak one word, or she might lose all sense of control. Her emotions were too close to the surface, and it took all her energy just to hold them at bay.

Michael pulled her back and placed the softest kiss on her lips. Then he stepped away. "There, I'll be able to sleep now. Thank you again for coming for me, for finding me."

"How could I not?" Sophie said. "I mean, everything I believe in is wrapped around you." She spoke the words with conviction, realizing they were true. The people she'd grown to love—their fate—all centered around this one man. If Walt was right, Michael controlled the gold that could bring them victory . . . or ensure their defeat. The thought caused a shiver to race down her spine.

"Good night then," he said, turning and walking away with the slightest bounce to his step. "We have a big day ahead tomorrow."

Sophie nodded, realizing Michael spoke the truth. *If he only knew . . .*

❖ ❖ ❖

Weather grounded Ritter on the day after his crash landing. But for the first time ever, he didn't feel much like flying.

He rubbed the bandage where the Russian's bullet had nicked his forehead. It hadn't done much damage, except for grazing the skin. The doctor confirmed it was the stress of the situation, not the injury, that had caused Ritter to black out. He was more embarrassed about it than anything—until the news of his successful landing started circulating.

After that, he'd retold the story at least a dozen times to pilots amazed at his ingenuity under pressure. As far as he knew, it was the first successful landing with damaged gear in Spain. Any others who had attempted it were no longer around to share their stories.

But his story wasn't the only one being discussed at length.

Rumors circulated from the main office that cable after cable had arrived from international reporters eager for any bit of information on who had bombed Guernica. Their sergeant-telegraphist offered the same response to each.

Ritter had personally talked to the man this afternoon.

The telegraphist always cabled back, *We have been grounded for days because of the weather.* He gave no hint of their mission. Or hinted that the "we" could include German pilots.

Ritter sat next to the radio in his private room and turned on the radio and listened as the Nationalists issued their first disclaimers. As he did each night at ten o'clock, General Queipo de Llano gave his official report. No matter what else was happening, Ritter knew that all over Spain, people would pause what they were doing to listen to the general, who was more like a radio star than a military leader. Some cheered and chuckled. Others most likely fumed at his rugged, clear voice. They loved him and hated him, but all were entertained.

Ritter remembered one of his quips during the massacres early in the war. "Tonight I shall take a sherry, and tomorrow I shall take Málaga," he had boasted.

Now, in line with the other communiqués from Nationalist headquarters, he simply dismissed the Guernica bombing as a myth. "The reports of German bombers are completely false," he declared.

Tired of hearing the general's voice, Ritter turned off his radio. A moment later, there was a knock at the door. Ritter opened it, and a timid-looking soldier stood there with his hand outstretched, offering Ritter a slip of paper.

"Herr Agler, telegram for you. I'm sorry, sir; there were so many cables coming in today, we almost missed it. It looks important, sir. It's from Göring himself."

Ritter took the note, only mildly interested. The news of his recent air victories must have somehow reached Berlin. Göring no doubt wished to congratulate his friend's nephew for a job well done. As if that would make any difference to his mood. As if that would make him want to go up tomorrow.

The messenger left, and Ritter sat at his desk to read the telegram.

OBERLEUTNANT RITTER AGLER STOP YOUR UNCLE TOLD ME ABOUT YOUR WORK ON THE GROUND AND HOW YOU OUTSMARTED THE ENEMY STOP RETURN TO BERLIN AT ONCE STOP HERMANN

Deion kicked at the dirt with his big, booted foot. Then, without removing the boots, he eased himself onto the bed—a straw tick with rough sheets and blankets. The scent of slightly moldy straw almost comforted him. He hadn't grown up with those fancy mattresses or feather beds like some of the other guys in the brigade. One doesn't long for what one never had.

The driver had dropped Deion off near this area and told him he'd join the men protecting Bilbao. Philip had continued on with the truck; his assignment was near Madrid with another group of the Internationals.

The driver had been too impatient to allow the men more than a quick handshake as they said good-bye. He was trying to cover as many miles as possible before darkness fell on the land.

Deion wondered if he'd ever see Philip again, or Sophie, for that matter. Still, it was good to be around the other volunteers and know that he was back doing his part in protecting the Spanish people. After all, that's why he'd traveled all this way.

He rubbed his sore leg, reminded of the injury that had taken him out of the action for a few months. It still bothered him and was still weaker than the other—giving out every now and then. But he didn't tell anyone that.

Not that he'd had time to talk with any of the other men. He arrived just in time to sleep. Or to lie in bed thinking about sleeping, as memories of the last few months replayed in his mind. And somewhere outside, the sound of a guitar drifted through the night air along with the scent of wildflowers and fresh grass on a distant hillside.

One memory was most vivid, and it seemed to hover in his mind at all times. It was the look of the injured woman's face as he opened the door to the basement, rescuing her from beneath the debris of the tailor shop in Guernica.

The appreciation had been evident in her gaze; and her trust, when she handed her infant over to him, was unlike anything he'd ever experienced. His chest grew warm just thinking of it. That one moment alone made the whole trip worthwhile.

"Hey, you schmuck, stop snoring," one American called to another, interrupting his thoughts.

Deion knew it wasn't the sound of the snoring that bothered the other soldiers. Everyone had gotten used to sleeping under any conditions. What they objected to was that the snoring drowned out the Spanish love songs the guitar played from somewhere outside. No one got up to gaze out the window, but if they were like him, the other men were no doubt picturing a handsome guitarist strumming and singing to a fair Spanish *señorita* under the light of a golden moon. Deion didn't usually put much stock in all that romance business, but somehow after what he'd witnessed over the last few days, it had a special appeal.

He thought about the olive groves outside the windows. They belonged to the people now. According to the peasants who'd welcomed them, the owners hadn't been around much, and now they wouldn't come back. He tried to imagine what that would be like if such a thing happened in the American South. If the rich landowners were gone, and the people were in control of their land, their destiny. It was hard to imagine.

Hours later, still unable to sleep, he strolled outside to the campfire where the guitarist had played. Though a fire had licked the air just a few hours before, the ashes were now cold, the night air silent. He picked up a stick and poked it at the pit, stirring the ashes as one would a pot of stew.

Suddenly a sound startled him, and turning, he caught the image of someone behind him. The shadowy image carried a rifle, that much he knew—but at an awkward angle, as if fearful of it.

This was no soldier. Perhaps a young boy, a friend of Franco, with dreams of becoming a hero by taking out volunteers for liberty. Without thinking, Deion was on his feet, chasing the lithe form by the light of a half-moon.

The figure ducked into the olive groves, with Deion right behind. Darting under low branches, four long strides later, Deion tackled the figure to the ground. A cry pierced the air. The screech of a girl.

Surprised, Deion scrambled backward onto his haunches and peered into the dark. Just in time to see the barrel of the rifle leveled at his chest. The barrel swayed slightly as if the weight of the gun was too much for the girl's arms.

He slowly raised his hands, speaking in a low voice and wondering if his few Spanish words spoken with a Mississippi twang made any sense to her.

"Easy now, *señorita*. I won't hurt you. I thought you were someone else. A soldier."

The trembling of the girl's arms increased. She sat up straighter and shook her head but didn't respond.

They stood there for a minute, maybe two, Deion trying to think of the right words. Words to convince her that he wouldn't hurt her, in fact, could help. Her eyes perused him, as if wondering just what stood before her. Had she never seen a black man? From the look in her eyes, he assumed not.

He opened his mouth to speak, and another small cry escaped her lips. Her arms, tired from the weight of the rifle, dipped

115

slightly, and Deion took the opportunity. With one swoop, he snatched the rifle from her hands and tossed it onto the ground. With two more steps, he swept her off the ground and pulled her tight to his body. She struggled but didn't make a sound. Suddenly a pain shot up his arm as she bit into his flesh. Surprised and hurt, he released his grasp; and before he knew it, she was gone. Darting again through the trees.

Deion thought about following her but changed his mind. It would only scare her. What would he do with the girl anyway? He'd only wanted to stop her from doing something stupid or hurting someone. Dragging her back to the barn would only achieve one thing—waking the rest of the sleepy men.

Instead, he took a closer look at the rifle and realized it was one of their own. She hadn't come into the camp to hurt anyone, but rather to steal a rifle. Maybe for protection. Maybe to hunt for food. Either way, it didn't matter. Deion had a sneaking hunch that the girl was alone and in trouble.

And as he slowly made his way back to camp, he knew that he'd get no sleep. As soon as dawn brightened the horizon, he wanted to be out there looking for her. From the thinness of her frame and the desperation of her actions, he suspected she would try something equally drastic again, and perhaps the next guy wouldn't be so friendly.

Chapter Fourteen

Petra wiped her face and spit again, disgusted that she'd actually broken the man's flesh as she bit his arm. She knew he hadn't meant to hurt her. At least that's what he said. For the first time in her life, Petra was thankful for all that time inside the cold and quiet house taking English lessons from a tutor.

Still, even if the man wouldn't harm her, he could keep her from getting to her destination.

With a soft grunt, she pushed a large rock over the hole she had dug to stash her food. She didn't want any wild animals to get it—although they were the least of her concerns. She had spent enough time roaming the hills outside her family's home to know that wild creatures were more scared of her than she was of them. It was the soldiers she had to watch out for.

That afternoon she had left Guernica in the back of a truck loaded with injured men and women and a few children allowed to ride along. Three soldiers rode up front, including the black man she'd encountered in the night. Her biggest concern had been finding a way out of town, and she was relieved to catch a ride.

She'd monitored the truck's progress by peeking out from the canvas flap. As soon as it headed the wrong direction, she'd planned on jumping from the back and looking for another ride. Amazingly, it had taken her nearly to the town of Bilbao—not far from her destination.

Petra stood and brushed her hands on the maid's clothes. Then she scanned the area, trying to figure out the best place to hide. Spying a hill that might give her a better view of her surroundings, she ran toward it and climbed it to the top.

In the moonlight, she could barely make out the large building the soldiers used as barracks, but her position on the hill provided no hiding place. Instead she spotted a nearby olive grove, and decided to wait in one of the trees. From childhood, she had always loved scrambling up trees and hiding in their branches. This would give her a wonderful vantage point, where she could keep an eye out for danger.

She found the tree with the most foliage and scaled it as if she had just shed ten years of her young life. Once settled into the curve where two branches joined, she scanned the adjacent fields, roads, and buildings. She thought of the map she'd torn out of one of the books in her father's library and hidden in her room. Dozens of times she had plotted the best route to visit Edelberto.

It was hard to believe it had been two years ago since she'd seen him, so vivid were her memories. They'd met at an outside concert in Madrid. He had been with his family, and she with hers.

He had told her of the place his family owned west of Bilbao. Edelberto said his family raised some of the finest horses in the country, and described them in vivid detail. They talked as they sat on the blanket between their families, until they were shushed by those around them. Then, with her parents' permission, they had walked to a nearby fountain—still in her father's full view, and she had talked about their land in La Mancha. In that short time, a friendship was born. A friendship that could have been decades old.

As the day turned to afternoon, and their families prepared to go their separate ways, they'd exchanged addresses, and even wrote once or twice a month. Petra hadn't heard from him since the war broke out, and she hoped he was still safe.

She supposed she'd find out soon enough. When she'd first

arrived, in the fading light she had scanned the distant hills and estimated that she could make it to his house in a few days' travel—staying off the main road for safety. She'd failed to keep the gun she had stolen for protection. She'd have to wait it out and try again. No one, not even the colored man, would believe she had enough courage—or as they said in English, "enough guts"—to return.

She had already succeeded in stealing an armful of food. She ate enough to stop the rumbling of her stomach, but knew she needed to make sure it would last. The rest was hidden, and she knew more would be needed for the journey. She'd have to find out sources as she went and eat as little as possible. She had a long journey ahead, as soon as the morning dawned. But in the meantime, she leaned against the tree limbs cradling her and let her weary eyes close.

As soon as he had enough light to make his way through the hills surrounding their barracks, Deion headed out, wondering what the others thought of waking up and not finding him there. Did they think he had sneaked away to meet with a *señorita*? Or perhaps decided to run from the fight?

Hungry, he hunkered down to lean his back against an olive tree, squirting water from the wineskin he'd brought. The slightest hint of fermented grapes gave flavor to his drink. Some dripped down the side of his face, and he wiped it away with the back of his hand. Drinking from a wineskin was trickier than it looked. The first time he'd used one, he'd tried to squirt it in a stream into his mouth, but that hadn't worked. He now knew to hold the spout to his mouth, cupping the opening with his lips. Next, he stretched the skin high above his head and let gravity take over.

Above him, through the branches of the trees, the sky was pale. He was taking another long drink when he heard a crashing sound above him. He jumped to his feet and looked up just in time to see a thin body falling through the branches.

Deion chuckled to himself. He had hoped he'd find her, but still, he didn't expect her to drop in his lap.

He stretched out his arms to catch the girl. It wasn't until he held her, gazing into her terrified face, that he realized it wasn't a girl at all, but rather a woman—a young one, but clearly a woman. She sat motionless, her chin quivering with shock.

Deion tried to think of reassuring words. The Spanish he'd picked up—*plaza, agua, churros, niños, casa*—none of those words would do. Then he remembered another. *Iglesia*—church.

"Me, *iglesia* . . ." He made the sign of the cross, hoping that his effort would show that he was a man of faith—at least some faith, and would not hurt her.

She frowned and pushed back from his chest. Deion set her on the ground, but held her arm gently, willing her not to run.

"I won't hurt you. I . . ." Then he remembered a word. "Me *amigo*. A friend."

"I do not know an *amigo* like this." The woman tilted her head and offered a cautious smile.

"English? How in the world does a peasant girl know English?"

Her eyes widened, and fear again filled her gaze. She mumbled something under her breath.

"What did you say?"

"Nothing, nothing . . . *nada, de nada.*"

He released her arm and pointed back to the barn where the soldiers bunked. "Come. I'll take you to camp. For . . . help. You need help, don't you?"

She didn't respond, but she followed, taking cautious steps.

Deion hadn't brought his rifle with him, but his satchel hung on his shoulder, hitting his leg with each step. Remembering what was inside, he slid it from his shoulder and paused. The woman paused too. Reaching inside, he pulled out a *churro* from yesterday's dinner.

"Sorry it's cold. The best I can do."

She eyed it; then her eyes locked on Deion's. With a quick movement of her hands, she took it from him, then took a large bite. She chewed, then took another bite. This time a piece crumbled and fell to the ground. Stooping to retrieve it, she suddenly paused, picked up the piece of bread, and glanced back up at him. Embarrassment tinted her cheeks pink.

"It's okay." Deion shrugged, wondering if she could understand all his words. "This war has changed all of us in some way. I know what it's like to be scared. To be hungry."

She stood and started walking toward the building, and Deion followed. He wanted to ask this woman her story. Where had she come from? Did she have anyone left?

As he watched her, he wondered how many others the war had ruined. How many Spanish women had lost everything. How many now begged and stole to survive.

And though Deion's faith was growing—something his comrades would never understand—he wondered how God allowed this. Just as He allowed the killings of Deion's own people.

Despite there being some things about the communist movement he questioned, he resolved to continue the fight. It was a good way, a better way at least, to live than anything else offered to this people.

At least communism would bring equality, he reasoned, and give them all a chance....

In the morning Sophie dressed, then hurried downstairs, scolding herself for not waking up sooner. After all, it wasn't as if she were on holiday and could waste the day away. Just the opposite. The sooner she could find the information Walt needed, the sooner she could leave Michael behind for good.

Sophie followed voices to the patio behind the house. The yard and garden had seen better days, and she could tell that it had once been a beautiful garden. Now it was quite overrun, and the only area not overwhelmed with foliage was the tile patio where Michael and five others now sat, sipping their morning coffee.

She couldn't help but smile as its aroma met her nostrils, and she wondered just what they did to get the real stuff, instead of the poorly flavored ersatz everyone else around the country drank.

The conversation stopped as Sophie appeared, and a half-dozen faces turned to her.

She took a step back. "I am sorry. I did not mean to interrupt. I was just looking for Michael, but I will leave you to your business."

Michael stood. "No, it is fine. What you will hear is nothing that will not be on the radio tomorrow. Come, *Divina*. Have a seat by me. If you care to listen to war stories, that is."

Sophie followed Michael, noting the surprised look on many of the men's faces.

"We don't have to worry about our words making the press," he explained. "All Sophie told her supervisor was that she is waiting out the fighting in Bilbao, and they do not expect anything from her."

Two of the men looked at each other with lifted eyebrows. Still they did not speak.

"Look at her," Michael commented. "This is my fiancée; does she not appear harmless? She is here with me . . . and has no official duties." Michael wrapped his arm around her shoulders.

Sophie smiled, hoping it didn't appear too strained, and settled her cheek against his shoulder.

Finally one man cleared his throat. "As I was saying, the Italian Brigade has been ordered to take Guernica and the heights northwest of it. The Reds have left their positions west of Deva. Unfortunately, the Italian Brigade marched from Guernica to Bermeo along a valley road that is only a little above sea level. Fools. They did this without securing the heights west of the road. Things are not looking well for them. They are surrounded by heavy fire, but they are holding the position. Sperrle and Richthofen responded by sending their fighters and bombers through the thick clouds, but it will do little good."

Sophie tried to appear uninterested, but her mind worked to record all the facts. After a few more minutes of attempting to remember troop units and positions, her memory had filled to capacity. Then she recalled Walt's request. She was only here to get one set of information—and that was about the gold. So far nothing they'd said about troop movements had anything to do with that.

"And what is the response of the Basques?" Michael asked, patting Sophie's hand on her lap, but otherwise ignoring her completely. From the even tone of these men's voices as they conversed, it was hard to determine just whose side they were rooting for.

"The Basque president Aguirre pleads for help," another man said. "In a radio message to Valencia, he admitted their situation was serious. He is calling all men to bear arms."

"Does that mean we are not safe?" An older gentleman stood and paced toward an olive tree in desperate need of pruning. He peered cautiously over the brick wall, to the mountains outside of town, as if expecting the enemy to advance over the next hill.

"So far I have heard the fortifications are safe," Michael commented. "There have been diversionary attacks near Miravalles, about seven kilometers due south, on the edge of its Iron Belt fortifications. Yet I worry about the soldiers. The German bombers and other air groups dropped heavy bombs in daily attacks, from morning until night—on hill positions, tunnels, command posts, artillery positions, and troop concentrations."

Sophie's mind immediately went to Philip. She wondered if the Abraham Lincoln Brigade had been sent to help with those fortifications. Perhaps he stood under attack even now.

"Do you think we'll be asked to fight—if it comes to our town?" the older man asked again.

"That is the least of our worries," said another. "If they come here, it means our most precious treasure is in danger."

Sophie tensed, and Michael patted her hand again. She tried to still her breathing as he continued.

"If they come, there are always our wives and our children to worry about." He motioned toward Sophie. "More than land, it is our families that we must protect. And I for one will give everything to make sure the one I love is guarded. Is anyone with me?"

Chapter Fifteen

$\mathcal{P}$hilip joined the men of the Abraham Lincoln Brigade just after they arrived from the front lines at the town of Alcalá de Henares. He soon discovered most of the men had been fighting for three months straight since February.

He eyed the bombed-out church where the men lounged and attempted to unwind. He scanned the faces, looking for anyone familiar. Seeing no one, he realized it seemed like years, not mere months, since he'd been part of their unit.

It was hard to believe he'd once again been dropped off within thirty kilometers of Madrid, and even closer to where Attis's body lay in its eternal rest. Even now it was hard to believe his friend was dead. He'd give anything to see that boyish grin one more time.

He found a place to sit near the front steps of the church and tossed his duffel bag to the ground near his feet.

An officer strode by with long steps. "Rest is over, men. We'll be assembling in thirty minutes. I hope you're all cleaned up. You all got those free showers and shaves as promised, right?" He laughed.

"*Sí*, and a nice dinner with steak and lobster too!" a soldier joked from somewhere in the back.

All the men around Philip chuckled.

"Wonderful." The officer nodded. "We're ready then—special guests for the town's local May Day parade."

Philip quickly changed into his uniform, then fell in with the others. He chatted with a lanky cowboy from northern California and a sailor from New York. Then, just before they marched into town, he felt a tap on his shoulder.

He turned to see a short, stocky man with a thick moustache.

"There you are, Charles," the man said to Philip. "I wondered where you've been. Haven't seen you since breakfast." Then one of his eyebrows darted up in question. "Wait, you're not Charles."

"No, but we met back at Albacete—or wherever that training was. Guys there said we looked like brothers. I haven't seen him since Soph—since that woman showed up in our foxhole. Is Charles here?"

"Well, he was this morning."

Philip scanned the crowd and spotted someone just his height with the same blond hair. "There he is." He cupped his hands around his mouth. "Charles!"

Charles hurried over, and his eyes widened when he saw Philip. "I don't believe it. You're still in Spain. You're alive." The two men embraced.

"I never heard anything about you after that lady showed up on the front lines," Charles continued. "You have to tell me the whole story . . . later. Right now it looks like we're going to a parade. Stick by me and we can catch up."

"Lady on the front lines?" The shorter man shrugged. "I'm Antony, Antony Meyer, by the way." He shook Philip's hand with a firm grip; then all three hurried to catch up to the others.

Spanish music played and cheers rose from the crowd as the men marched through the center of town. The intensity of the cheers grew as they approached a plaza packed with people. Somewhere on the other side of the plaza a band played. In the center the statue of a man stood above the crowds.

Philip marched past, looking up to view it.

"Miguel de Cervantes Saavedra," Charles said. "He was a novelist...."

"I read *Don Quixote* with my students. That seems like a whole other world. I remember thinking I'd like to visit La Mancha after reading Cervantes. Funny how life turns out."

Charles slapped Philip's back. "Maybe once we win back control of the country from the Rebels we can travel there. Care to join us, Meyer?"

The shorter man nodded. "Of course. Maybe it will be sooner than we think. I hear Steve Nelson is coming. He's our new commissar of the battalion and one of the great leaders of the Communist Party in the States."

"That's good news. But I hope he gives us time to see the sights around town first." Charles wiped his mouth with the back of his hand. "I'm getting mighty thirsty."

When the men were dismissed, Philip followed along as they whistled at beautiful *señoritas* in the plaza and downed liquor at the local taverns. But his heart wasn't in it. His thoughts kept traveling to Sophie. Where was she? Was she safe? He pictured every detail of her face, keeping it ever present in his mind's eye.

Within two hours, news circulated among the men that they were wanted for an assembly back at the plaza. When they finally made it back and stood in ranks, not quite as well ordered as their first assembly, Steve Nelson stood before them. Philip smiled to himself; he'd heard Nelson's Croatian name once, although he never could have pronounced or spelled it. It was no wonder the man had Americanized it.

As he began speaking in his thick Croatian accent, describing his journey to Paris with other volunteers, the men fell silent, rapt by Nelson's oratorical skill. He told how they had traveled to southern France and embarked on a passenger ferry across the Mediterranean Sea. Their cheers over their first sighting of the Spanish coast had been interrupted by the sounds of a rapidly closing diesel engine. French border officers arrested them and treated them like common criminals. And after a trial in Céret, Nelson and the other volunteers received three-week jail terms for attempting to cross into Spain, since the borders were closed to all outsiders.

"We were then kicked out of the country," Nelson told the group. "Fortunately, no one watched which direction we took."

The men roared with laughter; then they cheered.

Nelson lifted his hands, and when the voices quieted, he continued. "You should be proud of your efforts, men. Fighting the antifascists is a benefit to our homeland. Our world! Even in the United States, the CIO labor unions heard of your fight, and it presages an increasingly sympathetic political climate. What you are doing here will benefit the lives of generations to come!"

Philip glanced at the men around him, noting how Nelson's words affected their fighting spirit. They drew their shoulders back and stood taller at this man's respect; in a matter of minutes they were transformed from a group of jovial men who wanted nothing more than to drown their memories of battle with liquor to a solemn group whose pride beamed from their faces.

Philip glanced over and saw tears streaming down Charles's face.

After Nelson's speech, they returned to the burned-out church for dinner. The men nearly talked over each other, discussing their part in recent battles and their hopes for those to come. But their voices stilled as another officer approached.

"We've just received word, men, of an imminent Fascist attack. Down the rest of your food. We leave for the front lines right away."

Philip scanned the men's faces. He could see a mix of disappointment and acceptance. Steve Nelson's words had not come a moment too soon. They could handle the adversity ahead.

As they began packing for their return, he was thankful to head back into danger. Danger drew the attention of correspondents. Maybe even Sophie.

Philip smiled as he swung his duffel over his shoulder, imagining Sophie finding him there—wherever "there" happened to be.

Father Manuel never had a chance to meet the one reporter Walt had asked him to talk to. Instead, as he stepped off the train in Paris, a mob of reporters greeted him. He turned to Armando,

128

but another man stood next to him. Then he remembered that his friend had exited at the border, and he was alone.

"Padre, Padre!" the numerous voices shouted.

Father Manuel scanned the crowd. Were these people all here to meet him? Had the man in the hat sent word ahead that a priest from Guernica would be arriving on this train? The bombing had been in everyone's conversation on the train, and no doubt across the border, too.

Doing his best to remember every detail, Father Manuel related the events of the day, three times. He spoke in Spanish and wondered just how much they understood.

Even then the reporters weren't finished throwing questions at him, yet he wearily held up his hand. "Please, I can answer more questions tomorrow. Tonight I must rest."

Like the Red Sea parting for Moses, they let him pass. One young man, a Spaniard like himself, even offered to carry Father Manuel's small suitcase. Father Manuel looked at the man warily, unsure how to act in this strange new place. The man looked friendly enough. He not only carried the case; he led Father Manuel to an inexpensive hotel and convinced the manager to find "one more bed." Paris, it seemed, was filled to the brim with those attending the World's Fair.

Father Manuel had hardly undressed before he drifted into a fitful sleep. The memories of bombs and cries woke him through the night. It was then he prayed, and he couldn't tell if his prayers were part of his dreams or his wakefulness.

He'd just drifted off to sleep when a pounding on the door woke him.

"Padre, come quick," a voice said. "It's me, Berto."

Father Manuel opened his eyes to see morning light flooding into the room. He quickly dressed, then opened the door. The young man who had helped him yesterday stood there.

"Come and see. This May Day they are marching—thousands of people, Frenchmen mostly, maybe millions—marching between the Place de la République and the Bastille in the largest workers' parade. They march to bring justice after the bombings, justice for Spain."

"Thousands?" Father Manuel stood, his knees trembling.

"Then they know about Guernica?"

"*Sí*, the story is all over the papers. Your words and others. Come quickly, and you can see for yourself! It is a May Day parade like no other."

Father Manuel followed him, but they didn't go far before they came upon a swelling crowd of workers filling the streets, their fists lifted in a high salute.

Berto brushed his hair from his eyes, speaking before Father Manuel had time to ask these questions. "They shout their abhorrence of the bombing. They plead for aid for the victims of Guernica. They beg their government to assist Spain's Republican government."

"My words helped to do this?"

The young man nodded enthusiastically. "*Sí*, Padre. Your words and the photographs taken by others . . . photographs of the city."

"May I see the newspapers?" Father Manuel raised his voice to be heard over the voices of the workers around them. "I met the female correspondent who took them. She was there in Guernica during the bombing."

The man shrugged. "I'm sorry, Padre, there are none of the bombing itself. Only afterward, of the destruction. Come. Come, and I will show you the photographs that the world sees of your town."

Chapter Sixteen

Sophie endured Hector's hospitality for what seemed like weeks, though only a few days had passed. She listened intently to the men talk about their families, their homes, all they could lose if the enemy gained ground. Not one of them gave a hint of anything dealing with the gold, and she was more than slightly disappointed. The sooner she could find out the information Walt needed, the sooner she could pass it on and find her way to the Abraham Lincoln Brigade.

Michael must have seen her boredom with the men's prattle. She tried to hide a yawn as they talked about everything from the bridges in the town to crops in the fields.

He winked at her; then he rose from the wingback chair, one of many that graced the elegant living room, and motioned for her to follow. "Care to go for a walk?" He stretched a hand toward her.

Sophie offered a sincere smile and took his hand. "I'd love to."

They exited the front door onto the sidewalk that lined an active street. Even here, near the center of town, the war's closeness was evident. In the distance artillery rumbled, and the acrid odor of gunpowder wafted by. It was scary, she realized, how well she'd come to recognize that odor.

They walked in silence, the tragedy of the homeless refugees and children they saw begging for food—the degradation—stifling their spirits.

One homeless man watched them from under a wide-brimmed cap. When Sophie looked toward him, he quickly looked away, and she could feel his shame of living on the streets.

Signs in every grocery store and restaurant read: *No Hay Nada.* There is nothing. Michael's eyes never wavered from their path, and in less than fifteen minutes they reached the port.

Sophie noticed his troubled expression, and they'd barely neared the waterfront when, with quickened steps, he turned her back toward the sanctuary of Hector's home.

As they began the return trip, Sophie noticed Michael repeatedly glancing to the side, furtively studying a large contraption—a bridge of some sort—spanning the river.

She eyed it curiously, then pointed. "What is that?"

"A transporter bridge. The automobiles drive up onto a roadway, and the framework of the bridge moves the road across the river."

"I've never seen such a thing."

"Yes, it's unique and fascinating. Hurry, though. Let's get back. I despise seeing this country in such a condition."

When they got back to Hector's house, Sophie studied the newspapers that Michael brought in, eager for any news of the Internationals. The news about Guernica was finally beginning to filter through the press. *Le Figaro* published the first photographs of the few standing walls in the stricken town—their window holes appearing like vacant eyes or open wounds.

Another newspaper printed a wrenching image of homeless Basque children. Reports from *L'Illustration* and *Paris-Soir* offered pages of photographs of the destroyed town of Guernica and the now-desperate victims of the attack. Sophie cocked her head, studying a photo of a burning church. It looked very similar to one she'd taken. She wondered if it was one of the ones Walt had promised to publish for her.

"Is something wrong?" Michael asked, noting the question on her face.

"No, it's just—well, this photograph seems familiar. Like one I could have taken. But that's silly. As you saw, none of mine turned out." She recalled Michael's disappointment at the photos she had offered him when they'd first arrived at Hector's house. Walt had taken the best. None she gave Michael, the two of them decided, were good enough to publish. "I'm a far better painter than photographer, I suppose."

She continued reading. "Listen to this. *L'Humanité* has printed Aguirre's first statement: 'Before God and history that will judge us, for three and a half hours German planes bombed with inconceivable destruction the undefended civil population of Guernica, reducing the celebrated city to cinders. They pursued with machine-gun fire the women and children who were frantically fleeing. I ask today of the civilized world if it will permit the extermination of a people whose first concerns always have been the defense of liberty and democracy, which the tree of Guernica has symbolized for centuries.' " She put down the paper and looked at Michael. "Sad, isn't it."

"Horrible," Michael commented, peering over her shoulder to study the photos himself. Then he breathed in, as if taking in the scent of her, and placed a kiss on her cheek.

Sophie ignored his advances and tried to keep her emotions under control. Seeing the photographs of the destruction was bad enough. Being this close to Michael and pretending that all was well between them caused her stomach to churn. But the report she read in the next paper made it all even worse.

Anger surged through her chest at the report written by a James Kimmel.

"Michael, you're not going to believe this. They're still spreading these lies."

"Let me see."

She handed him the paper, and Michael read aloud: "The fire burned up most of the evidence, but from my observances of the wreckage of the town that had once been Guernica, the incendiaries were caused by those on the ground. There is no evidence that any of the destruction of this town was accomplished by General Franco's aircraft. I have not seen any evidence of fragment bombs, and the craters I inspected were larger than anything a bomb dropped by an aircraft could accomplish."

Michael's voice was steady as he read, and though she tried to gauge his emotion, he showed none.

"It's safe to say these craters were caused by exploding mines on the ground," Michael continued, "most likely put there to destroy the roads and keep Franco's troops from passing. The Basques are a curious people—first destroying their town for their own protection, and then blaming their enemies for the destruction in order to gain the world's sympathy."

Sophie pressed her fingertips to her temples, sure her head was about to explode from its pounding. Tears sprang to her eyes. It was bad enough, what the people had faced. Now these lies . . .

She questioned again what she had done—destroying the paintings of the bombing and giving the photographs to Walt instead of submitting them herself. Yes, he'd published the one of the burning church, but what of those that showed the German planes in the sky? Why wouldn't he print those?

If she had sent them in herself, she would have known for sure she had done all she could to make certain the truth be told. Turning them over to Walt seemed the right thing to do at the time. It was for her protection, he had insisted. It would help her cover, too. Yet if she'd had any idea such lies would erupt, she would have thought of another way.

Now it was too late.

"Are you okay?" Michael took her hand. "I think it is too much for you to think about, Sophie. Maybe I shouldn't bring the papers home. Just as in Madrid, you wish to save the world, then feel helpless when you can't."

She met his gaze. "*Sí*, I wish I could do something—anything—to save lives. I would give my heart to do so." She jutted out her chin.

Michael took her fingertips and pressed them to his lips. Then he frowned, searching her eyes with his own. "I have no doubt you would. And I am glad you do not have that opportunity. I could not bear losing you again."

Sophie bit her lip, holding back her words, and forced herself to look away lest Michael see her anger at his part in using the wealth of Spain for himself, and not for the people.

"Maybe you should lie down." He stood and took her arm, helping her up. Then he drew her to his side, holding her close. "See, the afternoon siesta isn't so bad after all, is it? At least it gives Spaniards time to rest their minds from all the cares that press so heavily upon them."

Sophie gave Michael a quick squeeze; then she slipped from his embrace. Through the window she could see the small group of men congregating on the back patio. She had no doubt they waited to talk about any important information when she was out of earshot. Yet what could she do about that? Michael was right about this one thing—the weight of the world was too much to carry upon her shoulders. She needed space to think. Room to breathe.

"I'll see you in a couple of hours then. For dinner?" he said.

"See you then." With quick steps she moved to her room, closing the door behind her. Though she lay upon her bed, she could not sleep.

While the men lounged in the shade of the back patio, enjoying their afternoon conversation, a burden weighed heavily on her chest, as if pressing the air from her lungs. She stared at the whitewashed ceiling, attempting to push the images from the newspaper out of her mind, along with her own captured memories. She tried to forget the caring way Michael looked at her. Tried to forget all Walt had asked her to accomplish. She even tried to forget all the needs she'd seen today when they'd walked the streets of Bilbao.

With a heavy sigh, Sophie rolled to her side. She tucked her hands under her cheek. She told herself to close her eyes, rest her mind, try to sleep. Instead, her eyes spotted the Bible. She thought again of the eagerness of the nun as she offered the gift. And she remembered the letters within its pages.

Sophie sat up and gingerly grasped the book; then she flipped through the pages, looking for the handwritten treasure inside. There were over two dozen letters, and though dated, none of them had been sent. Some even seemed half written, as if the person who wrote them had become distracted and never returned to the task. Sophie flipped through them until she found the one that appeared to be the first written, and she started reading.

January 3, 1867
Dear Jeremiah,

Even though I know I will never see you again, you are never far from my thoughts. I am living in Spain, and I do believe I never will return to the life I once knew. While completing my social work in Paris, I met and married a Spaniard named Mateo, and he is a dear and caring man. So different from the boys I dated back home, yet the same in a way—with similar passions, hopes, and dreams.

Though the Spanish valleys are beautiful, the tortured geology tells another story. Mateo knows this. He works deep under the surface, where the coal seams are narrow and twisted. It's been said there are no coal deposits in Europe as irregular as those in Asturias. The veins run from one mountain to another, folding upon each other in the valleys. I thought that would interest you—you have always cared much for nature and all God's good gifts . . . haven't you, my friend?

If someone had told me five years ago I'd be the wife of a Spanish miner, scraping to live as he scrapes out the coal from the narrow veins, I would have laughed. I did not travel to Paris to fall in love, but I did. It is the second time, but this time, I hope, it will last until the end of my days. Yet I find myself needing so much from my husband. I realize this as the minutes pass by through the day and I await his return. I am strong about some things, not about this.

I've left everything behind for good, but I do not regret it. I have my Bible and my paper to write my thoughts now and then. I also have my Lord, and I'm finding He is enough.

It's a strange thing, because I realize that with no luxuries and no time spent climbing the social ladder, I have more time for God than ever. This is a very good thing, because my prayers here are not filled with foolish prattling as they used to be, but rather with the heartfelt concerns of a wife . . . and soon-to-be mother. Yes, I will be a mother. I am planning on telling Mateo tonight. And I have a feeling God will continue to draw me closer still, as I will depend on Him so much more from this moment out.

Love,
Eleanor

Sophie folded the letter back up, trying to remember what the nun had told her about the woman who penned these words. She said it was her grandmother's Bible—her American grandmother who had lived most of her life in Spain.

Sophie slid the envelope back into its place, feeling a strange yet comfortable connection with the woman who had lived and died as a stranger on foreign soil.

Though Eleanor's life turned out differently from what she'd planned, she didn't seem to regret her decision. Instead she sought God more than ever. Needed Him more.

Sophie rose and glanced out the window again, wondering if the person sent to watch over her was still there. She walked to her nightstand and pulled out a brush, running it through her hair.

Yes, I am fine. I am watched over. She moved the brush in soft strokes from her scalp to the end of the strands, letting the soft waves fall to her shoulders. Thinking about the woman's words, Sophie realized why she felt so uncertain about everything around her.

I need God more than ever, but have I sought to fill this need? Have I prayed about Spain's pain? About Michael? About the gold?

She thought again about the amazing and unexpected gift of this Bible and the letters inside. Obviously God had a message He wanted to speak to her heart. God had more connections even than Walt to ensure she heard it. He had a plan for her, even in this. He had to. If God wanted her somewhere else, living out another life, He would have found a way to take her there. Instead He had brought her to Spain. And He had brought her to a place where she could not go on without Him—she saw that now.

"I have a feeling God will continue to draw me closer still," Sophie said, repeating the stranger's words. Then she ran her fingers over the Bible's worn cover. "Yet I have a feeling that closer doesn't mean without struggles. Never has, never will."

She heard footsteps coming down the hall, and she turned to the door. A soft tap followed. Though Sophie had nothing to hide, she tucked the Bible into her satchel before opening the door. It was a treasure she didn't want to have to explain, only cherish.

"Darling, are you ready for dinner? We're meeting old friends."

"How many old friends do you have?" She took his hand and played the part of the adoring girlfriend, somehow strengthened and refreshed even though she hadn't slept. "It seems you know half the town."

"Well, I did spend every summer rather close to here. Not more than ten kilometers away."

"You mean the house you visited when you were a boy?"

"The very one. It's in a small village near here, Portugalete."

Sophie squeezed his hand. "Then can we visit? Is your family still around? I can't believe we are that close. Why didn't you tell me sooner?"

"Because I wanted it to be a surprise. But no, my aunt and uncle are in France. They thought it wiser to wait out the war there. We'll wait and see what happens before I make any promise of visiting. We are protected now, but you never know when Franco's troops will break through the line and overrun us. In fact, I've already planned our way of escape."

"You said *when*. Don't you mean *if* they overrun us?"

"I mean *when*. News is trickling down the lines that it won't be long."

"Then this may be my only chance, for a while at least, to visit your family's heritage."

He opened his arms and pulled her close, resting his chin on the top of her head. "You are right. If we go, then someday, when we have children, we can tell them that their mother too visited the property of their ancestors."

Sophie felt her shoulders stiffen. The thought of future children reminded her again of Maria. More than anything, she wanted to know if the other woman carried his child.

Michael didn't seem to notice her mood change. "Besides," he continued, stepping back. "There is something else I haven't yet told you—something about my family. A true treasure that is like none other in the world."

"You're talking in a riddle. The town is by the sea, this Portugalete. Did you come from a family of pirates?" Sophie chuckled, pushing Maria's face out of her mind.

"Not quite. But don't try to get it out of me now. I've waited over two years to tell you, and you can wait until tomorrow dawns."

Chapter Seventeen

José cast a brief glance back toward Portugalete, the small fishing village lying to the west of Bilbao. Most people wouldn't look twice at the surrounding hills if it weren't for the large house located there. Most people came to view the transporter bridge—one of the few of its kind in the world. José had ridden across the bridge more than once himself. Built over forty years ago, the car ferry was suspended by wires from a frame riding on tracks high above the cabin, moving the ferry from Bilbao on one side of the Rio Nervión to Portugalete on the other.

The bridge could be seen from the hill, but José hardly gave it a second glance as he hurried toward the barn. The house appeared empty, and he imagined the worst. Was his father well? Were the horses?

Growing up, he'd heard the horror stories of fine animals used for mere pack beasts or, even more tragically, for food. And though these horses were bred to carry military leaders to the far corners of the earth, he wanted nothing more than to protect them from the little men who attempted to carve out great empires.

A subconscious impulse made José touch the scar on his neck, remembering that in a strange way he had received the wound attempting to protect everything this place once stood for—honor and duty. Instead he'd found himself protecting a girl who'd fallen in love with the wrong type of person—someone who worked for the enemy of the people, yet tried to pass himself off as a friend.

Though Michael had visited this home every summer of his youth, obviously it hadn't been enough. For if he were truly a son of Spain, he would not have sacrificed this place, these horses, in an effort to line his own pockets.

"Halt!" a shaking voice cried out, and before José could utter a response, a shot rang through the air.

José fell to the ground and covered his head. Another shot sounded, and a bullet whizzed over his head, just missing his ear. "Stop, Pepito! Wait—it is I, José! Did you forget your glasses again?"

"José? What José? I do not know a José. The friend I knew is dead to me after he abandoned his own father."

José stood and continued toward the barn, knowing he was no longer in danger. All the anger in the world wouldn't cause Pepito to harm José, no matter how wronged he felt.

José scanned the open corral near the barn, then peered into the door of the large barn itself. "Pepito, where are you?"

"Up here." The voice came from above him, and José glanced up just in time for a puff of straw to tumble from the open barn window onto his head.

"Oh, it is a voice from the heavens. Pepito is an angel. I am so sorry to have missed your funeral." José brushed the straw away and scratched his head. "On second thought, you must be alive, for if you were to end your life on earth, the man I knew would hardly be first choice for an angelic being."

"Curses, and you had to return, didn't you?"

The voice was more distant now, and José knew that Pepito had headed toward the ladder, coming down to meet him. He leaned against the wall to wait.

"What are you standing there for, as useless as a statue? Come, hurry, you have arrived just in time."

José followed the man's short steps to the farthest stall, where an old man was holding the head of a dying horse. José acknowledged his father's gaze, thankful to see he was well, and moved to the beast. The horse bled from the neck, where a nail had pierced through the bridle. He could tell from the flow of blood that the jugular had been severed and nothing could be done in time to save the creature.

"What happened?" José asked, turning to Pepito.

Instead his father answered. "I offered to help haul a load of explosives for a friend. There was an accident."

José could hear sorrow in his father's voice, but he ignored it.

"A load of explosives?" José cursed. "This is not a simple farm beast. He is not bred for hauling loads."

Pepito cut in. "You do not know how things are. The house has been empty for months. They've gone to France and left us to fend for ourselves. We do what we can to make enough to feed ourselves and our charges. Do you think you can save the horse? If anyone could, it is you. . . ."

José stood, knowing there was no use in trying. He looked at the horse one more time, but he didn't answer the question outright. "Where are the other horses?"

"Two stallions and four mares are all that remain. They're in the far pasture. Shall we go see them?" Pepito led the way, his shoulders sagging in resignation. "Your father usually watches over them from the rear, and I from the front. But we are worried. We hear reports daily that the Iron Ring is not as strong as they claim. What then? I would rather kill the beasts than turn them over to the enemy."

José's footsteps slowed, and he imagined killing the horses. *Impossible.* He couldn't consider it. And that is why he'd come, to make sure the horses were safe—stayed safe—even if it meant facing those who believed he'd abandoned them for no good reason.

He had no choice but to keep the secret from them. Let them believe what they must. How could he explain that keeping track of Michael in Madrid, and discovering the truth, did more to protect them and the horses than anything else? All they knew is that José had abandoned them when they needed him most.

And the horses were worth protecting. Descended from the same bloodline as the Lipizzaner horse—the highly honored

Spanish stallions of Austria—José had spent most of his life learning to train these fine horses. Famous for their ability to perform a style of riding called dressage, the horses' muscular bodies, arched necks, and long manes and tails were as beautiful as any fine sculpture, even that carved by an artist as great as Michelangelo himself.

José and Pepito crested the nearest hill to find six horses grazing in the southernmost pasture. Two mares were pure white, and the younger ones brown and dark gray. All horses were born the darker color, and lightened as they grew older. The eight years it took for the color to change was also the time it took to train them. After that, the stallions were used to perform before audiences or in parades under the expert guidance of their riders.

José balled his fists, again considering how they'd been used to pull carts and carry loads. Inwardly he knew he couldn't blame his father. The old man loved the horses as much as José did. More than life itself. Things must be drastic to come to such measures.

Seeing the horses in the distance reminded José of the days when he commanded their complicated movements with ease. Powerful and graceful, riding them had been like floating on a cloud. Yet he too was forced to do what he must—to leave the horses as well as his father, so that he might protect Spain's other great treasures.

As they approached side by side, the farther stallion, Calisto, must have sensed José's presence. José's footsteps slowed, and the horse's ears perked. Then Calisto lifted his head and tossed his tail in greeting before cantering to José. José reached out his hand and held it there until the horse's nose nuzzled his palm. Then, as if sensing the injury, he moved his nose to José's neck. The thirteen months since he'd been in Madrid seemed to disappear. Feeling the hot breath from the horse on his neck, José knew he was home.

"Yes, boy, it is fine. I am well, and I have returned."

"Look," Pepito exclaimed. "It is a miracle. The light has returned to his eyes."

José ran his fingers through the horse's thick, black mane,

nodding and smiling. Yet he did not know if Pepito spoke of his eyes or his horse's.

❖ ❖ ❖

Petra's stomach ached—as it always did when guilt weighed on her conscience or when she faced uncertainty over a decision. This time she faced both. She felt horrible for running away from the colored man. She knew he had only tried to help her. Yet she didn't want help from him, especially since she'd forgotten her plan and spoken English. What peasant girl would be tutored in such a way?

This would be only one of many mistakes, she knew. Soon the International soldiers would discover her for who she really was—the daughter of a wealthy landowner. And then she would be their enemy. Just like that, her quest would end, and she'd never find Edelberto.

She'd walked all day, skirting anything that appeared to be dangerous and eating the last of the stolen food. The colored man's look of surprise had stayed with her as she walked. It was an odd gaze he gave her as she ran away—almost disappointment that she felt he couldn't be trusted. But the memory of that look faded as she neared the place she'd been seeking.

Petra had only asked one person for directions along the way. She'd stopped to chat with an old lady sweeping her front porch in the village of Portugalete. They'd discussed the approaching troops and the chickens the woman raised. The woman had even given her two boiled eggs. Nonchalantly, Petra mentioned she'd once heard of a family who raised horses in the hills above the seaside village.

"If you do not know where they live, then you have not been to Portugalete before." The old woman's voice had crackled, and she eyed Petra suspiciously. "You only have to look up the hillside to see it. It is the large white house, our own castle to watch over our town."

And now the castle stood before her. A beautiful house, with equally beautiful stables near the back. It was quiet, and no movement could be seen in any direction.

Petra clenched her fists. She hadn't thought about what to do or say when she got here. Did she expect to simply march up to the door and reintroduce herself to the young man whom she had met in a park in Madrid over two years ago?

She glanced down at her clothes, dirty from the trip. Her hem had been torn, and she didn't want to think about her smudged face or her hair. She ran her fingers through the rat's nest it had become and let out a low sigh.

"May I help you?"

Petra jumped at the old man's voice.

"I, uh . . ." She stood and noticed her height nearly matched his. She thought about running, but changed her mind. Where would she go? Instead Petra decided to tell the truth.

She sucked in a deep breath. "I am looking for Edelberto. I met him in Madrid, and—"

The old man's laughter interrupted her words. It was a deep laugh that reminded Petra of her own grandfather.

She placed her hands on her hips. "And what is so funny?"

"Only the fact that Edelberto has been gone since the first week of the war. His parents shipped him off to France, and then a month later they joined him. And still, nearly a year after he is gone, there is yet another female looking for him."

"Another? I am just one of many?" Petra tried to control her voice.

"Ten, twenty, one hundred maybe? I am not sure. All I know is that Edelberto has many friends. And you . . . "

Petra could see compassion in his eyes. They were the color of the gray marble that used to grace the floor of the entryway to her parents' home. They were kind eyes, and she felt at ease even if Edelberto wasn't here.

"Where are you from?" the old man asked.

Petra bit her lip, unable even to speak of La Mancha. "I came from Guernica. I was there—"

"During the bombing?" the old man interrupted. "My son, José, and daughter-in-law, Ramona, were too. Come, you must come inside. Surely things must be bad if you came to Edelberto for help." He took her arm and led her toward the house. "Did you lose everyone?"

Petra considered her cousins, but remembering their words and how they didn't even claim her, she knew they didn't count. "Yes, everyone."

"Oh, *sí*, *señorita*, then you must stay with us. Things are lean, but you are small. I'm sure you wouldn't eat more than a pea or one carrot. We will make a way, you will see."

And with quick steps, he led her through the front door of a house that drew Petra back to memories of her own home. As her sore feet padded over the gleaming surface of the entryway—tile the color of the man's eyes—she couldn't help but smile at the sweet memories that met her.

Chapter Eighteen

The sea of marchers strode down the Paris street before Father Manuel—waves of men and women in workers' clothes, hands upraised, crying out for his people in a language he couldn't understand. Yet God understood their words. And maybe their words would convince their leaders to take heart and offer assistance for the poor in Spain.

As he walked along with Berto, the crowd swept Father Manuel away with it. His feet hurried him forward to keep up. Pressed around him, men and women waved the printed newspaper images high in the air. Other bits of newspaper flew through the warm breeze, and more paper crunched under his feet.

As they moved forward, Father Manuel tried to get a better look at the city around him—the buildings all white and ornamental—fancy statues and showy fixtures that, in northern Spain, could only be seen on the inside of elaborate cathedrals, not outside on buildings and in public squares.

The young man tugged on Father Manuel's arm and spoke hurriedly. "We are almost there."

"Where?" Father Manuel felt his heart pounding as he

moved through the crowd, and he forgot for a time he wore the cassock of a priest.

Berto didn't answer; he just led Father Manuel to a building with a sign that read *The Society of Process Servers*. They moved past the offices to a set of spiral steps. Making their way upward, they came to a studio of some sort. A group of people inside were reading the newspaper *Ce Soir* and speaking rapidly in Spanish. The studio was in an uproar, and it was evident these men and women were fellow émigrés.

The door was partially open with a piece of paper taped to it. *C'EST ICI*. This is it.

Father Manuel followed his guide through two cluttered storage rooms. He noticed large paintings, one by Modigliani, on the floor. A large dog lay in front of them, as if protecting them.

Father Manuel opened his mouth again to ask why he was here. Then he recognized a name being repeated by many of the others. Picasso.

Could it be he stood in the studio of the Spanish master?

Another staircase led to the second of three levels, and an enormous studio opened before them. Women caressed the photos in the newspapers and wept. Others shouted and cursed. Father Manuel saw as much emotion amongst them as from the people themselves during the bombing, and his heart warmed to see so many other Spaniards. Though they were physically far from home, they were present there in heart.

Father Manuel paused, even as Berto continued forward. There before him was the man he'd seen many times in photos. Picasso was bald, and thinner than he appeared in pictures. He wore a blue-striped jersey shirt and paced the floor, outraged.

"*Señor* Picasso—" Berto interrupted his rant. "This priest, he was there. He shared his story with correspondents yesterday. I was making a delivery for my uncle at the train station, and I saw him come in."

The artist paused and turned to Father Manuel. "Is this true?"

All eyes turned his direction.

"Yes." Father Manuel's voice caught in his throat. "It is."

"Come, sit." A woman led Father Manuel closer to Picasso. "Tell us what you saw."

Father Manuel relayed the story again of the bombers. Of the fighter planes machine-gunning the people of the town. Of the cries and even the scared confusion of animals running through the streets.

Glancing toward Picasso, Father Manuel noticed the master had a sketchbook in hand. His pencil moved rapidly as Father Manuel spoke.

"Tell me of the people, of their fear," Picasso said, not lifting his eyes to meet the priest's gaze.

Father Manuel continued, forgetting that he'd already told the story numerous times, forgetting that others listened in the room; he shared his story with an audience of one. He spoke the images that filled his mind of those he loved and cared for— those who had occupied his prayers—running from the terrors in the sky. He shared their pain until his own aching gripped his heart and caught the words in his throat, allowing only sobs to emerge in their place.

Philip shifted painfully in the narrow trench and wrapped himself in his blanket. Two others sat beside him—Charles and a man Philip hadn't met before, and didn't have the energy to get to know. Antony had been there earlier, but Philip hadn't paid much attention when he left.

This man next to Philip cursed, and he felt like doing the same, only for a different reason. He didn't know if the pain in his chest was from cold or fear. Not for himself. The way he felt now, he could take on a whole hillside of Fascists if given the chance. He feared what was happening to Sophie, where she was, what she faced. Were there bombings? Moors? He feared the unknown, and his fingers grasped the stock of his rifle tighter as he waited for the promised assault.

"You know why we're out here, don't you?" The man next to him spat. "There is no Fascist attack. They needed us to fill a hole in the lines. I heard the Spanish troops had to be withdrawn to suppress insurrection in Barcelona. Isn't that just like our Trotskyite friends? We're risking our butts on the front lines, and they don't understand that for the Republican cause to succeed they need to fight Franco, not each other."

"Sometimes I wonder if it will ever happen." Philip tilted his head back and gazed into the sky full of stars. They twinkled at him, and he imagined them as flames carried by runners crossing the sky.

"If what will happen?" the man asked.

"You know. All we're fighting for. I mean, it sounds great in a speech that we're 'helping the people's civil liberties, assisting workers, and spurring land reform.' " Philip lowered his voice to mimic the commanders who regaled them with never-ending speeches at every opportunity. "But they're still fighting—among themselves. Sometimes it seems as if they don't want to be saved."

"Yeah, like the old saying goes, you can lead a horse to water, but you can't make him drink." Charles ran a cloth over the barrel of his spotless rifle. "But at least maybe they'll catch the scent of water and get a thirst for it. You know what I mean."

Philip nodded. "I suppose I do. And I suppose the scent of water is something I can fight for. The rest I'll have to leave up to them."

Antony stumbled toward them, blinking into the lantern light. He smiled crookedly. "They have fresh bread back there. And hot coffee. I'll cover for you if you want to go."

Without checking to see if the other two wanted to go first, Philip clambered out of the ditch and mindlessly moved through the darkness. Among a row of olive trees, he found a line forming. News spread fast when it came to food and letters from home. He smiled ever so slightly as a cook ladled hot coffee into outstretched tin cups.

As Philip lifted the cup to his face and breathed in the scent of the coffee—real coffee, not that fake stuff they'd been drinking—he remembered Charles's words. Sophie, to him, was like the scent of water. For some reason, God had led him to her—or her to him, really. He knew now that if he had the chance, he would take the plunge and confess every emotion he held inside, holding nothing back.

Göring had called Ritter back to Germany, and Ritter had no choice but to comply. As he prepared to leave the base, word reached them of the most serious loss of the war. Republican fighters had intercepted a Junker 52 carrying seven fighter pilots being transferred to another base. All were killed when it was shot down. It was a horrible loss. These were pilots Ritter knew and respected. Pilots eager to find adventure in Spain. Pilots he'd never see again.

And as Ritter flew away at the bidding of the most powerful man in the military, one German phrase ran continually through his thoughts: *Wo gehobelt wird, da fallen Spähne.* Where wood is planed, shavings are bound to fall. Death and destruction came to those who killed and destroyed, and somehow Ritter had missed both. For some reason Ritter had been called away. For some reason destiny had spared him . . . again.

Perhaps destiny offered a great task worthy of Ritter's skills. Or maybe it was a form of punishment for the pain he'd caused. Because even though Ritter lived and others died, he had a feeling that destiny's greatest trick was forcing Ritter to live with the pain of being unable to obtain what—or *who*—his heart wanted above all else.

Back in Berlin, Ritter walked the street, telling himself to turn the other direction, to find something else—anything else—to do in the two hours before he met with Göring.

Anything but hunt down Isanna.

Not that finding her was hard. Though Isanna embraced all the freedom offered to women in New Germany, she was traditional in many ways—such as the weekly visit to the hair stylist and lunch with her grandmother afterward. Ritter had joined them for lunch once, and that was enough. The two women chattered on about the latest news of this budding romance, or that new baby, or who was last seen with whom. It was enough to make a man want to fling himself off the large balcony in the hotel lobby.

He slowed his steps as he neared the large hotel. The doorman tipped his hat as he opened the door for Ritter. He paused inside the entry, taking in the polished marble floors, men in suits, women in dresses and hats, suited bellhops carrying their things.

Ritter straightened the lapel of his military uniform, wishing for some new medal or badge to signify his service in Spain. Unfortunately, the majority of Germany knew little, if anything, of their exploits. There were rumors of the Spanish war, but little more. And even those who knew about the fighting believed Germany was there to train and support Spanish pilots. If they had only a glimpse into Ritter's mind, they'd know otherwise.

He moved toward the dining area with sure steps, careful not to favor his weak leg. No one questioned him as he moved into the dining room and slid into a small table near the entrance. His heart pounded as her laughter met his ears even before he spotted her. Following the sound of her voice, he spied her at the table with her grandmother and another young woman. They sipped cups of tea and leaned close as the waitress brought in trays of finger sandwiches and small cookies.

His stomach churned as he gazed at her. She was more beautiful than ever. Her long blonde curls that used to hang around her shoulders were pinned to the top of her head in a stylish coif. She wore a white lace blouse with a high collar, and her cheeks were flushed pink.

Ritter knew he should stand and walk away, never to confront her again. Yet he couldn't bear the thought of living his whole life without knowing if his love had been one-sided.

Waving away a waiter who approached with a silver carafe, Ritter strode toward Isanna's table. He had almost made it to her side when she lifted her eyes and met his. Her mouth gaped, and with a clatter her teacup crashed to the table, shattered, and splashed hot liquid on her companions. Squeals of disbelief spouted from their lips as they rose, pushing back from the table and grabbing white cloth napkins to wipe themselves. A flurry of activity erupted around them, service staff rushing to their aid.

Still Ritter stood without a word, watching with pleasure as tears filled Isanna's wide eyes.

"You're—you are . . . here." She covered her mouth with her hands, and Ritter noticed the ring on her finger.

"And you're married." He spat the words, eyeing the ring.

"Ritter, I—"

"Could you have not waited one month, two, for my body to get cold in the grave?"

"Please, let me explain." She tossed her napkin from her lap onto the table and pushed back, rising.

It was then that Ritter noticed her round stomach. His jaw dropped open as he looked down.

Isanna instinctively placed a hand over her growing form—a protective hand.

His fists clenched and he stepped toward her, searching her gaze.

Ashamed, she looked away, glancing at her grandmother, who was still wiping at the brown stain on her cream-colored dress. "Please, can we go somewhere to talk? I—I have so much to say. I need to tell you the *truth*. . . ."

"No words are needed, Isanna. I see how much I truly meant to you. As I said, you wasted no time playing house while I was away fighting . . . for you."

She reached her hand toward his shoulder, and he brushed it away.

Then he cursed and turned, striding from the room.

"Ritter, please." And with her words came a low moan, followed by sobs.

Ritter refused to turn. Refused to offer one word of comfort. She had made her bed; let her lie in it. His heart ached every day for what had become of his existence. Let her deal with her pain, as he was forced to. Let her go home to her husband tonight with anguish in her heart. But even then, he knew, it would hardly reflect the agony within his own soul.

Chapter Nineteen

$\mathcal{R}$itter pushed all thoughts of Isanna out of his mind as he followed the security officer into Hermann Göring's lush office. The large man sat behind a massive oak desk. His eyes focused on a map spread on the surface before him, yet Ritter could tell the general's ears listened for his approaching footsteps.

When Ritter came within ten steps, Göring's head lifted, and a small smile curled on his lips. "Well, there, my son, there's the man I've been eager to talk with. Please come in; have a seat. I've read the debriefs, but tell me . . . what is it like flying over Spain? Was it everything you expected?"

Ritter chose his words carefully as images filled his mind. Explosions, clouds of smoke and rubble, men and women falling under the spray of his machine gun. The helpless feeling as his airplane spiraled to the ground.

"Oh, no, Herr General. It is not what I expected, but more. Oh, so much more."

As he settled into the plush leather armchair, another face filled Ritter's thoughts. Sophie's warm smile. The way she cocked her head and lost herself as she focused on the canvas before her.

"The fighting is intense." Ritter crossed his arms over his chest. "And the enemy far more deceptive than any of us anticipated."

For the next few hours, Ritter told Göring details of the true war in Spain. He was shocked to learn his reports were different from the battle reports Göring received. Ritter had flown the planes. He knew how their aircraft compared to enemy planes. He'd seen firsthand which strategies worked and which failed.

Ritter left out a few details—not about his job as a pilot—but about how easy it had been during the month he was stranded to foster friendships with the enemy.

"You have done your job well. You even handled your time behind enemy lines with quick thinking and cunning." Göring rose from his chair and heaved his massive frame across the office to the wet bar, pouring both himself and Ritter a scotch.

Though usually not one to drink, Ritter swallowed it down, then watched Göring do the same.

"I am impressed with your quick thinking. It not only saved your life, but ushered you into enemy headquarters," Göring continued with a twinkle in his eyes. "Most airmen do a fine job following directions. Yet there are few who can work so well under pressure. There are few with quick enough wit and resourcefulness to turn the worst of circumstances into a win. That is why I have summoned you. I've been looking for a special man like you."

"You have another assignment for me in Spain?" Ritter leaned forward in his seat.

"Not exactly. I wish for you to retire your pilot's wings for a time. The wings, but not the knowledge of flying, nor the mechanics of the aircraft. Have you heard of the Abwehr, Germany's secret service?"

"A little. Aren't they the secret security forces—spies, if you will? Spies for our country and our Führer."

"Spies? I like that, a man who says it like it is." Göring rose and moved to the window, lifting the velvet curtain slightly to peer down into the Berlin street below.

Even from two stories up, Ritter could hear the busy sounds of automobiles, the whistles of traffic cops, the jiggle of the trolley bells. So different from Spain.

"Yes, Germans pride ourselves in our espionage efforts. And

some believe that more has been done for our New Germany behind the scenes than will ever be accomplished on the front lines. And, in the matter I'm requesting your help with, I tend to agree." Göring lifted one brow and locked eyes with Ritter.

Ritter squared his shoulders, refusing to look away. He knew Göring was sizing him up, and he determined to prove himself worthy.

"First, I must ask you," Göring continued. "Are you willing to give up all you have and know for a time? To give up flying, all contact with your uncle and any other important people in your life?"

"To die to all I know, is that what you ask?" Ritter leaned forward in his chair, resting his elbows on his knees.

"In a sense."

"And this mission, if you will—it will benefit you, benefit our Luftwaffe?"

"More than you can ever realize."

"Then count me in. Nothing matters to me now, except serving our Führer and our great country."

"Good. That was exactly the response I hoped for." Göring moved from the window and glanced at his watch. "But unfortunately, now is not the time to discuss this. My wife requests I be on time to dinner tonight. It seems she's having a dinner party for many important people." Göring chuckled. "More brass will be seated around the table than amongst our serving dishes."

"Tomorrow then? Should I meet you here again?"

"Pff, I will not consider such a thing. I wish for you to join me. Besides, there is someone I wish you to meet." Göring glanced at Ritter with a twinkle in his eyes. "Someone who could be very useful to your next assignment." Göring's deep voice almost purred.

"By the tone of your voice, I assume this isn't some military commander or the like?"

"No, not quite. But, son, I believe you won't be disappointed. She is quite lovely."

Ritter nodded and walked side by side with Göring through the offices of the German high command and toward the shiny black sedan waiting out front.

Ritter's mind churned as he wondered just what Göring had up his sleeve. And even though he was on German soil, it was hard for Ritter's mind to wrap around the fact that he wouldn't return to Spain. As of tomorrow, he'd have a new assignment.

It both delighted and troubled him that a female would be involved. For while they gave him ultimate pleasure, those creatures also caused the greatest pain in inner places, pain for which even his military training could not prepare him nor from which it could protect him.

The stallion moved under José's body with power and agility. It felt like home—not this place, but this saddle. José knew that before he led the others up into the mountains he needed to see just what awaited them; much had changed since the start of the war, and places once considered safe were no longer so.

With sure steps, Calisto moved up the hillside that José knew better than anyone. After ducking his head under low-lying branches, he came out of the forest to a small valley. The sun hit his face as they entered the area, and José flipped the reins ever so slightly to the right to bypass a fallen log.

Calisto tossed his head as if denying José's request and instead leapt over the log with ease.

"Oh, so you want to play?"

José clicked his tongue. Pressing his legs lightly against the stallion's side, he gave the signal for one of the most difficult moves taught to the Lippizzaners, and one José had perfected with Calisto. He tried the passage first, which was similar to a trot. With a gentle grace, Calisto held one front hoof and the opposite back hoof in the air for a split second. With José erect in the seat, it seemed as if the horse below him floated upon the green meadow grass. José's hair bounced against his forehead, and he closed his eyes, imagining he was in front of the adoring fans once again—just him and the horse dancing on the air.

Next he tried the piaffe. He gave the signal, and Calisto pranced in one spot. José imagined music, and Calisto must have too, since his movements were in perfect rhythm.

Finally, the pirouette. With grace Calisto lifted his forelegs and turned in a circle.

Falling back to all fours, Calisto whinnied. José patted his neck. "So you miss it too, I see. Too bad things like war have to get in the way of poetry on horseback."

Before leaving for Madrid, José had worked with Calisto on and off for eight years, mastering some of the most difficult moves. José had planned to go further, teaching the stallion tricks that few horses, even the best, would ever achieve. Yet instead of moving forward with training in the battle leaps, or what they called "airs above the ground" in Austria, he'd left Calisto behind, moving to Madrid and renewing his friendship with Michael.

"Beautiful, my friend. You perform just beautifully. You have not forgotten—nor have I," José whispered as he urged Calisto on through the mountain passes.

José knew that the moves he'd taught Calisto were actually moves of war. Centuries earlier, when a rider was attacked, his stallion would leap into the air over the enemies' heads. Some stallions even learned to strike out with their hooves from midair. José had only trained one other horse in such a way, and was thrilled by the raw power and control.

If only men could be trained and controlled as easily. If only their actions were as sure, he thought.

It took most of the morning for José to plot out their route to the pastures in the mountains beyond their property. Endless mountains that he hoped would provide them safety. It wasn't a perfect solution, but it would save the horses for a while.

Now, if he could only find help to get the horses up into the safe places where armies didn't fight. Depending on his father and Pepito was out of the question. Both were too old to walk very far, let alone guide the sometimes-temperamental stallions. He thought about traveling to Bilbao and finding Ramona, but he doubted his wife would leave the patients to care for a half-dozen horses. Though he loved her, and she loved him in many ways, she didn't understand his passion for the horses. Besides, he still wondered if danger would find him, even here. Once his motives for getting close to Michael were discovered, there would be many who wanted him dead. For his wife's safety, it was better she remain where she was.

If he had to, he'd do it alone, somehow. Anything to keep the horses from falling into Nationalist hands. He would not lose them to war . . . or dinner.

The sun was high in the sky by the time José made his way through the back pasture of their property toward the house and stables. He knew something was wrong when Pepito and his father met him at the door to the stables.

Calisto stopped before the door, and José dismounted. "Well, what is it? The Nationalists haven't broken through, have they?"

"No, nothing like that." His father glanced toward the house as if expecting to see someone there.

"You were out late last night." It was Pepito who spoke this time, removing his hat from his head and twisting it in his hands.

"I was burying a dead horse. Not an easy task to do by one's self."

"*Sí*. And you left early this morning," Pepito responded. "Juan and I didn't know where you were."

"Off to check out the mountain pastures. You should have guessed. My father should have guessed."

Pepito nodded. José knew he understood.

"We have company." José's father met his gaze, and José saw compassion there.

"A young girl," Juan continued. "She was in Guernica during the bombing. She came here looking for help."

José released the girth and pulled the saddle off Calisto. "A kid? What are we supposed to do, open an orphanage?"

José heard a whinny behind him and turned to see a *señorita*—not really a girl—leading two of the horses toward the stable. She chatted with the horses as they walked along, and José was awed by the way the two young horses had taken to her. Their shiny tails swung gently as they walked, and to José it looked as if they actually smiled at the feminine attention lavished upon them.

José's jaw dropped. "Now why is she here?" Then he crossed his arms and tilted his chin. "Don't tell me she came looking for Edelberto."

Pepito nodded his answer. Then he pointed to Juan. "*Sí*, and *he* said she could stay. He's as softhearted as a hen with her chicks."

"She has been with the horses all morning, asking all types of questions about their care," his father cut in. "She is a natural, as you can see."

José met his father's gaze, and though neither spoke, they both knew that perhaps she was just the answer José looked for.

Chapter Twenty

It was rather a dull evening, one filled with pomp and circumstance, in which little men in pressed uniforms boasted of the strength and skill of their troops and training. As if these officers were the ones flying across the skies or developing and using the new machines that would protect and provide for Germany.

Most disappointing was the fact that, even though Göring made sure Ritter was by his side at all times, he said nothing of Ritter's time in Spain or his exploits. This confused Ritter, especially when he knew Göring usually was eager to share news of the Luftwaffe with anyone who would listen.

It doubly confused Ritter when Göring introduced Ritter as an international consultant. But he just nodded his head in agreement and allowed Göring to do all the talking.

Ritter's questions of his new assignment fell into the back of his mind when Göring introduced him to Monica Schull. Though she was similar to Isanna in coloring and physique, she carried herself quite differently. Her eyes held an unusual intelligence, and she seemed bored with the prattle of the women around her. She eagerly engaged Ritter in conversation.

"So, Ritter Agler, *ja*. I've waited weeks to meet you. General Göring can speak of no one else."

She spoke with a smooth accent, which Ritter first thought to be English; but from the way she stood with a relaxed stance and nonchalant attitude, he quickly changed his mind and guessed she was visiting from the States.

"So how does it feel to have a perfect stranger thrust upon you like this?"

Her gaze traveled from the toe of his shined leather shoes to the top of his head. "Humph. I have a feeling you're far from perfect, stranger." She chuckled. "Although my uncle Hermann seems to think so from the way he speaks."

"Your uncle, really? I didn't know our general had American relatives. Does the Führer know?"

The woman's burst of laughter surprised him. "Please, sir, you surely know he's not really my uncle. He's an old family friend, one my father has worked with often."

"Really? In what fashion?"

"As a consultant like yourself, of course." The coyness in her answer suggested she rather enjoyed membership in Göring's inner circle.

Ritter cocked one eyebrow and tilted his head, hoping she'd expound.

Monica leaned in close and whispered to Ritter over her champagne glass. "He's interested in aeroplanes, like yourself. In fact, he works at a manufacturing plant in New York."

"Really?" Instantly he was intrigued.

In Spain Ritter had spent his first months helping ground crews assemble their planes from a stack of boxes, joining piece by piece. Yet he knew better than to mention anything of Spain, or what his international consulting involved. He also knew better than to tell this woman how much her mannerisms reminded him of another American woman—one he'd lied to and should have killed when he had the chance, to keep her from helping the enemy. And, perhaps, to keep Sophie from haunting his thoughts.

"As I told Uncle, I'm sure my father would love to meet you. You have a similar passion. And a similar goal."

Ritter knew in due time he'd learn exactly what this goal was, but for now he knew better than to waste such an opportunity. "That would be nice. I'm eager to meet your father. But honestly, do you think we should waste the best part of the evening on talk of work?"

"The best part?"

Ritter took the woman's hand and spun her slightly, causing her champagne to slosh over the edge of her glass. She turned a full circle, and he still held her hand as she stopped before him. "Such a beautiful woman and an empty dance floor."

Without a word, the American placed her glass on the nearest silver table and allowed him to lead her to the floor.

As Ritter led her around the room, he thought again of Isanna, wishing she could see another woman in his arms. Wanting her to feel the same ache he felt. Yet also wondering how closely his new assignment would allow him to work with this American, and just what personal benefits he'd receive.

José breathed a heavy sigh as he led the last horse to the corral. And though his footsteps were quick, the young woman, Petra, stayed by his side.

He rubbed his temples, feeling a headache start to radiate just above his ears. Did the girl's questions never cease?

"When did it all start?" she asked. "How was it that these horses were chosen?"

He pondered her question, then took in a breath. "Well, in 1562 the emperor of Austria was looking for good horses. He found them in Spain. The Spanish horses were fast. They were strong enough to carry a soldier in heavy armor. They could jump high and make quick turns in small places. So he bought as many as he could and took them back to Austria."

"Where to?" The soft breeze blew strands of Petra's hair into her face, and she brushed them away.

"The emperor bred them at his farm at Kladrub. After ten years, he started the Spanish Riding School in Vienna." Then he hurried on, anticipating her next question. "The point of the school is to learn how to handle horses and how to fight on horseback."

"So you know German?"

"*Ja,*" he said with a smile. "And you?"

"No, only English and a little French. Languages bore me." She ran her hand down the horse's thick mane. "You're not planning to use *these* horses for battle, are you? It seems like the sound of fighting grows louder every day."

"No, of course not—even though that is what they were originally bred for. They are too valuable—"

I'd rather die than see them killed, he wanted to add.

"I've heard of the horses from Austria, though I never imagined seeing one," she continued, kicking at a pinecone in her path. "What is Lipizza like?"

"I've only been to the school in Austria, not to Lipizza, but I hear the land around the farm has rocky limestone. This actually helps the horses develop strong hooves and bones. Lipizza also has a harsh climate. They say it produces a hardy horse."

"Are you saying that hardship strengthens us?"

José cocked his head as he peered at the young girl, amazed to hear such wisdom coming from one so young. "I was speaking of horses and not men," he said after a minute.

"Of course," she commented, rushing ahead to open the gate.

Though José had considered getting to know the girl a little better before asking her for help, the pounding of the artillery caused his chest to tighten, and he knew he didn't have time to wait.

He also knew that heading further into the mountains meant journeying farther away from Ramona. With each step he felt his anger toward Michael build. If it hadn't been for Michael, José would have more time with his wife. And perhaps Ramona would have spent more time with the horses and learned to love them as he did. Perhaps she would be by his side even now.

Instead of giving voice to his anger, José shoved it down deeper, hoping it would remain there. Yet the small pricks of heat at the back of his neck told him his emotions remained too close to the surface.

Despite that, he focused on the task at hand.

So as they headed back toward the house, he turned to Petra, digging his hands into his pants pockets. "I need your help." He hoped she understood the urgency in his voice.

"What do we need to do? I can clean out the stalls if you'd like."

"I have to move the horses. We need to lead them away from this place. It's the only way to keep them safe."

"I agree. I remember my tutor telling me about how the Lipizzaner horses were protected before the Great War. The royal family saw that the Lipizzaner herd was in danger, and they decided to split them up. They knew if the enemies captured the horses at one place, others would be saved somewhere else."

José looked closer at the young woman, wondering how she could know such things. It was obvious she wasn't a peasant, even though she dressed like one. Well, they'd have time to swap stories once they made it to safety high in the hills.

"You are correct. They split them into three groups. Some of the mares and breeding stallions went to a farm near Vienna. The foals went to Kladrub. A third group of breeding stock stayed at Lipizza."

"Personally I would pick Vienna. When do we leave?"

Though she sounded serious, a glance at her smile told him she was being humorous.

"No, *señorita*, it is the movement I speak of, not the location. I need you to help me move these horses, but we need to go in two groups—in case one of us gets captured."

"But I have never ridden a horse like this. Nor do I feel worthy to protect such creatures."

"I am sorry, but that is not what matters."

"Why not?"

"I have no other choice. The job is yours."

Petra glanced at José with a smile as she placed her foot in the stirrup and threw her other leg over the horse with ease.

"Let me guess; you have been tutored in riding too?"

Petra shrugged her shoulders. "Some."

"Watch out," he warned, cautiously releasing the bridle. "This one is jumpy. It usually takes two years for a young stallion to fully trust his rider. That is why at the riding school only experienced riders are allowed to work with the young horses. It is important for them to get to know and trust each other."

Petra ran her fingers through the horse's mane. Even in these hard times the stallion was well cared for, and his mane glistened under the sun. "What is his name?"

"Erro. It's an old family name."

"And it sounds like *arrow* in English." She nodded. "I like it. Has this one been trained much?"

"Enough to know basic commands from its rider."

Erro moved awkwardly under her, as if he were getting used to having a rider on his back once again.

"He is a little clumsy still," José commented.

"Yes, but I know your horse can do more." She peered down at José and allowed the horse to walk her around at his leisure. "I can tell even by the way Calisto feeds in the pasture that he is well trained. It is almost as if his cocky attitude shines through even when he is at rest."

"*Sí*, but it does not matter now. All that matters is getting them to safety." José walked beside them. "Look at him. He's starting to get more comfortable. Tap your heels ever so slightly, and let us see how Erro responds."

Petra did, and the horse immediately started into a soft trot. She bounced ever so slightly in the saddle. "Good boy. Good Erro. Look at you."

She turned the reins, and the horse turned sharply. With the quick movement, she felt herself sliding in the seat.

"Easy," José called behind her. "He is trained well. The slightest nudge will move him in any direction you want to go."

Petra turned her head toward José, and she couldn't help laughing as he approached, excitement glowing from his face like a father watching his baby's first steps. "Well, I don't know who will lead whom, but if you have a plan to get these horses up in the hills, count me in."

She flipped the reins slightly, and suddenly the stallion bolted upright under her, kicking his front feet high into the air. Before she knew it, the saddle was no longer beneath her, and she flew through the air, letting out a scream.

She landed first on her hip, then on her back with a *thud*. Her head smacked the ground, and pain seemed to shoot through her from every direction. She tried to suck in a breath, but nothing happened. Sitting upward, she reached to José for help.

Instead he ran to the horse, attempting to settle him.

Pepito and Juan must have heard her cries, because both hobbled toward her.

A shooting pain filled Petra's chest, and finally her breath came.

The two older men kneeled beside her.

"Look at him," she managed to spout. "He didn't even check to see if I was all right."

Juan shook his head. "If you spend any time with José, well . . . you must know . . ."

Before Juan had a chance to finish, José strode over. "What did you do? You scared Erro!" he shouted, leaning down close to her face.

"I scared *him*?" Petra managed. "I'm the one on the ground."

"The horse should toss you off for giving him such confused signals. What were you thinking?"

"I did not know I was giving him any signals! You just told me to get on, remember?"

Without responding, José grabbed the reins, and with angry steps he led Erro to the nearest corral.

Juan clicked his tongue. "It's not you he shouts at," he mumbled. "You are only a substitute."

"Well, I would hate to be the person he *is* mad at."

"Me too," Juan said. "And just think, that person used to be his closest friend."

Chapter Twenty-One

𝒜 lone candle flickered on her bedside table, and Petra wondered how long it would take before the sun rose again. She hadn't slept more than a few minutes at a time. Her mind raced, trying to take in all that was happening to her and rethink all she knew to be true.

She thought of José. At one moment he was cheerful and kind, the next he was yelling at her for being tossed off the back of Erro. She wanted to be angry at him, but couldn't. Mostly she wondered what had caused him so much pain.

Above José's shirt collar was a jagged scar on his neck. Whatever happened to him had most likely been life-threatening. Yet he spoke to the horse gently, as Petra had witnessed her father doing with her mother on numerous occasions—with tenderness that only came from a heart of love.

She rose from the bed and leaned her forehead against the window, looking down into the village below. Beyond the village was the edge of the sea. And though no lights could be seen in the town, the moonlight on the water cast a lovely glow.

Petra had thought things would be easier once she left Guernica. Even though Edelberto wasn't here, there were two old, sweet men who seemed to enjoy the distraction of watching over her.

Yet instead of causing her to forget, this momentary sense of safety caused memories of the past to overwhelm her. They danced about her brain, reminding her of another world, one in which she was surrounded by family, not alone. Not so very alone.

She looked down at the long nightgown she'd been given. It reminded her of one of her first memories. Spring had come, and Easter was a time of celebration in her village. Her brothers had been in suits, and Petra wore a new, store-bought dress. Her father's eyes had sparkled as he lined up his offspring to get a closer look. He nodded with approval, stopping before each one and whispering a secret into their ears.

His grin broadened as he'd reached Petra. "My daughter, you are the most beautiful girl in the world. As lovely as the lilies in the field," he'd whispered.

As she grew older, and became uncomfortable with herself, she always thought back to her father's words. She'd clung to them every time she felt uncertain. *My father thinks I'm the most beautiful girl in the world*, she'd murmur to herself whenever those unsure feelings arose.

But what did that matter now? Who cared that she was pretty, or that her family had come from a long line of noble people? It mattered not at all. The things that mattered now were if she had enough to fill her stomach and a safe place to rest for the night. And now there were the horses. They were a nice distraction—a way to help her forget all she'd lost.

Petra touched the bruise on her thigh and winced, the blue flesh still sore from her tumble. Yet it was a small pain compared to the greater one she carried inside. The more she thought about her father's kind eyes, the more her head throbbed, and she soon felt sick to her stomach.

All she wanted was to curl into a ball on this borrowed bed, throw the covers over her head, and never have to remember or hurt again.

❖ ❖ ❖

During the summer, the sun was well up in the sky by seven o'clock in the morning. It reached its heat by one or two in the afternoon, but few were on the street during those siesta hours.

Sophie had never known what it was like to rest during the afternoon siesta. When she painted, her brush didn't pause just because the clock ticked a certain hour. And since she was an American, no one thought it unusual to find her sitting in the kitchen with a book and a glass of cold well water during the daily siesta.

From her place near the kitchen, she noticed Cesar sitting outside the front door. He reminded her of an American cowboy with his black moustache curled up at the ends and his black hat pulled low over his eyebrows. He'd arrived just a few hours ago, along with another man from Madrid. He whittled a piece of wood as he puffed on his hand-rolled cigarette.

Because of their arrival, Michael didn't take Sophie to his family home as promised. Nor did he tell her the secret about his family that she'd wondered about through the night. Instead he spent more time talking with the other men, beyond Sophie's range of hearing.

Months ago Sophie wouldn't have thought much about Cesar. Now she thought he must be a guard of sorts, making sure no one entered or left the house without his knowledge. And she was certain that the other man from Madrid had something to do with the gold. From the first time she saw the tall, lean Paulo, she knew he was up to no good.

Sophie watched Cesar for a few minutes more, and her stomach churned as she worried about just how she could leave the house if she ever did find anything to tell Walt. Her instructions were to find her way to the closest church with any information she thought worthwhile, but how could she do that if she couldn't even walk around the house at leisure? Surely, if she made the excuse that she wanted to go for a stroll, Michael would join her or insist on an escort. Things outside the home were far from safe.

Sophie rose and strode again to Hector's matador cape, remembering her first day in Madrid and Michael's comments. *All honorable young women have an escort through town,* he had said. Now she knew even better why the men of Spain wanted to keep the women accountable—not only for their safety, but perhaps to see to it that the women didn't innocently come upon what the men hoped would never be found out. For as much as the men spoke of their wives, they also talked of their mistresses and other sordid affairs.

While the men slumbered, except Cesar, Sophie returned to her room and pulled the Bible from her satchel.

February 29, 1867
Dear Jeremiah,

Sometimes when I'm working around the house or shopping at the market, I find myself carrying on a conversation with you in my mind. I think you would be uninterested in the daily events of the market, but if you were here, you would love to visit the mine.

The mine is not only a place for Mateo to work, it is a place for him to fight. He battles with new technology, although he was the first to welcome the idea. He fights against extended workdays. He fights for his income. He fights the man who desires to take everything from him, claiming a need for a greater profit.

Some men in the mine are skilled and highly paid. These blasters develop a great amount of experience. They use dynamite and powder. They work in the opening of tunnels and galleries. Mateo hopes someday to rise to this position.

Mateo is a picador, which in English means hewer. He cuts the coal at the face using a pick. Because the seams are usually inclined, he attacks the coal while lying on his back. He has an assistant who helps with timbering and removing cut coal and waste from the stall, but Mateo rarely talks about the young man.

Once, he had an assistant that he loved and cared for as much as a younger brother. Assistants start at the ages of ten or eleven, some even younger. Mateo's first boy died in an accident, and now he refuses to speak of him. In some ways I feel as if there are parts of my husband's heart as hard to penetrate as the black coal.

The letter ended there, and Sophie wondered what had kept the woman from continuing to write. Had her husband arrived home? Had she been overwhelmed with emotion?

The sound of men's voices filtered to her room, and Sophie

quietly opened the door and moved down the hallway. Although they could not see her as she pressed herself against the white-washed wall, she could hear every word.

"So, is everything going as planned?" It was the voice of the tall stranger, Paulo.

"Yes, I've heard from my contact, and all is well." Michael spoke with authority. "The shipment is safe, and I plan to visit Madrid soon. Just a short stop, of course."

"Madrid?" the man asked. "Good. Maria Donita asks about you."

Michael's words were interrupted by heavy footsteps. Before Sophie had a chance to turn and hurry back to her room, a large hand caught her arm and pulled her into the room. All eyes were upon her, and a voice boomed near her ear.

"Is this what you call secure?" It was Cesar's voice.

Sophie refused to fight him or even look Cesar's direction. She refused to wince as his hand gripped on her shoulder.

Michael turned to her, a look of confusion filling his face. "Sophie, were you . . . spying on us?"

"What are you talking about?" She tried to hide her trembling hands by pressing them together and against her chest. "I was walking from my room when I heard someone mention Maria." She couldn't stop the words from tumbling out, or the tears that followed. "I've been afraid to ask you . . . but now it's confirmed." Sophie pulled against Cesar's grasp, but his fingers only tightened.

Michael stood. "Let go of her."

Cesar released his grasp, and Sophie rubbed the sore marks left by his fingers.

Michael lifted Sophie's chin with a soft hand. "Sophie, I'm sorry, I didn't mean to accuse you. What are you talking about? What were you afraid to ask me?"

She glanced at the other men. She realized that in order to save her skin she was going to have to ask the question that had been burning inside her.

"In Madrid." She sucked in a breath. "At your funeral, I overheard two women talking. . . . They said that Maria was pregnant . . . with your child. Michael, is it true? Are you in love with her? Do you have a child?"

She watched as the color drained from Michael's face. Then the silence of the room was interrupted by Paulo's laughter.

"Woman problems? Oh, dear friend, it seems they cannot escape you. . . ." Paulo turned to Cesar and patted his shoulder. "She is not a spy, but a woman scorned. Yet . . . I do not know which is worse." He laughed again.

"Sophie, can we talk about this in private?" Michael's green eyes focused on hers.

She took a step back and pulled her face from his touch. "Answer me, Michael," she said, narrowing her eyes.

"I was seeing Maria for a while, before you arrived in Spain. A month before you came, I broke things off. We were not lovers. But you are correct; Maria was with child. She had a son just two weeks ago, but he is not mine."

Sophie cocked her head.

"That is the truth," he hurriedly said. "She carried the child of a banker, and they are married now. If you don't believe me, then we can see them when we go to Madrid. I'll introduce you to Emilio, her husband."

Michael turned to Paulo. "You are right. Woman troubles. Would you excuse us for a moment?"

Taking her hand, he led her out the back door to the patio. After shutting the door behind himself, he turned to her. "I'm sorry, *Divina*. So sorry you had to find out this way. I wish I had done things differently while we were apart."

"Michael, did you think I didn't know that you were involved with someone here? A woman always knows these things. I could read between the lines in your letters."

The lies spilled out of Sophie, and she felt her heart pounding. She hadn't known, of course. If she had, she surely wouldn't have come—but she couldn't tell him that. She refused to let him know the depth of the pain he brought upon her.

"I suspected it," she continued, crossing her arms tight to her chest, "but I ignored the signs because I knew you'd have to make a choice once I arrived."

"*Divina*. If I hurt you . . ." He placed a hand on her cheek.

She stepped farther from his touch. "You think you hurt me?

Well, you can't. Because I made the decision not to hurt a long time ago."

"Sofía . . . this wasn't how this day was supposed to turn out. I . . . I went to town and found some things for you. I know how hard it is for you to face everything that's happening when you don't have a chance to express yourself with your paints."

He turned her toward the overgrown garden, and for the first time she noticed an easel and canvas set up under an overgrown olive tree, just beyond the patio.

She opened her mouth and felt her heart do a double beat within her chest. Then she turned back to Michael and wondered if what he said about Maria was the truth—and if all the things he'd done that had hurt her had actually been intended to protect her, just as he said.

Chapter Twenty-Two

As she lay in bed that night, Sophie remembered the first time she really looked at art from the eyes of an artist. When she was a child, she thought that if a scene or a person looked "real," then the artist had done his job. Good art consisted of pictures she could understand—Monet's idyllic garden scenes or Leonardo da Vinci's portraits.

As she began to study art, and became a painter herself, Sophie's perspective changed. It was a change as vivid as looking at a single red poppy in comparison to a field of poppies. The art hadn't changed, but she'd gotten closer and noticed more of the intimate details.

The same was true of Spain, of the war, and of Michael especially. He hadn't changed, but she had. Because of her assignment, she took in every detail and found him to be more real and complex than she'd previously thought. He was kind and respectful to the men he interacted with, and they in turn asked him for advice. He wasn't raised solely in Spain, but she could tell he felt like one of Spain's sons. And the way he treated her lately . . . his tenderness and care reminded her of all she had longed for when she first came to Spain. Yet when his mind focused on other matters, it was easy for him to push her off to the side. It seemed he could only deal with one of his loves at once—either Spain or her. With each day her eyes of understanding deepened. And in a way, Sophie felt she knew Michael better than before.

Strangely enough, Sophie's perspective on herself had changed, too. As she noted her every action and reaction, she realized how often in the past she'd let her emotions affect her. Now she was forced to do just the opposite—unless an emotional outburst was the best response.

Her cheeks grew red every time she considered the way she'd reacted in front of the men that afternoon. It had worked for her advantage, this time. Once she was caught listening, it helped her cover to act like a lovesick girl. But from now on, she had to be more careful. Sophie knew she could display no emotion until she concluded it was the best one.

Even though she regretted looking so childish in front of the group, she knew the information Michael allowed to slip was of vital importance. Maria had married a banker—who worked perhaps at the very bank that had previously held the gold.

If the gold were moved, those inside the bank would be involved. And when a simple man, even a key bank employee, was in love with a beautiful woman like Maria Donita, any secrets he knew would be hers. In the Bible, Sophie knew, Samson had given away his secret to an alluring woman who confessed her love. Would a Spanish banker be any stronger?

Still, she didn't understand why Maria's sister would lie about Maria's pregnancy. Unless it wasn't a lie at all. And marrying the banker was simply another way for Maria to cover up the truth . . . and get the information she needed for Michael.

Petra sat under the shady tree watching José work with the horses. She had dozed off for just a minute, and awoke with almost a sweet taste in her mouth . . . as if she eaten the sweet images and digested them into her soul. She didn't dream of a handsome lover, but of a handsome land. A land under cultivation, with earth and sky, leaves and stalks, olives, orange groves, creeks and ditches. And she knew forgetting would never be possible.

Her family's large house in La Mancha had overlooked the hills, a winding river, and the small white walls and thatched roofs of the workers' houses. In her dreams, the sights mingled with the scents. She even dreamt of the friendly greetings of peasant men and women as they ambled over the land they knew so well. It was a pleasant dream.

Such images were commonplace growing up, but she no longer took them for granted. Instead, she carried them like a photograph inside a pocket in her mind. Yet she hoped that as time went on, like any photos they would fade, grow thin, and crack. Maybe then the pain would ease.

The images visited her too easily. The eggplants in straw baskets. The clusters of red tomatoes. The braids of garlic hanging in the pantry. Her family in their fine clothes gathered around the table.

Yet some things had already slipped away, and as she sat under the tree, she realized she'd missed the first Sunday of May. If she had been home, she would have watched the peasants whitewash their houses, as they did every year. To them, it was a tangible vision of renewed life in Christ. It was as if the white radiating from their homes would somehow make up for all the dark sins they carried in their hearts.

Not that she was any better. The only difference was that Petra did no whitewashing. Instead she covered all her frailties and insecurities with a smile.

Every day as she walked to school, Petra had smiled at everyone she passed. The villagers often asked how her father was and told her to give him their regards. She always replied the same, "Oh, thank you. My father is well." Then she relayed their messages and watched his face light up in a smile.

Not that the people had truly cared. They'd killed her father at the first opportunity. But maybe it was her smile that had saved her life. They could have searched for her and found her. Yet for some reason they hadn't seemed as intent on killing her as they had the others.

She glanced down at the simple skirt and dark blue blouse she wore to protect her secret. She felt safe with these men, but what about the others she would encounter? What would happen if they learned her identity?

She studied José and again was reminded of the man who cared for the horses at her father's estate, in his trim suit and smart leather gloves. The man back home seemed to be the same age as José, in his late twenties or early thirties. But José had lines around his eyes that told her he had seen much for his age. Amazingly, those lines softened around the horses, as if they helped him to forget.

Today José wore a cap that reminded her of a Hollywood gangster.

"Is everything going well?" he called to her, noting she had awakened.

"*Sí*. It is well." She crossed her legs and spread her tattered skirt over the ground. Though José hadn't apologized, she could tell by the way he looked at her he was sorry for yesterday's events.

He approached and squatted down before her. "I am going to Bilbao today. I need to find my wife, make sure she is well, and see if she will go into the mountains with us."

"Your wife?" Petra sat up straighter.

"Yes . . . Ramona. She is a nurse. I will be back before nightfall."

"And if you aren't?"

"If I don't return, it means the Nationalists have broken through the lines. In that case, take Erro and ride into the mountains. Untie Rafa and Lope. I think they will follow without straying. Hide until I come to you."

"What about Calisto?"

José shook his head. "No, he is too strong willed. Too stubborn."

"Oh, so he needs someone more like himself to ride him to safety." Petra grinned.

"*Sí*, that is right. Exactly." And with a smile and nod, José strode away.

Ramona glanced up from the hospital bed, expecting to see more aid workers carrying men on stretchers. With the front lines nearing, there were no field stations, and medics brought the injured soldiers directly to the hospital. Overworked and exhausted nurses and doctors now worked on patients who would have died if the hospital were any farther back. Worse yet, the medical staff lacked critical supplies to care for the men—most of whom were terribly wounded, all in severe shock.

Instead of seeing another stretcher, Ramona sucked in a breath as she saw her husband standing in the doorway. He looked sun-kissed and healthy compared to the dozens of white-faced men lining the walls. She bolted to his arms, and José wrapped his hands around her waist, pulling her close. He was strong again—fully recovered from his injuries.

She pulled back and studied his face. She wanted to tell him a hundred different things—share her heart concerning the war, confess her love, tell José how much she missed him and longed for him—but other words spilled out first.

"How are the horses, José? Are they well?"

His face fell, and he glanced away. "Then you knew where I went?"

"I knew from the first minute you said you wouldn't be traveling to Bilbao with me . . . though you have been very close this whole time, have you not?"

José's eyes darted to hers, then to the injured men again, as if it was easier to look upon their pain than hers. "Yes, the property is not too far from here. That is why I have come. To make sure you are well. And to take you with me. I have found a way out of this valley, into the mountains. We will be safe there."

"Oh, José." She glanced into his face and saw such hope there. "You think those horses will save you? Save us? Is that your excuse for going there . . . for doing all you can to save them? They are animals. When will you understand that?" She waved her hand around the room, motioning to the injured soldiers. "How can I leave these men to help four-legged creatures?"

Ramona made the sign of the cross. "Heaven forbid I ever leave the duties our Lord has called me to."

"It is not only the horses I worry about." José's voice was sharp. "I have come to take you to safety."

"Oh, dear man." She patted his cheek, smiling into his dark gaze. "I know you care. And I will not compare. But I just cannot do it. I cannot go."

José took her hand and pulled her to a side room that held surgical equipment. He pushed her softly against the wall, then placed both hands on her face. "Look at me, Ramona. I know there are injured men. But there will always be more. Let others care for them. Before long this town will not be safe. You are my wife. It is my duty to care for you. I have found a way to safety for us. When the Nationalists break through—"

"*If* they break through," she interrupted, "then I will worry about that. I am sorry, José. I love you, but I cannot leave. And if you truly knew the woman you married, you would not ask this of me."

"And if you knew my heart, and trusted it, you would know what I plan is for the good of all." José shrugged. "Although I have to say I am not surprised. I just wanted to give you a chance. Give us a chance to be together."

Ramona pulled back from his touch. "I cared for your injuries. I helped you heal. How could I deny that to others?"

"I suppose you cannot. But I hate leaving you like this."

"And I hate being left." Ramona wrapped her arms around herself as if giving herself courage for the words she was about to say. "But I suppose we have come to an impasse. We both have a calling, José. How can we turn our backs on those things . . . the things we care for the most?" Ramona tried to hide the pain in her voice. But from the look in José's eyes, she could tell he was not fooled. And she saw the same heartache she felt reflected in his look.

Sophie glanced into the backyard where a tangled but fascinating garden needed rescuing. Who knew how many generations ago it had been planted? But judging from the daisies that grew in every direction, leggy and untamed, they had taken over and ruled this patch of dirt for some time. Ivy crept along the back wall of the house and wrapped around the trunks of olive trees. The trees stretched out a protective canopy over the flowers, like a lover spreading a blanket of tranquility over his bride.

The strange thing was that instead of having the urge to paint the scene, Sophie had an unimaginable desire to tame it. Everything in her life was out of control—her duties, her thoughts, her emotions. She had information she needed to get out, and no idea how to do that either. She needed to feel some measure of control—to put something in order.

She noted a small shed in the back corner of the yard. From the look of the rusty hinges, the door hadn't been opened in years. The door gave a squeak of protest as she tugged it open and peeked inside. Everything was covered by a layer of dust and cobwebs. Noting a small bucket of tools on the ground, she poked around until she found a pair of pruning shears. They were slightly rusty, but they'd do the trick.

First she attacked the dead twigs on the trees. If only Spain's wayward ideals and power-hungry rulers could be tamed as easily as dead branches and leggy shoots. Only then could the new, fresh life grow.

As she worked, she thought of home. Only a block from where her father managed one of the finest hotels in Boston, the park of Boston Commons had been like a second home to her. She loved exploring the grounds and hearing how the land had been donated so that everyone in the city, from the mayor to the lowest servant, could raise livestock for his own use. If only Spain could grasp that freedom and equality.

Those thoughts propelled her attack on the overgrown plants. Sophie didn't know how many hours had passed, but by the time the sun was lowering in the sky, she was sweaty and dirty, and her whole body ached from her unaccustomed stooping, stretching, pulling, and hacking. Wiping her brow with the sleeve of her blouse, she stepped back and appraised her work. A smile spread across her face as she took in the look of new life that she had breathed into the old garden.

Tucking the pruning shears under her arm, she hobbled over to the shed, rubbing a sore spot on her back. She opened the door again, noticing how the afternoon light now beamed directly into the room. Sophie moved to put the shears back into the bucket, and then paused. A large wooden box with a lid sat on the left side of a shelf in front of her. Although it looked as old as the others on the shelves, there was no layer of dust. Looking closer, with the added light, she also noted the faintest footprints across the ground toward it.

Sophie stepped into the shed and reached for the box. Glancing behind her, she made sure no one was there. Still, she shut the door slightly, giving herself just enough light. Sophie pulled the box from the shelf, placed it at her feet, opened the lid, and gasped.

Inside were stacks of photos, obviously Michael's. The one on top was of a ship in the harbor. Underneath that was a picture of a young man Sophie didn't know. She moved to look at yet another.

She stopped herself, noting the haphazard way they'd been laid out in the box. To the common observer it would seem as if someone had just tossed them in. Yet she knew Michael too well. Michael did not toss anything. She remembered again how Walt had showed her how to place a piece of thread across the zipper of her satchel to tell if it had been disturbed. These photos, she had no doubt, had been laid out in this pattern for that very reason.

Sophie bit her lip and returned the top two photos exactly as she found them, then returned the lid and placed the box back on the shelf as close to its original position as she could remember. Then she backed up and retraced her steps, hoping she had not left any marks.

Walt had told her more than once that it wasn't her job to dig through any information or leads she found. Instead, she just needed to inform her contact where it was. Sophie just hoped her eagerness hadn't messed things up.

She readjusted the shears in the bucket and left the shed. And this time as she glanced at the garden she saw something else— clear evidence that she had ventured where she didn't belong, and touched and seen what she had no right to know.

Chapter Twenty-Three

*P*etra sat on the corral rail watching Erro prance about and laughing at his antics. It wasn't until she heard a man's laughter merge with hers that she realized Pepito had walked up beside her.

"It seems he has a crush on you. He is showing off."

Petra tucked a strand of hair behind her ear. "*Sí*, I like him, too. I always wanted a horse of my own."

"Oh, so you think he is yours now?" Pepito lifted one bushy, gray eyebrow and peered up at her.

"No, but I still like to imagine it." She hopped off the rail and plucked a long blade of grass growing near the fence post, twirling it in her fingers. "I have also decided that once this war is over I will follow in José's footsteps and train horses."

"Really, now? The training of a stallion requires long and careful planning. Highly bred and intelligent horses make great demands on the skill and understanding of their trainers. They require abundant patience and careful treatment."

Petra smirked. "Are you saying I am not patient?"

Pepito glanced at the saddle perched on the fence rail. "Going somewhere?"

"Well, I did get things ready. Just in case. You never know when the enemy will break through the lines." She shrugged.

"Yes, that could happen. But does the horse trust you?" Pepito asked. "You can saddle him, but do you truly believe he will let you lead him far from all he knows? The more he understands your character, the more likely Erro will follow your lead."

Pepito whistled between his teeth, and the stallion's ears pricked up. Then with a happy trot, the horse approached the older man.

"Let him know you're not upset due to yesterday's tumble," encouraged Pepito. "Give him a pat on the neck and show him you are friendly."

Petra did, smiling at the warmth of the horse's muscular neck under her hand.

Pepito walked to a nearby tree and pulled at the stalks of tall grass growing around its base. He approached the horse and held out a handful. Erro tugged the strands of green alfalfa from the old man's hands.

"*Sí*, I can tell by the look in his eyes that he understands all is forgiven," he commented.

Petra walked to the tree and pulled two large handfuls. Returning to the corral, she held them out to Erro. His black lips eagerly gathered the next mouthful. He finished all she had pulled and whinnied as if asking for more.

Petra opened her palms, showing him she had none, and Erro nuzzled them. He then neighed with a shake of his head. Finally, he struck the ground with an impatient hoof.

Petra looked to Pepito. "Shall I get more?"

He shook his head. "No, not yet. Just wait."

Petra watched, and the horse locked eyes with her; then he stepped backward a couple of paces and bowed down on his knees. Petra sucked in a breath. Then laughter spilled from her lips.

"*Sí*, now you can give him more." Pepito clapped his hands, and Erro stood to all fours. "And I encourage you to continue to feed him, pet him, and stay a constant presence. War horses are trained to dedicate themselves to their riders, and someday you may need him to do just that."

Sophie stared at her plate of baked fish and fresh tomatoes, forcing herself to take a bite even though her stomach knotted at what she must do next. Seldom a day passed when a group of five or six men didn't meet in the back patio after dinner. And Sophie counted on that happening this evening.

No one ever invited her to this gathering, and Michael had explained once that these men helped him with his work. She figured it had more to do with the theft of gold than with his duties at the newspaper.

She needed to talk to her contact about her suspicion. To tell him about Maria's husband and Michael's connection with them both. To tell him about the photographs in the shed.

"Sophie, I see you didn't get much painting done today. But the backyard looks better than I have seen it in years." Though Hector's words were kind, his gaze pierced her.

"I'm sorry; I should have asked first. I just got this crazy idea. . . ." She felt the heat rising to her cheeks. "Well, it seemed like a fun thing to do at the time, but, boy, does my back ache." She rubbed it, feigning laughter.

Hector nodded and chuckled, but she saw him exchange a look with Michael.

"It was thoughtful, Sophie, but unnecessary. It appears we won't be around much longer," Michael said. "We'll be leaving for Madrid in two days. Our friends here have found a way through the lines, to safety."

"But your family's home. I thought we were going there. Does this mean we will not get to visit?"

Michael sighed. "I am afraid not, and I did want to show you our family's most prized possession."

Sophie's eyes widened. "It sounds exciting."

Michael lifted his glass of wine and sloshed it around, winking at her over the rim as he took a sip. "Tomorrow perhaps. I'll tell you about it, about *them*, then. There are a few more arrangements for our trip we need to make tonight."

Sophie smiled, then yawned. "I understand. I'm thinking about turning in early. This Spanish custom of one late night after another is leaving me ragged. Unless you need me for something?"

"Not at all. I see dark circles under your eyes. Get some rest, and I'll see you at breakfast."

She stood, kissed him on the cheek, and ran her fingers down his shoulder, giving his arm a squeeze. Michael gazed up at her adoringly, and she blew a kiss over her shoulder as she strode down the hall to her room.

Once inside, Sophie lit the lamp and acted as if she were getting ready for bed. She took the camera from her satchel and placed it in the window—a sign to the person who watched that she had a message she needed to relay. And instead of brushing out her hair, she twisted it into a bun and tucked it under a scarf. Then she climbed into bed and waited.

The window was open, and she could hear the low murmur of voices carrying from the back patio. Minutes ticked past, and although Sophie still couldn't make out their words, the voices rose in volume. Soon laughter filled the air, and she knew they now drank the hard liquor—warming up for the night of relaxation after their serious conversation ended.

Usually, the laughter was her signal to join them. Michael always welcomed her to sit by his side once their talk of business ended. It was Cesar's signal, too. Every night when the drinks flowed, he moved from his place near the front door and joined the others out back.

Sophie rose and slipped on her slacks and a sweater. Then she hurried out of her room and down the hall toward the front door. She hadn't thought ahead to what she would say if anyone saw her. Perhaps that she couldn't sleep after all, and hoped Michael would join her for a stroll.

She moved to the kitchen first, which offered her a view of the front door. Sure enough, the chair was empty, meaning Cesar had already joined the others in the back. Without hesitating, she exited the front door and hurried through the night, lifting her eyes to the church steeple that glinted in the moonlight. She kept her eyes on it as it guided her way.

Sophie was nearly halfway there when she heard footsteps behind her. She glanced back, but no one was there. Whoever was behind her hadn't rounded the last corner. Her heart pounded, and she changed her mind about the meeting. She knew she needed to hurry back and get into bed. If she were caught, all she'd learned would be lost.

She remembered Walt's warning. Finding information wasn't the hard part. It was getting it to the right people. She must turn around and play it safe for the time being.

Sophie looked around again, then moved in the opposite direction of the steeple. She jogged down a narrow alley behind a small business district, hoping she wouldn't meet other threats in this part of town. When she was sure she'd lost whoever followed her, she darted into a deep doorway and waited. Fear gripped her chest, and she closed her eyes—too frightened to peer out and see if she was indeed alone.

Sophie's fingers trembled as she pressed herself as tightly into the corner of the doorway as possible. She took slow, shallow breaths, questioning why she'd taken such a risk. Maybe she should just forget it all—leave Michael and find Philip as planned. Who knew if anything she had found out could be of help to Walt? Perhaps she risked all for nothing.

Her ears were alert for any sound, but her pulse pounding in her ears made it hard to distinguish. Finally, after what seemed like fifteen minutes, she dared to peer around the doorway. But instead of a view of the moonlit street, a dark figure waited. Sophie gasped and turned to run. She'd hardly taken two steps when a hand reached out and grabbed her shoulder. Someone pushed her against the wall, knocking the breath out of her. Sophie opened her mouth to scream, but no sound emerged as she struggled to catch her breath.

"I wondered when the little mouse would come out of her hole," a deep voice growled in her ear. "It seems the little mouse isn't as innocent as she lets on. Anyone sneaking out at this hour has something to hide."

She recognized the voice. *Cesar.*

"Please, I do not have anything to hide. Let me explain."

A warm hand that smelled of sweat and wine wrapped around her mouth. "Silence!" Cesar's other hand cranked her arm behind her shoulder. "Did I ask you to speak? You'll have your opportunity to talk, and I'm sure your lover will be quite interested in your words!"

He pulled her arm higher, lifting her slightly off the ground. Pain shot through her shoulder, and Sophie was certain her arm would tear from her body. Yet instead of fighting, she went limp, knowing it was over. Knowing she'd been discovered. Knowing she'd failed.

Cesar took two steps back, pulling her along. Then suddenly a loud cracking sound filled her ears. Cesar lurched and released his grasp. Sophie felt herself falling backward, but another set of arms caught her. She turned to look, but a hand moved up to hold her face forward, still toward the wall.

"No, don't look. Just run home." She recognized the voice from somewhere but couldn't place it. "Run, Sophie, and don't look back. Pretend this did not happen. Whatever news you had to deliver is not worth your life." The man cleared his throat, trying to disguise his voice, and then he continued.

"Tomorrow night, a visitor will come for dinner. A man with a moustache and a cleft in his chin. He will ask to see the painting you are working on. Tell him what you know, and he'll advise you what to do next. Now, go—run. And don't look back."

He let go, and Sophie didn't hesitate. She propelled herself forward, down the alley and through the empty street. The sound of a struggle arose from behind her, and the cry of a man roaring in pain. Sophie didn't know if it was her defender or assailant whose scream of pain filled the night air. But she refused to look back, instead urging her feet forward.

Within a few minutes she reached Hector's house. As quietly as possible, she hurried inside and down the hall to her room. Quickly undressing, Sophie slid on her nightgown and crawled into her bed. Then she pulled the covers over her head as the sounds of the struggle replayed in her mind. Had a man died tonight because of her? Had she done something wrong to cause such a thing?

Suddenly a soft knock sounded at the door, and Sophie nearly jumped from her skin. She placed a hand over her pounding heart, trying to still its wild beating. Then the knock sounded again.

"Hmmm . . . " She mumbled as if being awakened by the knocking. She pushed back the covers and slowly walked to the door. She opened it a crack. Light flooded into the door, and she blinked, then peered outside. Michael stood there, and he seemed surprised to see her there.

"What's wrong? Is something the matter?" She yawned and rubbed her eyes.

"No, I'm sorry. I didn't think you'd be asleep already." He pushed the door open slightly and eyed her bare feet.

Sophie wiggled her toes under his gaze.

"I was just checking to see if you needed anything. I'm sorry for waking you, *Divina*."

"You don't look well." She glanced up at him. "You have me worried."

He took a step back and smiled. "No, everything is fine. I'm sorry." He chuckled. "I should have remembered that you fall asleep as soon as your head hits the pillow. Sweet dreams, Sophie."

"Michael, wait," she called to him, and he turned.

"Since I'm up, I might as well have one last kiss good night."

Without a word he approached and pulled her close, and Sophie hoped he'd mistake the pounding of her heart as excitement over being in his arms.

He leaned down and offered her a kiss.

Sophie accepted it, then she let out a groggy sigh. "Thank you," she murmured.

"No, thank you," Michael said as he held her close. "Thank you for giving me another chance. I have a wonderful feeling that with you by my side everything will turn out as it was supposed to. Man isn't made to work alone, to live alone. I understand that now. And thank you for helping me to learn to trust again . . . so much more than you'll ever know."

Chapter Twenty-Four

The next day Sophie laid out her canvas, opened her paints, and prepared her palette. While she gracefully painted in the garden, her hand captured the colorful flowers and the branches of the olive tree as her mind replayed the horror of the night before.

Cesar did not appear. And the weight in her chest confirmed he'd lost the fight in the streets. She was thankful her unseen hero had won.

She'd nearly finished the landscape when Michael approached and placed his arms on her shoulders. "Your talent never ceases to amaze me. I remember the first time I saw your work. I had that meeting at the museum."

"A meeting? I thought you were there for a story." She placed her brush on the palette and turned to him. "Or did you just make that up?"

Sophie noted a hint of red rising to his cheeks. Her jaw dropped in surprise. "Michael, your look exposes you. Did you really lie when you told me you were writing a story on the place?"

He raised his hands in surrender. "You have pulled the truth from me. I was standing in the museum at the end of a boring business meeting when I saw this beautiful woman across the room. You were giving a tour to a group of schoolchildren, if I remember correctly."

"You were there that day? I thought you came the next day . . . for your story. You even told Hector the same thing a few days ago." The breeze moved the leaves above her head ever so slightly, causing the sun to filter through, blocking her view of Michael's face. Though Sophie didn't want to admit it, her heart warmed at the thought that he'd gone out of his way to meet her.

She stood, placing her paints and brush on the stool. "Now that I think of it, I never did see that story in the paper. I think you made up some excuse at the time, but now I know the truth. So," she added nonchalantly, "just what type of business deal were you working on at the museum anyway?"

Michael shrugged. "Nothing important. I can hardly remember it now. The important thing is the appreciation of art that I acquired." He glanced at the painting. "Just lovely. Will it be dry before we catch the train tomorrow?"

"The train? I thought it was too dangerous."

"Well, I have a friend who is trying to arrange it for us, but I will not bore you with the details." Michael took her hand and kissed her fingertips. "But come, we have a guest for dinner. He's a fellow English-speaking correspondent. From Britain. It should be a nice surprise."

Sophie's stomach tensed. She swallowed hard, remembering what her rescuer had told her the previous night. Sucking in a deep breath, she followed Michael into the house.

Seated in the living room was a man with a moustache and a cleft in his chin.

Michael shook the man's hand, then turned to Sophie. "Sophie, this is a friend of mine, Lester McGovern. He's been chasing all the right stories, and sometimes I find myself envious of his work."

"Lester," she said, hurrying forward to shake the man's hand. She recognized the name immediately. She remembered what Walt had told her about the agent who was onto something, then disappeared. "What a nice treat, having you here."

Lester wasn't very tall and was rather plain looking. His perfectly trimmed, dark moustache and large cleft in his chin were indeed his two most prominent, and handsome, features.

"It's wonderful I caught up with Michael here in Bilbao. And he did not know we have a common friend." Lester turned to Hector. "How many years have we known each other, *amigo?* Four, maybe five?"

Hector nodded his head enthusiastically. "Five at least . . . you wrote many stories about my bullfighting."

Lester smiled at Sophie. "You are a talented young woman. I have seen some of your art in pro-Republican publications— very moving, if I say so myself. The one of the International soldiers in the hospital brought tears to my eyes."

Sophie's mind filled with the emotions of pain that had been in that hospital room, and so many others like it. Yet her face also warmed as she thought about Philip at her side during those times and the strength he'd given her.

"It was a hard painting to work on—all the ones that I have done in Spain have really taken a toll on me. So much pain and heartache." She glanced at Michael, who nodded his head in agreement. "That's why this morning I decided to paint the flowers outside. Flowers are much easier on the mind and heart."

"Is that the easel set up out back?" Lester pointed out the window.

"Yes. It's not my best work, but—"

Lester turned to Michael, who had just settled onto the sofa. "If you don't mind, I'd love to see her work."

"Not at all," Michael said.

Lester clicked his tongue. "We'll only be a moment." He waved his hand toward the door. "After you, Sofía."

"Yes, of course, but it's nothing much, only something I started this morning . . . of the freshly pruned garden," she said, winking at Michael, hoping playful banter about the pruning would help him forget her mistake.

Sophie took slow steps to the doorway. "I think you will like this painting, Lester—with the olive trees and flowers, I feel it captures the complexity and beauty of Spain."

The door closed behind him, and Lester walked to the painting. He nodded. "It looks as if the colors in this garden were absorbed into the canvas. Beautiful. Now, do you have a message for Walt?"

Sophie's eyes widened, surprised by his forwardness. He did not waste time with small talk. "Yes, but . . ."

"Your guardian sent me. He said it must be urgent for you to have tried so hard to get it to us. Please, hurry now; we don't have time."

She sucked in a breath, then blew it out, hoping she was doing the right thing. "First, I think Maria Donita, Michael's friend from Madrid, is somehow involved. She's married now to a banker."

"From the National Bank of Spain? That would help her with inside information, now, wouldn't it?"

"I'm not sure if that's the bank, but it sounds a little too convenient to me. After all, what type of vital information might one share with a wife that he wouldn't think of sharing with a friend? The banker's first name is Emilio, if that helps."

"Consider the information passed on. What else?"

"Photos. I found photos, in the back shed." Instead of turning to look at the shed, Sophie focused on the canvas and moved her hands as if explaining the painting it to him.

"Are there any of tunnels, ships, or a harbor, perhaps?"

"Yes, I believe so. Are those important?"

"Very. I need you to steal them for me."

"Steal them? But if they—Michael, Hector, or Paulo—find out they're missing? Then they'll know I'm involved. They already know I've been in the shed."

"Do you not think I can take care of that? Tomorrow, an old friend will show up. Have the photos ready to pass off—anything that has to do with shipments especially. I'll make sure that what you've done will be covered up."

"But . . . an old friend. Really?"

"You must trust, Sofía. Tomorrow you will see him, and you will know. Just make sure you have those photos ready. Think of a creative way to pass them off. You can do it. I know you can."

❖ ❖ ❖

200

Walt set down his satchel on the floor as he entered the room of the Gran Hotel in Salamanca. Yesterday he had been another person in another city. As Walt Block in Barcelona, he had walked by the central Plaza de Cataluña, near the Telefónica, the telephone exchange. It had saddened him to see that the classlessness that the volunteer soldiers had fought so hard for in the first months of the war had all but disappeared in that city. Men called to each other with the more formal term of *señor*, and he wondered what had happened to the friendlier term of *camarada*. The blue *monos* were nowhere to be seen. Businessmen in suits had replaced them. Beggars had returned to the street, calling out to those who walked by for mercy and a pesta or two. Even more evident was the tension in the air, and it was clear the insurrection of one of the antifascist groups weeks ago had not ended to everyone's satisfaction.

Today, he was another man.

After his freelance contributions, which were published in numerous papers and were always on the side of Franco, James Kimmel was a welcome fixture to the pro-fascist groups that hadn't left Salamanca since the war began. In fact, the generals and businessmen he mingled with all thought of Kimmel's numerous travels as exotic and daring. They even envied the freedom he had to explore the country and witness the success of Franco's soldiers for himself.

A knock sounded at the door, and Walt opened it.

"Mr. Kimmel, there is a request for you to join the generals in the caudillo's apartment on the first floor of the palace, sir."

Walt shrugged. Then he scribbled a quick note and handed it to the messenger. "Can you tell them I will try? I have a story to get out as soon as possible. I am sure they understand. *Gracias.*"

The messenger nodded and Walt shut the door, amazed at how easily he could slip from one persona to another. Just after the war started, he'd traveled to Salamanca, making friends in Falange headquarters and with the newly arriving Germans and Italians. A week here, a week there, becoming familiar in Franco's circles had been a fun game to play. Of course, being entertained by the Fascist leaders came second to keeping track of Michael. And who won the war was a secondary concern compared to the treasure that had gained the interest of Walt's employer long before the undercurrents of war rippled through the discontented country.

Walt pounded out a news story concerning the most recent Nationalist victories and planned to turn in early, not giving the generals the pleasure of his presence. Tomorrow would be soon enough, after the press conference. He'd discuss some of the latest issues regarding the war, then turn the conversation to more interesting matters, such as well-protected shipments out of Spain. Generals rarely shared their secrets vocally, but Walt had been around long enough to read their facial expressions that often revealed exactly what he needed to know.

Just as he finished the story, there was a knock on the door. Walt opened it just a crack and immediately recognized one of his co-workers. "Wilson, come in." He swung the door the rest of the way and stepped to the side.

"We have heard from Lester. He's safe . . . and he's with the woman."

"Sophie?"

Wilson nodded. "He hoped her information would be important enough to risk reappearing. He was right." He moved to the window with sure steps, glancing down to the courtyard below.

Though he worked with this man, Walt didn't like how Wilson handled himself. The more vital the information he needed to pass off, the more Derrick Wilson acted like a scared rabbit, darting from here to there. And his dull brown hair was too long and curly for Walt's taste.

Walt ignored the man's movements and hid his own impatience. "Well, what is this information?"

"She found a solid connection between Michael and the gold pieces—it seems Michael's friend Maria is married to a banker in Madrid. We checked him out, and he was one of the four who held keys to the vault."

"Maria, of course . . . she would be able to charm one such as him." Walt's mind clicked through all the pieces that needed to fall into place for him to return to Madrid. And those he'd contact first when he arrived.

"There's more. She's found photos." Wilson fumbled with

the buttons on his shirt, unaware of his nervous actions. "Lots of photos."

"Any that we need?"

"It appears so." Wilson smiled as he moved to the door. "Our plan is already in motion. José is being contacted as we speak. If all goes well, the photos will be waiting in Madrid by the time you arrive."

"It's as if you read my thoughts." Walt moved to his bed and pulled his satchel out, already repacking for the trip.

Wilson scratched his forehead. "Yes, well, that's what you pay me for. A little now, a lot later, yes?"

Walt placed his black fedora firmly on his head, pulling it low over his eyes. "You know that's correct. You also know this could be just the break we were waiting for. And not a moment too soon."

José recognized the form of the man even in the dimness of the stable. He stood near the stall of Calisto, leaning with arms on the rail as if meeting up like this was the most natural thing in the world. José's quick steps slowed, and when he got within ten feet, the man turned.

"Lester. I wish I could say it is a pleasure to see you, but that would be a lie." José leaned his back against the same railing.

"I heard you found Ramona. I also heard she decided to stay at the hospital." Lester's voice mimicked compassion, but José could tell the difference.

José shrugged. "What can I say? She has a caring heart. It is hard for her to leave the injured."

"Too bad. I need you to find someone to help with your next assignment."

"And who said I was interested in helping? Besides, I have no one to help."

"Oh, you will be interested, all right. And I think the young lady will do just fine. What is her name again?" Lester snapped his fingers. "Oh, yes, I remember. Petra."

"No, I refuse. I'm not going to risk her in that way."

As if sensing José's anxiety, Calisto turned toward him and whinnied. He pawed the ground.

"Too bad, then. Sophie's death will be on your shoulders."

"Sophie? What are you talking about? Last I heard she was leaving Spain."

"She would have, if your car—without the accident, well—would have made it. Thankfully that didn't happen. She's been more valuable to our cause than anyone would have guessed."

"Where is she? How is she involved?"

"She's in Bilbao. She has only been there since after the bombing in Guernica. She was there during the bombing. She went looking for answers . . . looking for you."

"For me?" José ran his hand down his jaw, his heart filled with fear. "So where is she now? Is she at the hospital? With the other correspondents? Is she okay?"

"She's fine, and those are all good guesses. But she found an old friend—her fiancé, in fact. She's with Michael."

With two quick steps, José found his face within inches of Lester's nose. He grasped the man's collar and twisted it, catching Lester by surprise and nearly cutting off his air supply.

"Why? What is she doing with him?" José shouted.

"I am not the one who sent her back to him," Lester managed to croak. He squirmed, struggling for breath. "I helped you fake his death, remember? Who was the one who found the identical camera? Now if you care for her, let me go. She . . . she needs you to get the information and pass it on to her guardian. Within those walls, I am already under suspicion."

José released his grasp slightly and noted that Calisto pushed his chest against the door of his stall, as if trying to break through and help him. "Will you promise me that you'll help her get out?" José quieted his voice, trying to calm himself for the horse's sake.

Lester shrugged. "I'm sorry. It's not my call. But without your help tomorrow, let's just say her case is hopeless. She will be found out for good."

"Fine." José crossed his arms to his chest and paced back and forth. "Tell me what I need to do."

"Tomorrow. This all must take place tomorrow."

José listened closely as Lester relayed his plan.

Chapter Twenty-Five

Sophie wasn't sure if she closed her eyes during the night, so intent were her ears on hearing every sound within the house. Sometime when the night was darkest and not a sound could be heard, she dressed and quietly made her way out of her room, then to the back door. With the softest steps possible, she walked through the patio and toward the shed. Reaching the shed door, she sucked in a breath, then pulled the door. Slowly, slowly she opened it, cringing when the hinges squeaked in protest.

Pausing, she listened to see if the sound had been heard or if anyone had awakened. After a minute, when no one seemed to stir, she pulled the door again, wider. Another squeak, and more waiting. Finally she stood inside the shed with the door closed.

Thankful the shed had no windows, she pulled a candle and match from her pocket. With shaking hands she lit it and placed it upon a dusty wooden shelf. The light flickered on the antique-looking tools and bins, and she noticed more than one large insect scurrying to hide behind cobweb-covered buckets.

As carefully as possible, Sophie pulled the wooden box off the shelf. Placing it on the ground, she thumbed through the prints. Some were of Madrid. Others of ships in a harbor. Sophie made a small pile of any that appeared to involve shipping, including a photo of large crates that read *DINAMITA* on the side. There were others too, of a large tunnel. There were many men working there—dark-skinned ones being watched by Spanish guards. Sophie didn't have time to question what these photos involved. She took the ones she hoped were relevant, knowing that trying to pass off too many could risk everything. She returned the rest to the box.

When she was through, she put the lid on, knowing any fool would realize the box had been compromised. She then tucked the photos under her blouse, using the waistband of her trousers to hold them there. There were fewer then twenty, but their bulkiness would be evident to anyone who looked closely.

She placed the box back on the shelf, then blew out the candle. The sound of scurrying feet sounded across the floor, and Sophie guessed it was a mouse. She blew out a breath. She waited for the wick to cool and the wax to harden; then she slipped them back into her pocket.

In the darkness of the shed, all her senses seemed heightened, and as she listened again to hear if anyone was outside, she inhaled the dusty air and said a silent prayer that she would make it back to her room in safety. Then she retraced her steps, out the shed, across the patio, into the house, and finally into her room. It was only after she'd made it all the way back and shut her door that Sophie realized her whole body was trembling.

Instead of climbing into her bed, she fell onto her knees before it. Wondering once again why she'd been chosen for this task, she prayed that God would help her succeed.

Petra yawned as she watched José saddle up Calisto and Erro. "Are we leaving this morning?" she asked, tucking her shirt into a pair of boy's pants. They looked handmade and had large pockets on the side. They were small, but not small enough. She wore a pair of leather suspenders to keep them up.

"We have a short job to do; then we will head for the mountains."

206

"Yes?"

"It is something very important. I need you to trust me."

In the early morning light she watched as José tenderly adjusted Calisto's saddle. He'd come in from the stables yesterday full of anger, saying nothing, but stomping around the house as if he'd just been double-crossed by his best friend. He spent much time talking with Pepito and Juan too, as if seeking their advice. Petra didn't ask what was wrong. Instead she kept her distance, hoping that the new day would bring a different attitude.

In the morning José busied himself around the stables, working with determined steps. He seemed resigned to some action he could not avoid. Action that for some reason included her and the horses.

Finally, he'd approached her with the clothes, telling her he needed her to hurry and put them on. Dressed and ready to go, Petra still did not know what urgent task awaited them.

She smiled as she approached Erro and rubbed her palm on his nose, just as he liked. She didn't say a word. She knew José would fill her in when he was ready.

He tied a saddlebag to Erro's saddle, then turned to her. "We'll ride into Bilbao today. I have a meeting with friends."

"Into town? Are you sure? I mean, if the city is bombed or the Nationalists break—"

José's eyes narrowed as he looked to her, and Petra quickly bit her lip. "I am sorry. I didn't mean to question you. You know what is best for the horses, and for me. I know you've already weighed all the consequences." Without another word, she slipped her foot into the stirrup and swung up into the saddle. She patted Erro's neck as she settled in.

With her compliance, Petra noticed the tenseness in José's face ease and the worry lines on his forehead fade.

"Good. I am thankful for your help." His voice was low. "We will ride into town. When we get there, I will ask a friend for help. His family owns these horses. I believe he is the only family member left in Spain."

José mounted Calisto, but instead of urging the horse forward, he sat as if thinking over the words to come next. Finally he turned to her. "While we are there, we will meet a woman,

Sofía. She will give you some photographs. You must ask for them, take them quickly, and hide them in your pockets. No one else must know. Not even my friend. It is vital . . . to save everything. If we lose those photographs we cannot save these horses or Spain."

Petra had never received a request so shrouded in mystery. And though questions filled her mind, it excited her to think that José would trust her in this way. She quickly nodded her head.

"*Sí*, I will do this. Thank you for asking for my help. I won't let you down, José."

He clicked his tongue against his teeth, making a sound that informed the horses it was time to head out.

"Thank you, Petra," he said. "Thank you for trusting me."

Petra shrugged. "How could I not? You've given me only reason to trust."

José smiled, then looked away. But not before Petra saw heartache in his gaze, telling her trust was something he appreciated, and something he'd not always received. She didn't ask any more, for fear his brave face would crumble before the horses covered ten steps.

The smell of breakfast cooking in the kitchen caused Sophie's stomach to growl. Remembering her assignment, she sat up on her bed and looked out the window into the streets of Bilbao. Gazing at the scene of fearful people and a battered town, Sophie realized she didn't even see Spain anymore—only pain, only conflict. But the fact was, she was here, and she had a part to play. Surely God must have trusted her to bring her to this country and plop her in the middle of this mess. If He were a God of love, that meant His love had brought her to this place too. And perhaps, in the end, she would discover a purpose in it all.

Voices reached her ears, and she knew the others were rising for the day. She dressed and went about her normal activities. Most of all, she hoped Lester had followed through on his word. And hoped that the stolen photographs wouldn't be missed before the mystery person showed up.

If not—if no one showed—she knew her best chance would be to wait until tonight and make her way to the cathedral again. Getting there would be easier now that Cesar no longer guarded the doorways. No one had mentioned his disappearance, and she didn't ask.

Of course, what she'd done might be discovered before then. If so, the charade would be up. Michael would know for sure, and maybe she would disappear just as Cesar had—with no one asking questions. No one thinking much more of the American painter who had found her way into Spain at the wrong time and gotten involved with the wrong people.

Sophie flipped open the Bible again, but her mind was too occupied with her own concerns to read Eleanor's letters. Instead the pages fell open to Psalm 117. And in the margin Sophie noticed these words written out in Eleanor's handwriting: *A promise to cling to.*

Sophie whispered to herself the verses that followed: *O praise the Lord, all ye nations: praise him, all ye people. For his merciful kindness is great toward us: and the truth of the Lord endureth forever. Praise ye the Lord.*

His merciful kindness is great toward us. . . . Sophie let those words drift through her mind.

The truth of the Lord endureth forever. She smiled as she thought of those words too. God knew the truth of this whole situation. He knew Michael's connection with the gold. He knew if Walt's motives were pure. He even knew where the gold was hidden and whether or not finding it could change any aspect of this war. God knew if the photos were worth the risk. And He was *not* surprised at the situation Sophie found herself in now.

Sophie closed the Bible and held it tight to her chest.

God also knew her heart, her emotions. He knew the truth about her place in Spain. *And His merciful kindness is great toward me. Just as it was to Eleanor, whose heart is shared in the letters in this book.*

"Show me Your merciful kindness, Lord. Is that okay to ask? In some way, can I get a small glimpse of Your plan and place in this mess? It's a promise I need to cling to. I—"

Sophie's whispered prayer was interrupted by a knock at the

door. She placed the Bible on the night table and stood, trying to put on her poker face for Michael. Trying to hold on to the truth of God, even as she stepped out into the false role she played.

"Almost ready, sweetheart." She smoothed her blouse and opened the door.

Sophie froze as she realized it wasn't Michael who stood there. Her quivering hand immediately covered her mouth. Her eyes widened in surprise, and words abandoned her.

José stepped forward and grasped her free hand. Her eyes darted to the large scar on his neck, a reminder of their parting months prior. He'd come to her rescue many times before—offered her kindness when she didn't know where to turn. Seeing him there reminded her that she wasn't alone after all.

"Walt sent me to help you, Sophie. Don't worry," José whispered. "He used Lester to get the message to me."

Sophie heard footsteps and looked down the doorway to see Michael coming. Disbelief still coursed through her, and she knew she couldn't have hidden her surprise and relief if she had tried.

Sophie also knew that Walt wasn't the only one who had sent José. God had heard her prayer and had answered even before she'd whispered those words.

"*Hola*, Sofía. It is your friend, José, back from the dead, *sí*." José spoke louder this time. "I should have sent Michael ahead to warn you. You should have seen the look on your face when you saw me. I thought you were going to faint."

"Oh, José. You are well. I am so thankful." She wrapped her arms around his shoulders. "Thank you," she whispered in his ear.

Michael approached and slapped José on the back. "He certainly gave me a start. I've never been more relieved to see an old friend."

Sophie studied Michael's face, and though he said the words, his eyes betrayed them. How did it change Michael's plans, seeing José here? Sophie didn't have time to worry about that now. She just enjoyed the overwhelming feeling of relief that José's presence had brought in answer to her prayer.

And as she hugged José one more time, she felt the coolness

of the photos pressing against her skin. They still hid beneath her blouse, waiting for the right time. Yet a new confidence surged through her. She had done well, and she trusted the person she was to turn these photos over to. More than anyone else, she knew she could trust José. And once she handed them over, it would only be a matter of time. Her part would be done, and she'd be free to leave Michael—free to find Philip.

Or at least that was her hope.

José led them outside, taking the cap from his head and twisting it in his hands. "The truth is, I've come for help. Not for me, but for my friends."

Sophie didn't know what José was talking about. But she and Michael followed their friend, with his typical quick steps, no more than five blocks from Hector's house. It appeared to be a place where Spaniards from the country came to bring their food and livestock for sale. Only now the stalls were empty—few people bought and sold in Spain these days. Instead, some of the small wooden shacks had been transformed into shelter for the many refugees who had spilled into town, hoping to find safety.

Sophie glanced at Michael, but he said nothing. She could see the tenseness in his jaw.

"One thing I know about Michael," José said, speaking over his shoulder. "He connects with the people he needs for his photographs by bearing gifts of news and gossip. I do not have much news, but I come bearing gifts. Yet these gifts come with a request. To save these treasures, I need your help."

José met Michael's gaze. "My father heard from a friend that you were seen around Bilbao. Seen at Hector's house. He wondered why you stayed here when your family's home was so close. At first I told him we must wait—that you had work to do, important work, and that you could not be bothered by the treasures of the estate . . . but I'm sorry to say that the time has come when waiting is no longer an option. My hope is that by helping me, you can protect all that your mother's family once stood for. All they have protected through the years. This is what I offer . . . " José pointed to a small corral where two horses waited. Both were saddled, and they stood poised and beautiful, in statuesque stances as if they purposefully displayed their beauty.

Sophie saw a young woman standing near the corral. At first she thought it was José's wife, but as they drew closer she realized the young woman was barely more than a child, perhaps fifteen or sixteen.

"I don't understand." Sophie paused, taking in their beauty.

"You've brought the horses here?" Michael stood in a wide-legged stance, hands on hips, shaking his head in disbelief.

"They are safe for now, but maybe I should explain." José approached the nearer horse and ran his hand down its muzzle. The horse's eyes brightened at José's touch. "The other four are back at the stables."

Michael turned to Sophie. "This is what I was going to show you. But I thought by now . . ." His voice trailed off. "So many things could have happened to them. I was afraid they'd all be destroyed."

"I don't understand. Is this the treasure you grew up with?"

Michael nodded and opened his mouth as if to give an explanation, but no words came out. The anger in his face faded as he looked toward the animals.

Instead José spoke in an authoritative tone. "It all started in 1580 when the brother of the emperor of Austria bought thirty-three Spanish horses. They were a special breed, and generations of men have cared for them."

Michael approached the white stallion, and Sophie was certain she noted tears in his eyes. "Yet what many don't know is that in Spain the same breed of horses was cared for by one family. My family." Michael's voice caught in his throat. "Our horses were descendants of the same ones purchased by the emperor's brother. But instead of raising them for show, my ancestors raised them out of love. They even risked their lives many times to save these horses. But that is not the case any longer."

Michael turned to her. "I never told you much about my time in Spain growing up, but that's how I came to know José. My mother's family is the one who raised these horses all these years. José and his father were a few of those who cared for them, and I got to know him there. We have been friends ever since, and we found it amazing we both ended up in Madrid at the same time." He glanced at José, his eyebrow cocked. "And now here. Together again."

Sophie held up her hands in question, again feeling the photos under her shirt. "Why didn't you tell me sooner?" she asked.

Then she turned to José. "It's amazing that I didn't know that part about you either. You talked about being childhood friends, but left out so much. So *you* trained these horses?"

"*Sí*, and now it is my job to save them. That's why I have come for help. If I do not find a way to get them out of here, they will be lost for good. Soldiers are hungry—and they will do anything for food . . . anything."

Sophie shivered as she thought of these amazing creatures being slaughtered to feed troops.

Michael's voice was curt. "I don't understand. You know my newspaper work. You said yourself how important it is. You also know that the rest of my family has fled to save their own skin. What could I possibly do?"

Suddenly the sound of gunfire erupted around them, and an explosion sounded, hitting a building not far from the corral.

Without hesitation, José motioned to the young girl. "Sophie, hurry, take Petra. Run back to Hector's!" Then he turned to Michael. "I plead with you. Help me . . . these creatures do not deserve war. Or deserve to die. Help me find a safe place."

Sophie didn't wait to hear Michael's response. With an outstretched hand she ran to the young woman; then together they ran down the street, with more sounds of fighting behind them. They entered Hector's house just as the other men ran out the front door to see what the commotion was about.

"The photos," said the girl. "José asked me to get them from you. Hurry, before anyone comes."

Without even taking time to catch her breath, Sophie took the photographs from under her shirt and handed them to the young woman. With quick hands, she slipped them into a large pants pocket, buttoning it closed. Only then did the two turn to the window to see Michael jogging toward them down the street.

When he reached the door, he turned to the girl. "José asks for you. He told me to send you back."

"But the danger—she can't leave yet." Sophie touched the girl's shoulder.

"There is nowhere in Spain without danger, Sophie." He looked to the young woman again. "Go. It was foolish to bring the horses into the city. There is nowhere safe here."

Without a word, the young woman ran from the house and back up the street toward José and the horses. Only after she was out of sight did Michael's gaze focus on Sophie.

"So, you are not going to help José? Help save the horses?" She studied his green gaze and noticed the conflict inside. And instead of anger, her heart ached for the decision he was forced to make.

"Just because I cannot help does not mean I do not care. There are other things I have to consider. First, to guarantee your safety. If anything happened to you, I could not live with myself. And there are other considerations, things you cannot understand. Things I've wished to share, but cannot." His eyes were tender, and Sophie knew he told the truth. Yet there was also something else she noticed in his gaze—suspicion, as if trying to figure out a deeper meaning to José's visit.

She opened her mouth to plead with him to open up, to tell her the truth, when another explosion shook the ground. This one was closer, vibrating the house. It seemed to come from the backyard.

And even before Sophie turned to look, she knew what had been hit. As she walked to the back window, she knew she would see the small shed going up in flames.

Chapter Twenty-Six

*I*t took one day's travel for Walt to reach Madrid. And after that only two hours before he had Maria's husband, Emilio, in his custody. It had been simple enough. He approached the older Spanish man outside the bank just before the lunch hour. Displaying his press credentials, he asked Emilio into his private press suite for an interview.

Thankfully the man was as prideful as he was foolish. And these two traits, which had made it easy for Maria Donita to capture him in her web, also led Emilio to the hotel room where Walt's brandished pistol had him promising to give Walt anything.

Walt considered the man on his knees on the patterned rug, and then pulled a cigarette from his shirt pocket and handed it to him. "Honestly, *amigo*, I do not wish to hurt you. I simply need some information for the good of Spain. In fact, I plan to reward you for your efforts."

"Reward me?" Emilio placed the cigarette between his trembling lips and allowed Walt to light it.

"You have a wife and a new son, correct?" Walt blew out the match and tossed it into the wastebasket.

"*Sí*, a baby born last week. Surely you would not deny him a father."

"No, of course not. In fact, I can offer you passage out of Spain—to Morocco or France, if you wish. You better than anyone know that Madrid will not be safe for long. After all, *señor*, you have a family to protect."

Emilio pushed his glasses up the rim of his nose. He blew out a lungful of cigarette smoke, then placed the cigarette in the ashtray on the side table next to him. "What do you wish to know?"

"Get off your knees. Relax." Walt motioned to a high-backed chair. "I only wish to know about the shipment of gold in October."

"The Republican plan was to move the treasure southeast . . . to the coast," he hurriedly said. "I was one of the 'lock men' from the bank's staff—for this second shipment."

"Lock man . . . what does this mean?" Walt noticed sweat form on the man's brow. He sat down across from Emilio and placed the pistol on his lap, out of sight, lest the man have a heart attack.

"The move was supposed to take place with utmost secrecy. My job was to hold one of four special keys for the ammunition-storage caves in a mountain just outside the port city's naval base."

"What city?" Walt leaned forward in his chair.

Emilio lowered his head. "Cartagena. But you have to understand; this was the only way. All of us knew it. It was the only way we could beat Franco. The gold could fuel the war."

"At that time, did you realize the gold was not safe? That, in fact, there were many who wanted to steal it?"

The man's eyes widened.

"You don't need to tell me; I've heard all about it." Walt readjusted his fedora. "It seems that although most of the commoners knew nothing about the treasure, every politician or commander saw it as an opportunity to help his own cause. Isn't that right?"

"Yes, many rumors were circulating around the city. We knew we couldn't keep it safe for long. That's why we sped up the gold's transport to Cartagena," Emilio said. "We knew once the gold reached the Russians, they had to ensure its safety. Also, the sooner the gold was in their hands, the sooner we'd receive the promised weapons. Also, it helped to make certain that no one else would attempt the same."

"*Sí*, that must be quite troubling, to be in charge of so much—as if the weight of the souls of Spain rested on your shoulders. In fact, I heard the head cashier was so nervous, he committed suicide. . . . It must have been hard, keeping the gold's shipment a secret from everyone except the few in charge of the locks and the transport." Walt grinned. "What I don't understand is how you managed to fall in love and marry when so much was happening."

The man ran a hand through his graying hair. "Maria and I met a few months prior. It was an immediate romance. And once I found she carried my child, how could I not marry her? With war all around, one tries to find happiness in the few places he can."

Emilio stood and paced. "But it seems you know as much as I. . . . Perhaps there are others who have told you what you need to know? If so, I do not see why you need me."

"*Sí*, there are others. But this is where my information ends."

Emilio paused and turned. "I am not sure what you need of me. . . ."

Walt stood, placed his hands on the table, and leaned close. "Just answer two questions. Has the gold been shipped?"

"Yes. It is in Russia."

"Was any of it stolen?"

"Not that I'm aware of."

"Fine. But now I want every detail of how the shipment took place."

"I swore not to tell . . . besides, it's over. Done. There is nothing we can do to change what is already finished."

Walt shrugged. "Then what does it matter? The gold is gone, and in exchange you obtain protection for your family."

"Fine. But, please, can we leave soon? I will protect my family at all costs. I worry about the bombers. I worry our luck will expire."

"Of course." Walt smiled. "I can make sure you are safely out of the country by tomorrow afternoon."

Walt tried to picture what ten thousand white wooden army ammunition boxes had looked like eight months prior, before the October transport, as they filled the circular vault. He had visited the vault under the National Bank of Spain once when he had written a story on it. And though he'd promised the head cashier all the details would be left out of the news story, Walt remembered every one. And with Emilio's information, he now had a complete picture.

The vault sat a hundred feet underground, behind concrete walls and all-but-unbreachable steel doors. Emilio claimed it had taken twenty-five bank employees to pack the boxes, and once packed, each box weighed about sixty-five kilos.

The ammunition boxes full of gold had been carried to the elevator by a crew of some fifty handpicked soldiers. The men worked in three shifts and ate and slept in the bank until the job was complete. Walt wondered if they had believed the lie—that artillery had been stored in the vault. Then again, how would ordinary soldiers know such treasure existed? Most of Spain had no idea of the amount, nor its worth.

Walt strode to the window, watching Emilio climb into the black sedan Walt promised would be waiting. What would Maria think, he wondered, when Emilio arrived home to tell about their trip out of the country? What would Michael think when he arrived in Madrid and found she had disappeared? Walt knew he'd have to watch that play out, but until then, his mind returned to the gold.

On his tour of the bank, he'd ridden a slow elevator to the vault. The vault itself had been twenty-five meters in diameter and surrounded by a protective moat six meters wide. To approach the gold, he'd crossed a bridge of wooden planks. It seemed rickety at the time, and he imagined how it must have sagged precariously every time two soldiers crossed balancing a box of gold.

Once inside, Walt had expected to see gold ingots, but he was told there were very few solid bars—maybe thirteen boxes full, once loaded. Instead, he saw millions and millions of gold coins—dollars, sovereigns, gold pestas, currency from at least a dozen countries. The most appealing were the Aztec gold, louis d'or, and other ancient coins with numismatic value far exceeding their weight in fine gold.

The man had urged Walt not to print any of this in the newspaper, of course. But like King Hezekiah in the Bible who showed his wealth to neighboring kings, the man's pride was greater than his wisdom.

Walt's employer had been right. Spain did not realize the treasure it guarded in its vaults. As Walt followed Michael, he had discovered the truth. Though Michael's cover had been a photographer, his role in Spain involved stealing the most valuable gold pieces—Aztec gold and louis d'or coins—ones that would make any collector proud.

Michael believed his efforts would protect the finest pieces from being melted down in Russia with the rest of the gold. He also believed that by turning the gold over to Franco he would save some of Spain's most priceless treasures.

Walt knew otherwise. Franco had a war to win, a country to command, and would use any resource possible to help his efforts.

Walt knew only his employer—who could care less about who won in Spain—could maintain the gold's safety. Walt's employer was a lover of fine art, who understood that such treasure must be protected at all costs. But he was also a businessman, looking to make a profit by selling the coins to the most influential museums in the world. And though his boss favored no side over the other, Walt offered his services on one condition—part of the income would return to the Republic, providing more help and weapons than Russia alone could provide.

While he had first come to Spain years ago in search of this treasure, he had eventually fallen in love with the people. If the Fascists won, he knew things would get worse. And while Walt wouldn't call himself a Communist, their ideals were ones he could appreciate—ones worth backing up in any way possible, for the good of Spain.

Emilio's information had been vital. It took Walt one step closer to finding the lost pieces and saving them . . . before the gold—and the war—were lost for good.

Sophie's hands gripped the armrests of the seat as the train carried them from Bilbao. How was she so lucky to leave, when thousands wished for a way to escape to the relative safety of Madrid? The citizens of the town hid in fear, knowing the Iron Ring weakened, and in a matter of time the Nationalists would descend upon them. The people had heard stories of other over-run towns. As she looked out the window, getting one last glance of the coastal town, Sophie hoped they were just that—stories.

"Don't worry, *Divina*. We will be safe in Madrid before we know it." Michael wrapped a protective arm around her shoulders. "The fighting is getting a little too close for comfort now, isn't it? I mean, who would have guessed a handmade bomb would land in the backyard of Hector's home? What were the odds?"

Though his words were spoken softly, questions filled his gaze.

Sophie looked away. "The only thing that helps me at times like this is to get my mind off of it." She lifted her satchel from the floor and placed it on her lap, removing the Bible. She had told Michael before about the letters, but he had seemed mildly amused.

"We all need something now and then to help us forget—to give us distance," he said, his green eyes focused on her. "Sometimes my photographs do that for me. It's like the camera separates me from the pain. The pictures carry the burden for me, so I do not have it weighing on my heart or emotions." He sighed, removed his arm, then laid his head back against the cushioned headrest and closed his eyes.

Sophie wanted to ask him what weighed on his heart. Instead

she looked away. Her own emotions rose in her, and she felt a tenderness growing inside after seeing him so vulnerable. But then, she realized, she needed to protect herself too. The more time she listened to Michael's heart, the easier it was to care—something she refused to do.

Sophie opened a letter and began reading. She needed the distraction to still the dozens of questions that filled her mind, especially her worry that by leaving Bilbao she was leaving her guardian behind.

July 17, 1867
Dear Jeremiah,

Sometimes I walk to where Mateo is working, and I watch. The other women think this is foolish, but they've lived this same way as long as they remember. I like to watch as the coal tumbles from the chutes and falls into the wagons. It is then moved from the pithead to the sorting area. The wagons are pushed by men. They push them to where the women sort. Some of the women are widows. A few are married and trying to work beside their husbands for survival. They sort the coal by hand using a sifting screen. Two women work together. They work hard all day and have little to show for it.

I'm amazed by the independence of the people I now live amongst. The farmers live in their own houses and eat the food grown by their own hands. All households make their own clothes and even shoes—wooden madreñas, which they form in the leisure of winter. It is hard enough working to support oneself, but recently rich men have come into the area searching for a cheap, abundant, and subservient labor force. Now these farmers work twice as hard to enhance the lives of the rich.

Most miners do not live close to the mines, and some take an hour to travel to work. There are poor roads, no electricity, few schools, no washing facilities. The worst of all is the lack of water. I think back to the river behind my father's house, remembering how we used to laugh and play in its current during those hot summer days.

These are a wonderful people, I'm realizing. A people who center their lives around traditional and religious practices. That is not to say they are always friendly—they think little of outsiders. I saw this when I first arrived, but I strove to win over their hearts. And, I soon discovered, the people were easier to adjust to than the conditions of the environment.

Here there is no water and little beauty. Perhaps that is why I find myself in the chapel of the Minas de Saus as often as I can. It is a beautiful chapel decorated with elegant paintings, altar pieces, and sculptures.

Mateo heard there was a miners' strike in Langreo, but he won't tell me much about it. Perhaps he knows I would want to have our own strike. Sometimes I talk too much about men's right to be free. My husband tires of it. He should know better. When he married me, I was in Paris for a workers' strike. Did he think he married a quiet woman?

I know you would have agreed that something should be done. There should be an argument against the wage reductions, against the harsh discipline for the smallest infractions, and the overtime work.

Still, I'd rather live here without protest than not at all. Even when Mateo works long hours, he always comes home, washes up, and opens his arms to me. He's never too tired to listen about my day and the small things I enjoy sharing. He no longer asks about America, and I no longer tell him. He understands more than anyone what I gave up to be with him, yet he doesn't feel bad for me. My Mateo knows our love means more to me than anything America held.

When I first moved here, the villagers would ask me about America. At first I'd tell them all the wonderful ways of my homeland, but they looked at me as if I were relating the Grimm Brothers' fairy tales. Now I simply tell them that it's not unlike Spain, and in the deepest hearts, it is the same. People have the same hopes and dreams and desires. The only difference is that in America you can strive for them, whereas here you shove them down further and pretend they're not there.

I wonder what will happen when these people learn more about the outside world—when they realize it is not fairy tales that I speak of. Will they revolt? Try to change? Can things ever change here? It's hard to imagine this world any different.

I wish I could say something, do something. Instead, all I can do is pray for this people and this land. Pray that the outside world will take notice of their plight.

And just think. If you, my love, hadn't died, we would be married and living a peaceful life in America. Though I miss you, I know I am here for a purpose. Even if it is only to pray for a change, to pray for these people.

Love, Eleanor

Sophie didn't notice her tears until she refolded the letter and returned it to the pages of the Bible. Taking a handkerchief from her satchel, she wiped her face and blew her nose.

Michael opened his eyes. "Sophie, you're crying. Are you okay?"

"Just a sad letter." She patted the Bible and tried to laugh at her own sentimentality. "A letter from a woman I've never met, who died before I was even born. Still, it feels as if I've found a kindred soul."

Michael patted her hand. "Maybe it is simply a way to help you release the emotions you have inside. You try to be so brave, you know. Sometimes I wonder how you do it."

"I do it by thinking of the man I love." She looked at Michael as she said those words, but they caught in her throat.

For though he smiled and offered her a quick kiss on her nose, Michael had no idea she thought of another as she said them.

Chapter Twenty-Seven

Deion woke with a start—the face of the man he'd killed filled his mind. The Moor had died months ago in body, but he lived strong in Deion's imagination and dreams.

The nightmares started once Deion returned to the front lines. It wasn't the sound of gunfire that worried him. Or the bombing raids. It was the reality that Moors could silently infiltrate their position.

In Jarama the Moors had attacked with force, but Deion had heard other stories—more recent stories—that trickled down the lines. Rumors of soldiers waking to find all their comrades dead, throats slit and bodies mutilated. Some said these were only stories, but Deion didn't doubt they were true.

Alex hunkered down at Deion's left side, a Swiss named Weiner on his other. Both snored softly, almost in unison, and Deion wiggled his shoulders, wishing he could adjust his position without waking them. Suddenly he heard footsteps and spotted a figure running toward them. Snatching up his rifle, Deion was on his feet.

"Deion? For goodness' sake, what are you standing around for? Get those guys rousted. They're lining us up—you need to move or be left."

Within minutes others joined the three, and Deion pushed through the crowd of soldiers to try to hear the shouted orders.

"What's going on?" he asked the man who seemed to be in charge.

"We're moving forward—attacking."

As the men anxiously awaited their orders, small talk centered on other battles. They spoke of men who'd died during the months Deion recovered from his injuries and drove Sophie. They talked about attacks at Jarama, and anger filled their voices as they murmured about their losses.

Because of the slaughter at some of these battles, battalions had joined together. The Washington group joined with the Abraham Lincolns. The British joined one of the regiments of the Fifteenth Brigade. And somewhere near them, he heard, was a group made up of the French, Slavs, and a Spanish battalion.

"Do you remember a Scot named Ian something?" Deion asked as they waited. "I remember him from Jarama. Did he make it out okay?"

"Made it out, but not okay," said a short, stocky man. "His body was fine, but his mind went. He couldn't stop the shakes. Some say he ran away and was killed for desertion. Others say he went so loony they locked him up."

The man looked away, but not before Deion saw understanding in his gaze and the looks of the others. They all knew it could have just as easily been them.

Finally a man approached—a new officer Deion hadn't seen before. He had a high, wide forehead and large cheekbones that gave him a determined look.

"This is our last chance at protecting Bilbao," he said. "We're taking the far hill."

They marched, chatted, shushed one another, and talked again. Before long, they were all crouched in a vineyard, waiting for their turn to advance on a far hill. Deion was thirsty, but he knew his water had to last, so he refused to drink.

A small group of a dozen soldiers huddled under one tree. No one took charge. If there was a plan for their formation or what they were to do on the other side, Deion didn't know what it was. He supposed they waited until they were told to run, guns blazing.

Finally word came down the line. They were to dig in and wait. Deion hated the uncertainty. The anticipation seemed worse than fighting. He worried whether he'd be able to do his part, or if he'd fail and look like a fool in front of the others. And from the looks on the faces of the other men, it seemed they too just wanted to get it over with.

They dug as quietly as they could until they created a long trench large enough for all of them to fit inside. Deion curled his body and snuggled down tight in a hollow near an ancient olive tree. He pressed his hands to his ears, trying to ignore the cries that came from across the field.

He thought about the bespectacled student who had recently joined their ranks. The kid looked no more than seventeen. Just a few hours ago, the boy had a look on his face that was a mix of worry and excitement. Was he now fighting for his life somewhere across the darkness?

Lightning streaked the sky, followed by thunder a few seconds later, and Deion smelled the rain coming. His body trembled with cold. His teeth chattered so violently he was certain the clacking could be heard across enemy lines.

Grenades burst in, pink and green under the black velvet shadow. Soon, big fat raindrops fell, and a man in the next dugout muttered feeble curses. As if that was not bad enough, a whine shrilled through the air, ending in an explosion not fifty yards from Deion's dugout. And the rattle of a machine gun soon followed, crackling like popcorn.

And so they passed the clockless hours of the night, waiting for their orders to fight. Instead, another voice rang through the air as morning dawned. Deion recognized it as their commander's, though his voice wasn't as steady and sure as it had been hours earlier.

"Retreat! Retreat!" the officer's voice called from somewhere behind him, and Deion didn't have to think twice about following orders. He would live to see tomorrow. The only problem was that the Nationalist troops would spill into Bilbao by then.

To give up the line is to give up the town, he thought as they ran.

José rode up the ridge and glanced behind him to watch those who followed. Petra rode Erro. Pepito and his father were on two of the mares; the other two followed quietly. Behind them, Bilbao's skyline was visible in the deep valley below. From the rumors that circulated around town, the Ring of Iron had been crushed. The campaign in the north—the Nationalists' push to destroy the Republican stronghold—was over. And though Pepito and Juan had both insisted the invading army would let them be, José refused to take any chances. It was hard enough leaving Ramona. He just hoped the Nationalists would be as kind to the nurses as his wife believed. And he promised himself that as soon as he led his father to safety, he'd return for her, despite the danger.

They had left before dawn, heading into the mountains where the horses struggled up the steep, sometimes nearly vertical, hillside. The horses were bred to be showpieces, yet José took pride in what they'd accomplished. Calisto led the pack with confidence, as if he'd been a guide horse his whole life. And for some reason, with Petra on his back, Erro too behaved his best, making the trip possible. With the two stallions in the lead, the mares followed without question.

The plan was to save the creatures, but José also knew it was the creatures who saved them. Without the horses, the trip would be impossible for the two old men and the girl. Without the horses, their only choice would have been to submit to the Nationalists and beg for mercy.

By this afternoon, José expected that the soldiers would march into Bilbao's Plaza de Arenal on the bank of the Nervión. The Republicans had evacuated the city without a fight, leaving the people to meet the horror of the arriving enemy troops.

From José's position on the hill, he saw the Nationalists erecting pontoon causeways to take the place of bridges blown apart by retreating troops. He only hoped Sophie had escaped in time.

He'd done all he could for his friend. Petra had done her job well; not only had she brought him the photographs, she had done so without question, trusting his decisions and motivations. Together they'd passed the photos to Lester. And though Lester seemed out of sorts, José did not stay around to find out what had unnerved him. Then the explosions of the bridges started, and José knew time was short. With no rest for him, Petra, or the horses, they raced to the stables, got the others, and headed for the hills.

Nearing the top of a wooded plateau, José slowed his horse. From Calisto's pricked ears, he knew they weren't alone in these mountains. He climbed from the stallion's back and waited for the others to approach.

With tired eyes, Petra looked down at him from her mount. "Is everything okay?"

"We'll soon find out. All of you, stay here. There must be soldiers in these hills, and we don't want to come upon them by surprise."

While they waited in the trees, José walked a half mile toward a clearing. As he neared the edge of a cliff, he fell to his knees and crept closer to the edge, gazing down the hill. Then he sucked in a breath, noting the sea of troops below. There had to be a thousand of them in the valley where he and Calisto had frolicked just a few weeks before.

He pulled the binoculars from his jacket pocket and took a closer look. Before the troops stood a priest wearing a scarlet beret with a purple tassel. If José was not a religious man, he thought, he would find that the vividness of those made the man a perfect target. He patted the holster that held his pistol. It was an ornamental piece—a gift from a friend. But who knew when it would come in handy in these hills?

The talking of the troops ceased as the priest began mass. In the silence his voice carried to José's ears. "*¡Contra Dios no se puede luchar!*" he cried. Against God it is impossible to fight.

José crawled backward until he was out of sight, then stood and headed toward the others, mumbling to himself. "So they have God on their side, do they?"

He thought of the people in Guernica and those in Bilbao

too. Did the destruction they faced mean that God had turned His back on them? Or . . . like the numerous times in the Bible when His people strayed, was God only trying to get their attention?

Or perhaps their pain was due to the sins of others—men who hungered for power and control. José believed that was true above all else.

He found Petra, Pepito, and Juan sitting on the ground, eating lunch and chatting, unaware that less than a mile away the enemy prepared to descend upon the coastal valley. The soldiers would never take this high path where they rested, but still José didn't want to wait too long. He took his water skin from Calisto's saddlebag and took a long drink, curious at what Petra and the men could be talking about with such serious expressions on their faces.

"Edelberto's family fled, I know, to save their lives. It is amazing his cousin Michael still remains." Petra leaned close to the men, as if fearful of speaking too loudly. "But I do not understand . . . why did the people target the rich in the first place? Wasn't it these landowners who provided for them all these years?"

Juan cleared his throat. "There has always been strife between the *dons* and the people. When Don Garcia bought tractors to help with the harvest, the people tore them apart. Then, when their demands for better wages weren't heeded, they refused to gather the harvest. Much was lost that year."

"I've seen men burn the barley in the fields," Pepito added. "Some of the men were arrested and beaten."

"But I don't understand," Petra said. "Wouldn't a tractor have made their lives easier?"

José eyed her curiously. He'd known since he first met her that she was more than an ordinary peasant girl . . . but by the way she talked . . . he could see the truth.

"Yes, Petra," José said, interrupting. "But one tractor driven by one man can do the job of ten men. How will the other nine feed their families? It is hard enough for them to care for their wives and children as it is. The killings were wrong, but the people simply lashed out against the oppression that has for so long burdened them."

He squatted before her and held out his hand.

She looked to the bread in her hand, refusing to meet his gaze. Then she broke off a piece and handed it to him.

"The killing was wrong," he said again. "Surely they could have found another way." Then he stood and took a bite of the bread. "But these are things we can discuss as we travel. We still have a long way to go."

"And just where is our destination?" Juan asked, rising with slow movements.

"Away." José looked into the distant hills, wishing he could offer more than that. "Far from the troops and the fighting. To a high mountain pasture somewhere, I hope, where we can sit out the war."

He looked at his father, realizing his words did not satisfy. His father, more than the other two, no doubt had questions about where they'd find shelter and replenish their food supply, but for those things José had no answer. Finding safety was all he had to offer. He had to trust that after this first thing was accomplished, more answers would come.

What Jose didn't tell them was that by a place where "we could sit out the war," he meant "*they*." For with every mile traveled, he made a promise to himself to return and find Ramona. True, she did not want to come, yet he should have forced her. For a time, his being apart from her had brought her safety. But now she needed his protection.

Chapter Twenty-Eight

$\mathcal{P}$hilip counted up to the tenth day when it was his turn to travel from Alcala, on the outskirts of Madrid, into the city itself. Preparing for an afternoon of leisure in the city, he sifted through his things, looking for something halfway clean to wear. Under the stack of letters from his father, he came upon the navy blue windbreaker quite by accident. *Olimpiada Popular* stood out in a circle of white lettering, and he thought back to the days when he'd come to Spain for the races. A second windbreaker had been tucked inside his duffel back next to the first, and Philip pulled it out and slid it on. He put his hand in the pocket and removed an empty cartridge. Attis's souvenir, no doubt.

Feeling his chest tighten, he removed Attis's jacket, returned it to the duffel, and replaced it with his own.

After cleaning up, he walked toward Madrid with a small group of guys. Charles chatted as they walked, keeping within five feet of Philip at all times. Antony was on the other side—his short legs stretching to match Philip's stride.

The outskirts of Madrid were similar to many of the villages around Spain. Grain fields filled the landscape, and on the edge of town was an ancient church. Next to the church, a group of women clustered in a pool shaded by poplars. They busily scrubbed their clothes on flat rocks, then spread them in the tree's branches to dry.

As the men followed the tree-lined road, three burros tromped passed, prodded forward by an old man with a wide-brimmed hat. Following him, a woman lagged behind with a shawl covering her head, protecting it from the sun high overhead.

"*Adios,*" the man called to the soldiers with a nod as they passed. His words came out of habit, Philip knew. *Go with God.*

Around the woman's neck hung a chain with a large cross. Philip had heard some of the other men talking about that very thing the previous night. Their Christ still ruled over the country, even though there were no priests. Even though their church had been refitted as a mess hall for foreigners. Their children learned songs from the Republicans, and they were taught to read and write in order to keep informed with socialist and communist papers. Still, their religion could not be pried from their hearts.

The other brigade members considered their faith to be a weakness, but Philip wasn't certain. During his time locked away in the jail cell, faith had helped him through. Finding Sophie again had also caused him to believe that God was watching over them both.

And as the most recent days passed, and the fighting on the front lines never materialized as expected, Philip sometimes questioned if God had protected them, or if it was just dumb luck. Either way, a small measure of faith had served him well.

As if reading his thoughts, Charles cursed under his breath. "Fools. Why can't they use *salud* like everyone else? Don't they realize the church has robbed them blind? If God does exist, then it is clear He only cares for the affairs of the rich."

Looking around, Philip could understand how the poverty of one-story adobe houses could seem like evidence confirming Charles's words. So too the barefooted children with hungry, pro-truding stomachs. And the freshly dug graves in the cemetery near the church. Still, Philip wasn't ready to stop believing just yet.

When they reached the train station on the edge of town, Philip saw new volunteers sitting around the station, looking for a ride to wherever their next destination would be. Their clean, well-fitted uniforms and stiff boots betrayed the fact they hadn't seen a battle yet. Of course, Philip's ragged uniform and unkempt hair didn't necessarily mean he'd seen anything worthy of a story in the hometown newspaper.

A line curled toward a building near the train station where steaming soup was ladled out of black kettles for the new troops. Philip fingered the pestas in his pocket, debating whether he should eat here or in town. He turned a questioning gaze to Charles to get his opinion and noticed his friend's eyes fixed at the tree line near the church. A stone house stood there, fancier than the rest. Philip could see mixed on Charles's face longing and disgust.

"It's a good thing the rich were killed. The people deserve better than to be treated like slaves by cruel masters." Charles glanced at Philip, his eyebrows lifted as if waiting for Philip's agreement.

Philip didn't comment, but instead moved to the lunch line. It was easy for Charles to talk about death. It was harder seeing things such as the destruction of Guernica and remaining as passionate.

On just the other side of the lunch line, a speaker touted the communist cause, listing the many ways it could help the people. He spoke of a free government and reform, and his hands moved with his words as if he conducted an orchestra. The speaker's voice rose above the sounds of a train whistle nearing. The only ones listening were the soldiers. Many nodded their heads in agreement.

A few Spaniards settled under the nearby trees. They were given a free lunch in exchange for a listening ear. Yet with bellies now full, most pulled their wide-brimmed hats lower over their eyes and slept—their siesta coming a little early today.

Unimpressed with the speaker's words, Philip turned his attention to the train, wondering if more volunteers would spill out, and questioning if in the end their efforts would do any good.

He eyed the windows of the train, and his attention settled on the front passenger car where men and women gathered their things to disembark. It was the dark hair that caught his attention first, and the simple way the woman brushed her hair behind her ear.

Sophie.

Handing his bowl and spoon to Charles, Philip darted toward the train, relief flooding over him. She was safe. She was here. And in a moment, she would be in his arms again.

At first Sophie thought she was seeing things. The tall man in the white and blue jacket couldn't be Philip—it just couldn't be. It wasn't until she focused on his face, the way his eyes lit up, his smile, that she knew it was. She paused as he lifted a hand in greeting. A sea of men separated them.

Sophie lifted her chin slightly in acknowledgment, and then Michael's hand tightened around her waist. Philip's eyes darted from Sophie to Michael, and a look of confusion filled his gaze.

Her feet refused to move forward. And her heart started to ache, remembering their time together. *Philip.*

More than anything, Sophie wanted to push Michael's hand away and rush into Philip's arms. She could see in his eyes he wanted the same thing. Unfortunately, this thing was much bigger than she was. As it was, she barely held on to Michael's trust by a thin thread. If she left now, he would know she had double-crossed him. Not only that, she still had no idea if her protector was near. She needed Michael. Needed to stay by his side. Needed him to survive the mess she'd gotten herself into.

And so she turned away. Sophie grabbed Michael's hand and quickened her footsteps, praying Philip wouldn't follow. And when she climbed into the horse cab that waited for them, she glanced back one last time. He hadn't followed. But even from this distance, she saw pain in his gaze that cut her to the core.

"Is that someone you know?" Michael spoke, glancing back also.

"I think so. I'm not sure. There were dozens of men I cared for—so many injuries. And I'm sure they remember me better than I remember them. Funny, how the faces of men in pain all seem to look the same."

Seemingly satisfied, Michael sat next to Sophie and placed his arm around her shoulders. "I'm sure there is more than one soldier out there who has feelings for you, *Divina*. Maybe a few who would even say they are in love. The beautiful painter who shows the world what they fight for, who is also a compassionate nurse—their own angel of mercy." Michael squeezed her shoulder. "And I don't blame them."

Sophie chuckled. Her laughter was a little too loud, but it was all she could do to keep from crying. "Yes, perhaps that could be the case." She quickly changed the subject. "So tell me, Michael, what will we be doing now that we are in Madrid—safe from the fighting, at least for a time? I saw you received a telegram at the station in Bilbao. Will you be off on another assignment?"

Inwardly Sophie hoped that would be the case. If he left soon, maybe she'd have a chance to find Philip and explain. Besides, what more could Walt ask from her now? She hoped she had given him the information he needed to find the gold.

Michael cleared his throat. "The telegram was nothing like that. Just a note from my editor saying he received the most recent batch of photos. It's dangerous for the couriers, you know—risking their lives to make sure the photos get to the press offices."

The sun was high in the sky, different from the clouds that had been over Bilbao. Sophie felt beads of sweat on her brow and hoped Michael believed they were due to the hot rays of light.

"Who are these couriers?" She unbuttoned her jacket and slipped it off, as if this was the most casual conversation in the world.

A shout rang out from behind them as the horse carriage continued on. A man's voice, but Sophie couldn't make out the words. Her stomach ached, and she forced herself not to look back.

"The couriers? Just men who want to help the cause. They get paid for their work, of course. But more than that, they get the satisfaction of knowing they are helping our efforts."

Michael helped Sophie with her jacket. Then he folded it and laid it over his lap.

Sophie stared straight ahead at the cobblestone streets the horse cab carried them across. It was the same Madrid, but she saw it differently now. And though Michael was again by her side as she entered the city, she knew nothing would ever be the same.

"Sophie, are you okay? You look as if you've seen a ghost."

She sighed. "I never could hide my feelings very well, could I? It's just seeing those soldiers . . . it brought so many memories of the hospitals I worked at during our months apart. The men—their shattered bodies and cries for help. The way they faced so much on the front lines . . ."

The image of Philip, and how she first saw him in the foxhole as she ran to him, seeking his help. His arms around her. His caring smile as she painted. His sad eyes as they parted . . .

Tears trickled down her cheeks, and she thought her heart would split open. "I saw things, felt things I never thought I'd face. My heart breaks just thinking of all those men lost, all their pain."

Her hands covered her face, and Sophie felt Michael's arms wrap around her, pulling her toward him. She allowed her cheek to rest against his chest as sobs overtook her.

"Oh, dear girl, there is so much inside you that you don't let on. Did you think I would not understand? Go ahead and cry. I will not think any less of you."

And so she did. Sophie cried until weariness overtook her and she melted into Michael's arms. Only he did not know that she wasn't weeping for all those soldiers, but simply for one. One whose broken heart she saw in his confused gaze.

Sophie lay in the hotel room bed, feeling as if all energy had drained from her. The desire to head back to the train station and find Philip overwhelmed her. She had to explain to him why she was with Michael, and hope he would understand. If she let her thoughts spin long enough, she could almost convince herself that she should.

Surely the key to finding the gold wasn't all on her shoulders? There had to be someone else who could get any additional information for Walt. Did God really want her to live under false pretenses? He was the One who brought Philip into her life, after all. Would He be so cruel to show her what her heart desired most and then keep it from her?

But inwardly she knew she had done the right thing. Like Esther in the Bible, God had placed her in this position *for such a time as this.*

She also knew the Philip in her thoughts wasn't complete perfection, as she set him up in her mind—just as she knew Michael wasn't complete evil. Instead, they were two men who loved her, each with strengths and weaknesses. It was just that she believed in Philip's cause, and despised the choices Michael had made.

Yet, Sophie also realized, if she had believed in the Nationalist side, Michael's choices would seem honorable to her—brave even.

Sophie rose and tried to press the wrinkles from her skirt with her palms. Michael had gone to a meeting and given her no time for his return. She washed her face with a towel that had been left with the pitcher of water and basin in her room. She didn't want to have to explain her tears. And she wasn't willing to lie to him about one more thing. She had lied so much that sometimes she forgot the truth.

Sophie pinned up her hair, and a nagging feeling came over her, reminding her that somehow even spotting Philip had a purpose. As she unpacked her satchel, looking for clean stockings, she came upon the Bible. Could it be that she was so focused on these men in her life, and the numerous emotions that stirred within, that she had forgotten about the most important relationship—her relationship with God?

It was easy to complain to Him. To question why she was the one put in this position. It was easy to ache for Philip, to grow angry with Michael. All those things were simpler than confronting her weaknesses. Or accepting her part in God's overall plan and trusting He indeed knew best.

A knock on the hotel room door startled her. Michael had

said he was heading to the Telefónica building, and she knew he couldn't be back this soon. Instead, Sophie hoped that somehow Philip had found her.

Quickly wiping the tears on her cheeks, Sophie hurried to the door. But the tears came again, even faster this time, when she opened it to find not Philip, but Walt.

"You," she spouted, trying to keep her voice from rising. "What are you doing here? What will you ask of me this time?"

Without hesitation, Walt entered and closed the door behind him. "I am sorry, Sophie. I hate to think of all you've been through. . . ."

"You have no idea what I've been through. Who I just saw." She crossed her arms over her chest. "I saw Philip . . . and he saw me with Michael. Can you imagine what that was like, not being able to explain?"

Walt only nodded, and Sophie noticed he didn't seem one bit surprised by the news.

"I need you to do something for me. I need your help . . . again. But this time we're close. In fact, it was your help that made the breakthrough."

"I'm sorry, Walt." Sophie shook her head. "I'm not going to do one more thing for you until you tell me the truth—the whole truth. You got me in the middle of this, and you owe me no less."

Instead of protesting, Walt moved to the window and glanced out, scanning the city street below. "Yes, I will. And I hope you're a quick study, because there is much you need to know. You're right. To continue, you need to understand the whole story. And once you do, you'll understand why I've asked so much of you."

Walt motioned for Sophie to take a seat on the small sofa in her hotel room; then he pulled out the chair from the desk and placed it in front of her, sitting down and leaning forward for emphasis.

"Sophie," he said with a sigh. "It all started the day Michael saw you in Boston."

Chapter Twenty-Nine

$\mathcal{F}$or the next hour Walt told Sophie a tale she found hard to believe—one that started years before the war with a group of men who wished to get their hands on the priceless gold artifacts previously held within the bank vaults deep under the city streets of Madrid.

"So you're telling me these men were interested in the gold before the war even broke out? Before the threat of losing it was real?" Sophie rubbed her temples, wishing her headache away and attempting to focus on his words.

"Spain has been unstable for a long time. And many of the generals have been unhappy with the influences filtering into their country. With the rise of numerous antifascist groups, and the election of a Republican government, they knew it was a matter of time before a civil war erupted."

"So these Fascists planned to steal the gold . . . in order to fund their cause?"

"As did many other groups . . . any leaders who wanted funds considered the gold their answer. Of course, the generals could not tell the people working for them they simply wanted an easy source of income. In fact, many involved in the plot believed the purpose was simply to protect the priceless treasures."

"Michael," Sophie mouthed. "Is that what he believes?"

Walt nodded. "Yes, Sophie. It is."

She stood and paced the small hotel room. "Why doesn't someone talk to him? Tell him the truth? I can talk to him. . . ."

Walt shook his head. "Some have tried. Michael didn't believe them . . . especially since the request to help was brought to him by his own parents."

"His parents? But you said it all began the day he met me at the museum."

"Michael's father called a meeting there. Other businessmen joined him to plead the case for the precious gold artifacts. The museum was just a cover, of course, a front for Fascist sympathizers." Walt removed his hat, setting it on the armrest of the chair. "Of course, they had no idea that Michael would see a lovely young American that day and fall in love . . . or that his fiancée would find her way to Spain and become the greatest hindrance to their goal."

Sophie blew out a heavy breath. "So what's next? I assume the missing gold includes those valuable pieces you've talked about, right? Are you any closer to finding the lost truckloads?"

"Yes. The photographs you stole seem to be just what we needed." Walt lowered his head. "Unfortunately, they were compromised. That's why I need you to tell me what you saw on them. To sketch it if you will."

"You mean José and his friend didn't pass them off?"

"No, they were passed off, but that is all we know. I'm afraid our two men in Bilbao were both found dead. We do not know what happened to the photographs after that."

Sophie assumed that Walt was referring to Lester. She also wondered if the second man was the guardian who had protected her all those days and nights. But she didn't ask. It would be one more burden for her to carry—and she wasn't sure she could handle all that weighed upon her as it was.

"So, do you think you can sketch what you saw? I don't know where else to look. We've searched all the ports near Cartagena, where the gold was shipped from. We know the stolen gold was taken to some type of cave, and we assumed it was one similar to the naval caves where the shipment was held. But from what we have searched, that is not the case."

"Well, as my mother always said, two heads are better than one." Sophie moved to retrieve her sketchbook and pencils from her satchel. "I'll do what I can, and you can tell me about the robbery, as much as you know. Maybe something else I've overheard will tie in—I'll never know until I hear the complete truth."

Walt tapped his fingers on the chair and then studied her eyes. "You say you saw Philip?"

Sophie nodded, opening the sketchbook to a blank page.

"And still you stayed?"

She nodded again, outlining on the page the shape of one of the ships she had seen in the photograph of the harbor.

"Okay, I will start from the beginning—when the gold first left the vault. I trust you, Sophie." He intertwined his fingers and settled them on his lap. "Besides, I have no other choice. The Republican troops are losing ground on all sides. If I can find the gold artifacts, they can be sold for far more than what the Russians paid—money that can help the troops. Not only that, my employer has promised they'll be sold to some of the most trustworthy collectors in the world—ones who can guarantee their safety, and perhaps will be willing to sell them back to Spain when this land finds peace."

Sophie set aside the sketchbook as Walt told her about the layout of the vault. But even as she forced herself to concentrate on Walt's words, the image of Philip's face didn't leave her. Her heart ached, but more than that, hearing the truth behind the gold confirmed she was doing the right thing—even if her heart told her otherwise.

"A dozen *carabinero* guards patrolled the vault," Walt explained. "Another two guards greeted the boxes and their carriers when they arrived at street level. The guards escorted the loads to police trucks waiting in the bank courtyard. The loaded trucks then left for the nearby Atocha railroad station—the one you arrived at this morning."

Where I saw Philip, Sophie thought.

"The lack of adequate security would have made Michael's mouth water," Walt said with a chuckle. "Can you believe only one *miliciano* driver armed with a pistol and one *carabinero* patrolled each load?"

"Surely word would have leaked out about the shipments. Weren't the bankers worried about that?"

"That's the amazing thing. Most of those who worked inside the bank truly believed it was weapons being transported. Premier Francisco Largo Caballero and Finance Minister Juan Negrin knew the truth, but most of the bankers believe their treasure is still locked inside the vault, including the louis d'or coins."

"You've mentioned those before—what are they, exactly?" Sophie asked.

"A very rare coin, minted in the seventeenth century. They are extremely fine pieces with the head of the French monarch Louis XVI on them. But that is just one example of the worth of some of the pieces they treated as equal to plain gold bars."

"The first convoy left with eight hundred white bags on September 15 at eleven thirty at night," Walt continued. "The rest followed at nightly intervals. The trip to Cartagena took more than fifty hours. Once there, the gold was tucked behind three solid doors. Each door closed off one cave and was secured by three locks. They had three lock men, one for each lock."

"How do you know so much?"

Walt's eyes twinkled. "Our friend Emilio was one of the lock men."

"Maria's husband?" Sophie felt her heart pound, understanding for the first time how vital her information had been.

Walt nodded. "The very one. The second week of October, the finance minister ordered the gold sent to Russia. The Spanish wanted a receipt, but the Russian in charge refused. No one wanted to be personally responsible. They knew if word leaked out, then one spark would ignite Spanish tempers. All those who disagreed with the exchange of gold for arms, or wanted it for their own means, would hunt it down at any cost. Those in charge of the shipment also worried about interception by anarchists on land or by Italian or German ships at sea. No one can be trusted when it comes to such wealth. The Russians told the Spaniards a formal receipt would be issued in Moscow by the State Bank."

"And they let the gold go anyway?"

"Most of it. At dusk on October 22, twenty five-ton trucks in two convoy shuttles transported the gold. For three moonless nights, from seven to dawn, sailors loaded the white ammunition boxes. Since there was no formal order and no receipt, it's no wonder some of the gold disappeared. In the confusion, no one even missed it. My guess is that the thieves took a box or two from each truck. The right number of truckloads were delivered, but no one checked to see if the correct number of boxes was contained in each."

Walt's voice rose as he spoke. "The ships sailed for Odessa at ten the next morning. A relay of Spanish warships guarded the convoy along the Mediterranean. The captains of the navy vessels were not told what they guarded. They carried sealed envelopes to be opened only if they received a special SOS code."

"You found out all of this from Emilio?"

"Yes, he was one of the few who joined the operation from beginning to end."

"And Maria no doubt knew every detail."

Walt cocked an eyebrow. "*Sí*, she is a beautiful woman who no doubt has her ways with men. We can assume as much."

"So the shipment made it to Russia, I presume?" Sophie asked.

"It arrived in Odessa in November, and when it was completely counted in January, it was worth over five hundred million dollars."

"And no one knows the rest of the gold is missing—or where to look for it?"

"We know it is held in a cave somewhere—which was confirmed by the photos you found."

"Photos we no longer have." Sophie sighed.

"We have searched all of the naval caves held in Nationalist territories, but came up with nothing. The photos will help, but it will take time to match all the clues. And our worry is that the longer it takes, the more time Michael has to get the gold out of the country. He's stalling, we know—trying to find the perfect way to ship the priceless treasures now that he has them in his possession. In fact, we are sure that is what he was strategizing in Bilbao with his friends. So if you heard anything at all . . ."

Sophie stood and crossed the room, searching her memory for any mention of caves, but the only thing that came to mind were the coal mines that Eleanor mentioned in her letters, and that was hardly a fit. Unless . . .

"Walt." She turned to him. "Have you thought about other caves? Maybe coal mines? They are all around the country, and many are quite developed, having been mined for years. Of course . . ." She thought out loud. "Coal mines aren't very often near the coast."

Walt jumped to his feet. "I think you're on to something. There are other places. . . ." Walt snapped his fingers. "Yes, Sophie, I think that is it. Grab that sketchbook and show me what you saw."

For the next thirty minutes, Sophie sketched the boats in the harbor. She sketched the interior of a tunnel and the large warnings on the wall that read *DINAMITO*. She tried to remember as much as she could, but she knew her drawings missed much.

"What about the land around the harbor?" Walt asked. "Is there anything that stood out?"

"Well, one of them had a large mountain of sorts."

"Really? What did it look like?"

Sophie sketched a triangular shaped mountain made of rock, looming over the bay.

"That's it!" Walt turned to her, eyes bright. "I have a feeling Michael will return today with news that he's been given an assignment to cover a story near the Strait of Gibraltar. I'll see what types of caves are in the area—other than the naval ones already searched."

Sophie remembered seeing the rock of Gibraltar in a painting. "Yes, I think that's the one. Why didn't I think of it sooner? So, if you believe that's where he's going, should I ask to join him?" Her heart pounded a little quicker, realizing how close they were to the gold.

Walt strode to the window and stroked his chin. "No, that won't work." He snatched his hat from the armrest and set it on his head with a flourish. "The Strait is in Nationalist territory, and you, Sophie, are a well-known sympathizer for the Republicans. You'd be a target for sure. You must let Michael go alone. Let him think you'll be staying where it is safe, in Madrid."

"Let him think? Where will I be instead?"

"With me. We'll travel down together. After all, you saw the photos. You can help me find the caves. You'll have to be in disguise, of course. It will be a challenge, but I believe I can have false papers made up by dawn." Walt stroked his chin. "Yes, I think it will work. There are Americans volunteering on the Fascist side too, you know—nurses especially. That will be your cover—an American nurse heading to southern Spain to volunteer. Tell me, Sophie, do you have a name you'd like to go by?"

"How about Eleanor?" Sophie said without hesitation.

"Is it someone you know?"

"Yes, it is. Eleanor was an American who was very much in love with the Spanish people. My kindred spirit. She couldn't find a way to help, but I think she'd be proud to know I can."

"Eleanor it is." Walt turned toward the door. "I'll be in touch. . . . If you can, find a way to change your look. Maybe do something with your hair?"

Sophie touched her shoulder-length brown hair, letting it run through her fingers. "I'll see what I can do."

Walt left, and Sophie moved to the satchel that held the Bible. Changing her look seemed like such a simple thing to sacrifice. That wasn't what worried her. But her stomach knotted as she wondered if she could pull off the charade. She'd taken chances before, but always as herself. How much would she have to change to be perceived as someone new? And just how did one go about inventing a whole separate life?

Chapter Thirty

*I*nstead of trying to hide his limp, Ritter emphasized it as he strode from the gangplank of the German ocean liner *Bremen* at Pier 86. New York City loomed before him—a skyline he'd seen many times in newspapers or newsreels, but never imagined seeing in person.

His steps were slower than usual, as he emphasized with his cane. His papers bore his name, but instead of showing any military status, his paperwork stated that he was the director of an export-import company, visiting New York on business.

The American woman strode by his side, her footsteps matching his. Though her arm wasn't entwined in his, she walked close enough to his side that Ritter thought anyone who took time to notice them would assume they were a couple— which, over the weeklong journey across the Atlantic—had evolved into more than mere acting.

Of course, Monica knew little about Ritter's past and his true motives for traveling to the States. While she knew of the arrangement between her father and Göring—to share their knowledge of aircraft to the benefit of both—only Ritter and Göring himself knew there was more to the trip than the exchange of ideas. Much more.

The sky was overcast, and it was cold for a June day. The customs inspector pulled thin gloves from his hands, his teeth chattering as he rifled through Ritter's things. He gave Ritter's suitcase the normal scrutiny and even took a quick glance at the cane.

Monica spoke quickly in English, and Ritter understood no more than a few words. The inspector waved them forward, and Ritter turned to her with a questioning glance.

"I explained how you were injured in a flying accident, but I don't think he cared much. I think he was most interested in pouring himself another cup of coffee to warm up for the rest of his shift."

"Excellent. Where are we off to first?"

"I thought you'd enjoy a tour of the weapons factory, but I'm not sure they'd let you in." She winked at him. "So instead, why don't we meet my father for lunch? He's eager to meet you."

"I'd love to, but are you sure you want that? I'm afraid you might get bored with all our aviation talk."

"Are you kidding? I love hearing about it. If I had my choice, I'd be working in that factory myself. Of course, my mother would never allow it. She thinks a woman's place is at a man's side. In fact, the only reason she allowed me to travel overseas at all is that she thought my world travels would interest an eligible bachelor."

"Then she won't be surprised to meet me?"

"Not at all." Monica squeezed his arm as they moved toward a waiting yellow cab. "In fact, you are exactly the type of person she hoped I'd meet. Someone educated, motivated. Someone who is involved in all the right circles."

"So basically, when it comes to both your father and mother, you've captured the perfect man."

"Captured? Not quite." Monica slid inside the cab and patted the seat. "This guy was thrust upon me by my 'Uncle Hermann.' But, yes, I think my traveling companion is worth knowing, especially since he doesn't think a woman's place is in the home and doesn't think aviation talk is above me."

"Not at all," Ritter said, squeezing her hand and ignoring both her little pun and the guilt rising within him. For not only was he not what she, or her parents, thought, but his intention was to use her for his gain.

As they drove through New York toward the high-rises, Ritter studied the crowded streets, taking it all in. He also replayed his plan.

Yes, he would talk about aviation with Monica's father, and even share some information in return for what the American offered. But the true purpose of Ritter's trip wasn't for the information freely offered to him, but for that which he would only obtain through trickery and theft.

Though they retreated from the Iron Ring around Bilbao, the sound of gunfire sounded closer than Deion anticipated. His arms shook with fear, but he refused to run into the woods as he saw other soldiers do. He refused to leave the fight.

He'd been under fire before, yet the memory of the bullet piercing his leg seemed like something that happened to another person long ago. He could remember that it hurt, but he couldn't remember the pain.

But fear, that was another thing. It came back to him the moment he picked up the rifle the first day he'd returned to the Internationals. And now that he was back under fire, Deion realized it wasn't bravery that kept his feet planted, but the fear of shame. Shame of being a coward among others who had faced much worse. Shame of being first to run for cover. Shame that he had lifted his hand high and signed up with great conviction, then come thousands of miles to fail.

He knew now how important the fight was. He'd seen what happened at Guernica and knew that the Fascists wouldn't stop there. Nothing would stand in their way, not even the very people—the heart of the country.

As they marched down the road, gunfire erupted around them. Deion dove toward the side of the road, throwing his body into the protective trees and boulders. He pressed his face into the ground and covered his head with his hands.

Bullets pinged against the rock like angry hornets, sending a shower of rock chips flipping through the air. Deion saw the man next to him crumble to his knees. As if in slow motion, the soldier's hand flew to his neck, and he opened his mouth to speak. Instead of words, blood spilled from his lips.

Deion jumped to help him when another explosion hit. Closer this time. He felt a jolt through his gut like an electric shock. And then only darkness.

It hadn't surprised Ritter when he first learned of his assignment. Ever since the end of the Great War, he knew Germany's military had been limited by the Versailles Treaty. They had not shut down everything, though, and even managed to create an illegal *Schwarz Luftwaffe*—black air force. Still, their efforts to keep up with technology had been handicapped.

The Black Luftwaffe had purchased what technology they could. But, Göring explained, what they couldn't buy they were forced to steal, since some things weren't available at any price.

Unable to carry any information with him, Ritter replayed in his mind all he knew about the Norden bombsight. Göring had passed on what he could; the rest was up to Ritter.

Ritter walked to the window. Just four months ago he was in a first-aid station in the heart of Spain; now he was staying at the Taft Hotel in downtown New York.

Tonight he had plans for dinner with Monica's family, but before then he had other priorities. Changing into a pair of slacks and a white cotton shirt, he left the hotel and took a cab to Brooklyn. Not speaking much English, he presented the cab driver with a written address.

Ritter was surprised to find that his contact lived in a simple apartment in a rumble-tumble building. He found the right apartment and knocked on the door. A thin man with hollow cheeks and several days' worth of stubble opened the door.

"Herr Kern?" Ritter said, stating the code word.

"Who asks?" the man responded in German.

"Your cousin from the old country has sent her greetings. Hilda asked me to look you up when I came to town." Ritter nodded as he finished the phrase, telling the man he'd come from the office of Göring.

"Hilda, *ja*, of course." The man's eyes brightened. "Come in. Would you like some coffee? Not as good as the stuff in the old country, but not bad."

For the next hour Kern told Ritter about his work in the Norden factory. Kern wasn't his real name, of course, nor was Anderson—the name he'd adopted when he came to the States.

"I could get a better job if I wanted to," Kern explained as he described the layout of the factory. "But I am of best use in the janitorial department. I'm allowed access into most areas, and no one pays me any attention."

"So you like living here?" Ritter eyed the small apartment.

"The United States has treated me well, but my heart remains with Germany. Most of my family is there, you know. I consider myself on assignment for the Fatherland. My work isn't for the money offered to me, but for the pure knowledge that I assist Hitler with his dreams."

"You are a fine German indeed." Ritter rose and moved to the window, glancing down at the street below and noting a passel of thin boys playing kick the can. "On behalf of Adolf Hitler, I thank you for your service. Now, how many blueprints of the Norden bombsight can you get me?"

The man laughed. "Why, sir, you waste no time getting down to business, do you?"

Ritter smiled as he turned. "We both know patriotism wastes no time with niceties. And I can assure you that you will be nicely rewarded for your efforts. In fact, I believe Herr Göring has already set up a New York bank account for your efforts, courtesy of the treasury of the Third Reich."

"I will get them to you, but you will only have eight hours at most to complete your task. Meet me here tomorrow night. Do what you must; then return them to me before dawn. I work a double shift the next day—both closing the plant and opening it. I must have those plans returned before the first workers arrive in the morning."

"Of course." Ritter turned and handed the man the cane he'd been leaning on. "I think this will be of use to you. It has a hollow center. I'm just so sorry to hear about your bad strain to your ankle. You should be more careful about moving so hastily up and down these flights of stairs."

Sophie waited most of the day for Michael to return. She'd put on her nicest clothes and fixed her hair just the way he liked. But from the moment she opened the door to his knock, she knew something was terribly wrong.

Michael strode inside and slammed the door. Without looking at her face, he approached quickly and pushed her into a chair. She fell back, surprised, her head hitting the backrest as she fell.

"So who is he, Sophie? The man you spent the afternoon with? Is he a lover? Or are you spying for the money? Is that it?"

Sophie's hands shook as she pushed her hair back from her face. "I ha–have no idea what you're talking about."

Michael let out a gruff laugh and tilted her face to his. "The man in the hat. You should know. He was in your room most of the day."

She pulled her chin away. "Were you having my room watched?"

"Yes. As I should have after the little incident in Bilbao. Tell me, did you set the bomb yourself that blew up the shed, or did you pay another?" Michael cursed. "You have no idea what you destroyed. Do you think this is only a game?"

"I'm not going to answer any of these accusations until you calm down. Why do you suddenly think you can treat me this way?"

Instead of answering her, Michael strode to the window. "Really, do you think talking to me like this is wise? Especially considering the fact that the man you love will be dead within thirty minutes . . . unless you tell me the truth—the whole truth."

"Walt's a reporter, a friend. He's the man who helped me into Spain. We talked, that's all. Surely you remember me telling you about him. We are just friends. I promise."

"No, not him. I figured out your friend Walt awhile ago. Hard not to when he seems to show up wherever I am. I'm talking about the man you *love*. I would have never known of your true affections if it hadn't been for the little episode at the train station today. I could tell something bothered you, but I didn't know what it was until our horse carriage rounded the corner and, according to one of my associates, the American volunteer started running after us." Michael laughed. "He's quite fast, you know, and was determined to talk to you. But I don't think that's possible now. He's a little tied up at the moment." Michael pointed to the street below.

Sophie couldn't help herself. She jumped from the chair and hurried to the window. As if watching the window and waiting for her to look out, a man . . . Cesar . . . pulled Philip, bound and gagged, out of the backseat. Sophie gasped as Michael grasped her arm.

"I'm not sure what surprises you most," he said. "To see your . . . Philip, is it? . . . or to see Cesar. You thought he was dead, didn't you? Cesar said that Luis knocked him out, but didn't kill him. The old man has too much of a soft heart, if you ask me. It doesn't fit with this work at all."

"Luis?"

"Surely you did not forget Benita's husband. He volunteered for the job—to live on the street as a homeless man in order to watch over you. Isn't that sweet? But thankfully Cesar got free and got my photographs back." Michael came close again, forcing her into a corner of the room. "So tell me, how did you know which were the important ones? Did Walt tell you?" He signed to Cesar, who shoved Philip back into the car and slammed the door.

Instead of threatening her again, Michael turned back toward the window.

Sophie placed her hands over her face, trying to think . . . think of anything to get out of the middle of this. Anything to save Philip.

Michael sighed. "That's okay. You don't have to speak. But unless I walk to that car in fifteen minutes, your Philip will be shot and dumped into some alley. My friends have done it since the beginning of the war, and they are quite good."

"And what if I tell you . . . then what? Will you let him go? Somehow I doubt it."

"I will let him go . . . let both of you go. I never got into this to hurt people, only to help. And if you tell me what you are in the middle of, and what exactly your friend Walt knows, I'll make sure you both live to see tomorrow." Michael glanced at his watch. "But you'd better talk fast. You only have thirteen minutes now."

Sophie took a deep breath and began. "We figured out where you have the gold . . . in a cave near Algeciras. I was going with Walt to find it. But if I don't, I'm sure he'll go alone." Sophie took a step toward Michael and placed a hand on his arm. "But you have to know that what he's doing is for the best. Walt is trying to get the gold into the hands of those who can protect it. Otherwise it will be lost for good."

Michael laughed. "And you believe that? How do you know?"

Sophie squared her shoulders. "And how do you know that what you're doing is best? Do you really think helping the Fascists is the best thing for the people of this country?" She strode to the window. "We can debate this later. I told you what you want to know." She pointed down to the street. "Go get Philip, will you? Make sure he's not hurt."

"Fine. And then you and I—we will take a little trip."

Sophie's jaw dropped. "But you said you'd let us go!"

"I will. I'm a man of my word. But I never said when. I'll let you go when I find my gold safe . . . and it is shipped off to my buyer." Michael shrugged. "This works well for me, actually . . . that the simple girl I fell in love with has become an important pawn."

Deion woke to find himself in some type of field hospital. A sharp pain radiated from his gut, but when he looked down, he saw no open wounds. No blood.

"You are lucky." It was a woman's voice, and it was soft despite the frantic cries from other men around the room. "It was the concussion of the artillery that knocked you out, soldier. You'll be up and back into the fight in a few days."

The woman wore an ordinary nurse's uniform, but her presence said it all. She was in charge of this field hospital, no matter what anyone said.

She reminded him of Roberta—a singer he'd known in Chicago. She was beautiful, to say the least, with skin the same color as his. Yet she did not carry herself as one caught up in her own looks.

Deion sat up in bed, watching her. His head hurt slightly, but other than that it was as if he was waking from a night's sleep.

The nurse was using all her energy to turn over a mattress on another bed—most likely to hide a large bloodstain.

"Ma'am, that looks difficult. Do you think I can, uh, help you with that?"

She shrugged. "If you'd like. I'd appreciate it. But only if you feel up to it, soldier."

Deion rose, forcing his legs to stay steady under him. He grabbed one side of the thin mattress and helped turn it. His eyes stayed on the woman the whole time. She smiled under his gaze and didn't look away. Her slim figure looked attractively feminine, even in the drab uniform. She wore a revolver on the belt of her nurse's uniform, and it seemed to fit her somehow.

She sighed as she glanced around at the other rows of bed already filled. "Here's a pretty kettle of fish," she said to no one in particular. "Any idea what we can do here? I have more injured men than beds."

Deion wasn't sure the nurse was talking to him until she looked directly into his eyes.

"Well, I think the problem is these bed frames," he finally responded. "They limit you to one person per bed. If we take the mattresses off and lay them on the floor, we could put three injured men to every two mattresses."

"Excellent idea. Can you help me with that, soldier?"

Deion felt his lips curl into a smile, forgetting why he stood in the aid station. The ache in his head increased, but he paid it no mind. "The name's Deion, and I'd love to," he said to the nurse, "if you'll tell me who it is I'll be helping?"

Chapter Thirty-One

There were more dark faces in Algeciras than Walt had ever seen. It made sense. This city on the southern coastline in Spain, had been founded by Moors in 713. And now they returned as paid killers.

Legionaries filled the streets. They spoke in excited, loud voices like boy scouts on a campout as they moved among their tents set up along the streets. Walt could tell from their eager movements they were ready to fight. Though the Moors had been unwelcome in Spain for many years, they now came for a distinct purpose—to fight for the Nationalist side and gain a fine payment for their efforts.

Of course, if the mercenaries actually received the money they were promised it would surprise Walt. The Nationalists said a lot of things they didn't do.

And if Walt had his way about it, the gold they planned to use to fund some of their efforts would soon be under his control . . . and he could send it to those who really cared for the concerns of the Spanish people.

It had taken two days to travel from Madrid to Valencia. From there he had taken a boat to Gibraltar. Now he strode down the street, scanning the faces of the dark-haired women, hoping against odds one of them might be Sophie. He had returned to the hotel only hours after he'd talked with her to find her gone. The clerk said she'd left in a hurry with a dark-haired man, and Walt had a feeling she was in trouble. The best case was that Michael had brought Sophie to Algeciras. He didn't want to think about the worst case.

Walt hurried through the streets, then slowed as the bodies pressed tighter around him. Out of the corner of his eye he spotted a figure with a hat pulled down low over his face. Walt slowed even more and moved closer to the nearest building, a small clothing store filled with Moors.

Walt paused at the window, pretending to look at the bolts of fabric displayed there. Instead, he looked at the reflection and got a closer look at the man who trailed him. Though he couldn't see the man's eyes, he knew that firm jaw and crooked nose anywhere. *Cesar.*

Walt removed his long coat and folded it over his arm. As cautiously as possible, he removed his revolver from his pants pocket and hid it under the folds of his jacket. He moved back into the street, realizing there was no way he could continue until he shook his tail. Seeing a group of schoolchildren ahead, Walt returned the gun to his pocket, knowing what he had to do. He took a deep breath and moved their direction.

Walt removed his camera from its case and approached the teacher. "What beautiful children. Are they enjoying an outing?" he asked in Spanish. "Such beautiful, smiling faces cannot be ignored. Do the children wish to pose for a newspaper photo?" Walt gently touched the heads of a few of those closest to him. "The people should be reminded again that the fight for our grand country is not for men who desire power, but for the future of the next generation, don't you agree?"

Immediately the group of children circled up and smiled his direction. Walt focused his camera on them; then he shook his head. "I'm sorry, the sun is too bright. It is right in their eyes. Is it okay if we turn the other direction?"

Obediently the teacher and her students turned, and Walt noticed Cesar standing near the door of a small café. Walt hunkered down, focusing the lens on the children, and captured a perfect frame of Cesar at the same time. Before he could snap the shot though, Cesar figured out what was happening and hurriedly moved behind a throng of Moors in order to hide himself. Seeing his chance to escape Cesar, Walt quickly snapped the photograph, then rose, glancing at his watch.

"I'm sorry, children. I have to run. I'm late for a meeting." And before his tail could see him leave, Walt hustled into a side street, then followed a path of small twisting roads until he glanced back and was sure he'd lost Cesar for good.

Walt hurried out of town, then slowed again as he neared the docks. It was here that some of the poor in town gathered to beg for alms. One woman, who appeared to be crippled, called to him in a whiny voice.

Walt approached, and the women's eyes warmed as she held out her fingers. Her dark hands were rough, and her fingers curled like talons. They were dirty hands and covered with sores, evidence of the woman's meager existence.

Walt reached into his pocket and pulled out a handful of coins. "I imagine, dear lady, you have lived here most of your life, have you not?" He placed one of the coins in her hand, but withheld the others.

"Oh, yes, sir, I was born in this town, as were my father and my father's father."

"Then you know this place better than any other, do you not?"

She patted her legs. "Before these limbs grew tired, I ran these very streets and knew every inch by heart."

Walt offered her a few more coins and a small bottle of water he pulled from his jacket pocket.

The woman's face was wrinkled and dark from the intense rays of the sun, and she eyed the water with even more eagerness than the coins. "I get mighty thirsty waiting under the sun for enough to purchase a bite of bread." She ran her tongue over dry lips. "But if I stay home where it is cool, I cannot eat."

Walt handed her the bottle of water; then he turned the conversation back to what he needed. "It's a shame that you are not able to get around now. I've heard rumors of a tunnel dug under the channel—a link to Africa. If you were still young, perhaps you would be able to show me around. Together, perhaps we could discover if such a thing existed."

"Are you a reporter?" she asked. She took a long swig of the water.

"Indeed I am, and it would make a wonderful story for my publication if such a tunnel truly existed. Some people think I'm a fool for believing that some of the Moors being brought over here have come to work in this tunnel—and not to fight."

"The Moors." She cursed under her breath. "I've lost two brothers in fights to keep the Africans out of our country, and then what happens? Franco declares our salvation will come from the Army of Africa . . . and not only that, but he shuttles thousands of them to our shores."

She finished the water and handed back the empty bottle and looked at him sharply. "I may not be able to run as I used to, but I have eyes and ears. I can't tell you exactly where the opening to the cave is, but if you can find it in your heart to fill that bottle with wine and bring it back, I'll point you in the right direction."

"Then it's not made up? Franco is really trying to build a tunnel underground to connect Spain with Africa?"

"Made up? I've visited the place myself. My mother used to have a cart and donkey, and we'd take lunch to my brothers who worked on that very tunnel. The donkey's name was Rosita, if you do not believe me."

"Oh, I believe you. It is wine you wish for? Give me three minutes and I'll be back." Walt handed her another coin—a silver one, and probably more than she usually saw in a month. "I think, *señora*, you have found a new best friend."

As promised, three minutes later, Walt offered the woman a bottle of wine in exchange for the information he needed.

"I do not like the tunnel," she told him, accepting the bottle. "There is enough Africa here without such an easy path. It is hard enough for those who have lived here their whole lives to find work; do we need to support the whole world? Besides, the Moors are not nice."

Then, as Walt listened intently, the beggar spoke of the railroad tracks on the outskirts of town. "Beyond the spur line is the road to the tunnel. You can't miss it. It is heavily rutted due to the large trucks that travel down."

"Thank you. That is exactly what I needed to know."

The old woman shrugged. "I am still not sure that information is worth a bottle of wine. There is no way you can get in, even when you find it. The compound is heavily guarded. No one gets in uninvited."

Ritter gazed at the New York skyline. *So different from Spain,* he thought. Then he took a cab to Kern's neighborhood, and walked the last block to the janitor's apartment.

As promised, Kern waited for him in the apartment with the blueprints hidden inside the cane. It was then the hours ticked down.

Instead of returning all the way downtown, Ritter rented a room in a seedy hotel. Locking the door, and pushing a chair against it for good measure, he spread the blueprints on the wobbly table next to the bed. His heart pounded as he copied them, taking time to trace each minute part. Yet, hours later as dawn approached, Ritter was discouraged to see he still had far to go, and he wondered how big the bank account would need to grow in order to make Kern willing to replay the same scheme during his next double shift.

Ritter rolled up the blueprints and slid them back into the cane, considering how easy it would be to simply steal them and be done with it. It would meet his immediate goal, to be sure—but he would be like the man who slaughtered the goose that laid the golden egg. It would jeopardize his contact on the inside and ruin any opportunity for future assignments.

No, it was better to follow this course of action the following day, or maybe two. Not that he would mind staying around longer. Although his interaction with Monica and her family provided little information of use to his Fatherland, it was enjoyable nonetheless. Just as he knew he needed to be patient in stealing the plans, so too he needed to use his time to woo the Americans.

Who knew what benefit they, too, could provide to him in the future?

The dirt road leading to the tunnel compound was dark, and from his place in the bushes Walt watched the Moors travel in small groups of two or three, coming back from their shift underground. After talking to more people from town, passing around a few more coins and a little drink, he discovered that the Moors worked in the mines for only a few weeks at a time. Most had come to Spain, after all, for the wages battle brought them and the booty they received upon capturing a town.

Walt wondered how many more would exit the mines. He then reconsidered his plan, trying to figure out if he could pull off capturing two Moors, when he saw a lone shape approaching in the distance. Quickly he splashed some vodka about his face and staggered onto the roadway. As he'd hoped, the Moor hurried his steps and approached.

"Where are you going there, *señor?*" The Moor spoke in Arabic mixed with Spanish.

"Just trying to find my way back to my automobile. I think I parked it down this way." Walt pointed a shaky hand toward the tunnel.

"I believe not, *señor*. I just came that way, and there isn't an automobile anywhere on this road. Tell me where you are staying, and I'll escort you home."

Walt mumbled something, and he felt the Moor slip the bottle from his hand. "Here, let me help you with that. You do not wish this fine liquor to go to waste."

As Walt continued on, his head lowered, he heard the man taking long drinks from the bottle. Walt's steps straightened as the Moor's became erratic.

The man moaned and placed a hand on his forehead, pausing in the center of the empty road. "I suddenly do not feel so well, *señor.*"

"Here, let me help you. I see a tree over here you can lean upon—"

The words weren't completely out of Walt's mouth before the man staggered and crumpled to the ground. He was amazed that such a large man went down so easy—he'd hardly added a pinch of the sleeping drug to the bottle.

Using all his strength, Walt dragged the man off the road, behind the tree, and to the vehicle he had waiting. Then he drove back to the small room he had rented and managed to half-walk, half-carry the man inside before the Moor fully awoke.

The man's eyes widened as Walt shined a light into his face, and he tugged on his cuffed hands. "What is this? Where am I?"

"You are about to get the opportunity of your life, my friend," Walt said with a smile. He nodded to the handcuffs. "I mean you no harm, really. I just need you to answer a few questions, and you'll be on your way with more loot in your pocket than you could get in five months on the front lines."

The Moor's eyes widened, the whites of his eyes seeming to glow in comparison to his dark face.

"Do you agree?" Walt asked, pulling the key to the handcuffs out of his pocket and dangling it before the man.

He nodded with a jerk of his head.

"Good." Walt circled around to the back of the man and released his wrists. Then he handed him another bottle. "Go ahead; it's good wine. And not drugged."

The man took a long drink.

Walt settled down in a seat across from him. "I need to know about the tunnel—everything you know."

The man shrugged. "That is no problem, but it isn't much. I have only been here four days."

Walt stood and lit a cigarette. "You may know more than you think. . . . Tell me how you get in."

Chapter Thirty-Two

José had lost track of how many days they had traveled through the mountains—two, maybe three? All he knew was that each day he could see his father's strength diminishing. They had to find a place to stay for more than a few days. And soon.

He glanced back to see Petra, walking and leading his father's horse. She told José that she enjoyed stretching her legs, but he believed she liked his father and wanted to be close to the old man.

They were chatting about wildflowers when suddenly Petra's cry pierced the air. "José, come quick!"

Somehow she had managed to jump into the saddle behind his father and was holding him erect. "He just slumped in his seat. I don't know what's wrong."

Pepito dismounted and joined José as they hurried back and pulled the old man from the saddle. Petra jumped down, dropping to the ground and cupping Juan's head in her lap.

Pepito reached for the water skin and mumbled under his breath. "His water doesn't have a drop gone. What a fool. He is tired of stopping to relieve himself, so what does he do? He doesn't drink . . . despite the hot sun."

"Will he be all right?" Petra's eyes were wide with worry.

José took the water bottle from Pepito and lifted it to his father's lips, not knowing what else to do. "*Sí*, he will be all right. It's just sunstroke, but we will need to rest for a while."

Juan reflexively swallowed the water poured over his lips, and began to stir. José reached up and felt his father's face. Indeed it was hot, his cheeks flushed.

"Look, we can rest over here in the shade." Petra took the reins of the horses and led them to the shade. Then she pulled her own blanket from her saddle pack and laid it out on the ground, smoothing it.

José and Pepito took Juan by the arms and carefully dragged him to the blanket.

"What happened? Where am I?" Juan's eyes fluttered open.

Petra leaned over him, offering another drink from the water skin. She laughed, and José could tell it was a laugh of relief.

"Don't worry. Your body decided to take a siesta, and the sun offered to help you sleep better." She took his wrinkled hand in her small one and lifted it to her lips. "But do not worry. Your son will care for you, and I will help."

She smiled again and cocked her head, turning to José and meeting his gaze. Her eyes were large and brown . . . and he forced himself to look away.

José saw a love there that overwhelmed him. And he'd seen it more than once as they rode side by side. She trusted him. She believed in him. And, he feared, she loved him.

José twisted the wedding band on his finger. He wished it were Ramona by his side . . . Ramona looking at him with such adoration in her gaze.

Ritter smiled as he eyed the last of the tracings. In two days he would depart for home on the same ocean liner that carried him here. But not only was he taking home plans that would enormously assist the Luftwaffe's work, he had also stolen the keys to a woman's heart.

Monica had a hard time hiding her sad eyes as she stood at

the docks, bidding Ritter farewell. "Must you leave already? I'm sure if you stayed a few days my father could dig up a few more tidbits of information on the American Army Air Corps that could be of use to you."

"*Ja*, I'm sure he could, but I have work waiting for me. I enjoyed my duties for the Fatherland, but a man who sleeps during harvest has no fuel for the winter."

"Who needs fuel when I could keep you warm?" Monica placed a soft kiss on Ritter's lips, and his mind flashed again to Isanna. He had catered to Monica, but he refused to offer her a piece of his heart.

She patted his hand on the top of his cane and tilted her head to the side. "Of course, if you insist on leaving, I just might have to book my own trip to Germany. Unless you'll be away on business?"

Ritter's mind darted to Spain, and he wondered how the other pilots fared. Though he enjoyed the new work his country called him to, he missed soaring above the clouds. A part of him wished he could return to Spain, while the other part feared the very thing.

"Actually, that may be the case. I might travel to Spain in the near future."

"Spain? Aren't they in the midst of war?" Monica brushed aside the blonde locks that the gentle ocean breeze blew in her face. "Why in the world would you want to travel there?" She could not hide the hint of interest in her eyes.

"Because during war people get desperate, and in times of desperation, a wise businessman can give people what they desire most, lining his pockets in the meantime."

Monica laughed. "I like the way you think, and I'm sure my father would like it, too. Who knows, maybe we both will visit you, showing up when you least expect it."

Walt studied himself in the mirror one more time, checking to see if the dark makeup covered every part of him that showed. It was risky to say the least, but if what the Moor said was true about the night shift, he should have no trouble getting into the tunnel. Like the Moor's, his eyes now seemed to shine from his face. Walt pulled a cap down over his hair, tucking it all inside and hoping security didn't look closely at his features, which looked nothing like those of his African friend. The Moor said that even if the moon was high in the sky, the road was dim, the entrance was dim, and even the tunnel was dim. He believed in the low light that Walt could pull off the deception. It was amazing how cooperative the man had been, when promised such a fine reward for his help.

Walt joined a group of other tunnel workers leaving the town, and followed a few steps behind them. His heart pounded as they approached the guarded gates, and his trembling fingers slipped the identity card out of his baggy trousers. Watching the others before him, Walt followed suit. As soon as one of the Moors approached the worker at the gate, he handed the card to the official. The official studied it, then called the name to his assistant. Without looking up, the assistant found the name and called out his confirmation.

Walt did the same, and the man read the name without even glancing at Walt's face. He let out a low breath as the card was returned to him. He then shuffled through the gates and joined the other men, who, he'd been assured, were all strangers and would pay no attention to Walt.

He was assigned to a small work party with six others and a Spanish foreman. No one talked much, and Walt used the opportunity to scan the tunnel as they walked. Trucks drove back and forth carrying out loads of dirt and entering with all types of construction materials. The walls of the tunnel were still rough, but he was amazed by the enormity of the project and what they had already accomplished, especially under these circumstances. If they kept at it, he had no doubt they would make their way from Spain to Morocco in no time.

As he walked, Walt noted a tunnel that swept to the side. The wall was painted with a warning of explosives. And at the end, no more than a hundred yards down, was a large door big enough for trucks to drive through. A smaller side door also allowed entrance to the area . . . just as Sophie had described. Just as she'd sketched from her memory of the photographs.

Walt worked alongside the other Moors loading rock and debris into buckets, thankful that they spoke little. The tunnel was cold and dimly lit, which helped him greatly. It would be obvious to any of these men, especially in daylight or under a strong lightbulb, that he wasn't one of them.

Their Spanish supervisor moved among them quietly, yet his eyes were on their every move. He wore a pistol at his side, and his hand was on it at all times.

The supervisor watched their progress for a minute, then moved among other small groups of workers farther down the line. Though he supervised a half-dozen groups, Walt was out of his sight for no more than thirty seconds at a time.

Walt's hands steadily moved bucketfuls of debris left over from the explosion of rock, yet his mind raced. His first question was how to get out of the supervisor's view long enough to check out the side tunnel and door.

Before coming into the deep cave, Walt had hoped that he'd only have to get into the tunnels once. Now he doubted that would be the case. Unless . . .

He scanned the few trucks that rumbled past toward the end of the line. Then he glanced to the truck parked nearest to them, where they loaded their buckets of debris. An explosion sounded from down the tunnel. Walt assumed the same trucks were hauling both explosives and debris, which meant there could be a chance that some explosives could be found inside the cab.

As he worked, he moved closer and closer to the truck, expanding the space between himself and the other workers. When the supervisor moved his direction again, he eyed Walt curiously, but said nothing.

The next time the supervisor got out of Walt's view, Walt made a dash for the door. He knew without a doubt the next thirty seconds would make or break his plan, so he didn't even look back to see if his movement caught the attention of the other workers.

With five steps he was at the door of the truck. He swung it open and glanced at the seats, then looked under them. He grinned as he noticed sticks of dynamite stacked underneath. He grabbed a couple, then took a Zippo lighter from his pocket. The voices of the other workers rose around him, but he ignored them and lit the explosive. Then, with a sure hand, he threw it across the tunnel to a wide area where none of the Moors worked.

Before the dynamite hit the ground, Walt grabbed another stick and sprinted toward the side tunnel. He'd taken no more than twenty steps when an explosion sounded behind him. He turned just in time to see part of the rock wall crumble. The cries of surprised and fearful men filled his ears, and soon they ran in every direction. He darted past a few other supervisors who were more concerned about the unexplained commotion than the lone figure running down the tunnel. Within a minute, he was at the side tunnel. Walt turned and started down it, noticing it was less well lit than he'd previously thought.

He pulled the second stick from his pants pocket, highly doubting the side door would be open. He ran to it and checked. Sure enough, it was locked.

Running backward twenty steps, he lit a second fuse and chucked the stick of dynamite toward the door. It hit against the metal, then clunked to the ground. Walt turned and covered his ears, waiting for the explosion, but then the scrape of the door opening caught his attention. He turned just in time to see the door open to reveal Michael standing there, looking down at the stick of dynamite with an expression of wild surprise.

Chapter Thirty-Three

$\mathcal{W}$alt watched in horror as the explosive crushed the side wall and crumpled the small door. He didn't want to think what it had done to the human body caught in the midst of its power.

Cries in Arabic filled his ears as waves of frightened men filled the tunnel behind him, running toward the entrance.

Walt darted to where the door hung on its frame and pushed it open. His gaze met the surprised eyes of Michael, lying on the ground.

"I know you," Michael said, barely above a whisper. "Your disguise doesn't fool me. You were the one working with Sophie . . . . " Michael moaned, and Walt glanced down and saw a chunk of metal the size of a playing card protruding from Michael's left thigh. Other than a layer of dirt covering him, the rest of him appeared untouched. The door must have absorbed the majority of the blow.

Without a response, Walt moved past him toward the two trucks parked within. He hurried to one and lifted the canvas. Stacks of white ammunition boxes filled the back. One crate sat partially open. Lifting the lid the rest of the way, he saw it was indeed filled with gold coins—antique coins—and his heart pounded in his chest.

Suddenly, he heard the sound of a pistol being cocked behind him. Walt turned just in time to spot Sophie. Before he could open his mouth, she pulled the trigger, and the gun fired. The sound of a bullet whizzed by, hitting the bumper of the truck just beyond his leg.

"Sophie, what are you doing?" he shouted. "Give me that gun." He snatched it from her.

"Walt?" She looked at him and took a step closer. "I thought you were a Moor."

"That was the point. How do you think I got in? What are you doing here?"

She crossed her arms over her chest. "It's not that I had a choice. I'm a pawn. But I haven't been a silent one. I told Michael that he was crazy to expect all the gold to be here."

"And were you right?" Walt asked, almost afraid to know the answer.

Sophie nodded. "There were two trucks of stolen gold. Now one whole truck is empty." She pointed to the truck before them. "This is all that's left."

Walt made sure the gold was secured in back and ran to the cab. "Sophie, get in the cab," he called.

Without hesitation she obeyed.

"Take me with you," Michael called. He had taken off his shirt and wrapped it around his leg.

Walt ignored him and swung the truck door open.

"You need me!" Michael yelled. "You'll never get out of here alive without me."

Walt heard the jingle of truck keys, and he turned.

"Sure, you can take the gold, but what about the entrance? Do you think they will let you drive out? Especially with that dark makeup? Do you think you'll fool anyone?"

"And just how can you help?" Walt climbed from the truck and approached him.

"I come and go from this place at will. They won't stop me." Michael pushed against the wall and stood. "You need me," he said again. "If you drive me out of here, I'll help you protect the treasure."

Michael looked to Sophie. "I'm tired of all of this. I'm ready to get out. Please. Take me with you. I can get us all to safety."

Walt glanced back at the door. Any moment, someone might appear. Though he realized he might regret it later, he hurried to Michael and helped him. Sophie ran forward and placed Michael's free arm around her shoulders.

Michael limped to the truck. His face was pale, and his body shuddered with pain.

Walt helped him into the passenger side of the truck; then Michael handed Walt the keys.

Michael turned to Sophie. "Do you see that large lever over there? If you flip it, the door will open."

Sophie did as he asked, and Walt started the truck. Then she jumped into the passenger's seat next to Michael.

"Drive toward the entrance," Michael ordered. "Just before you get there, you'll see another small tunnel to the right. It's a private entrance. It's guarded by only a few soldiers."

Walt drove the truck into the packed tunnel, and then followed the flow of men streaming toward the exit. Panic swept through the crowd. The guards called out to the Moors, warning them to stop and firing into the air.

The Moors parted for the truck, but not as quickly as Walt wished. The truck rumbled along, and a few supervisors glanced toward it, but most paid them no mind.

"Sophie, give me your jacket," Michael ordered. She did, and Michael covered the wound in his leg. "Up ahead, to the right. Do you see the other tunnel?"

Walt turned the steering wheel and followed Michael's directions, hoping he wasn't driving into a trap. The tunnel he drove into was far smaller than the main one, and he expected the rocks to scrape the side of the truck.

After a short distance, the tunnel opened up again, and Walt saw the light of the moon. Two guards waited there. Walt thought about gunning it, trying to outrun them, but he slowed as one of the soldiers stepped in front of the entrance. The soldier raised his hand and motioned for the truck to stop.

"Slow down. Stop for them." Michael must have known Walt's thoughts. "You can't outrun them, I promise you. They'd hunt you down if you tried."

Walt stopped the truck, noticing the look on the guard's face at his dark skin.

"What is this?" one guard asked. Then he spotted Michael.

"There is fire in the tunnels. We need to get this out as fast as possible." Michael's voice was firm.

"Fire? Is that what all the commotion is about?"

"Yes. Get on the line and call for help. In the meantime, we're taking these explosives to safety. I'll be back for more soon."

The soldier nodded and motioned to the other guard to let them pass. Then he turned to the telephone.

Walt drove the truck through the open gate, then turned in the direction of town. When he neared the outskirts, Walt pulled the truck to the side of the road.

"Keep going," Michael urged. "Are you insane?"

"I was just going to run inside for a doctor. . . . I know someone here."

"I know many people, too. Many who may have figured out my involvement. Or will soon. Keep going. I'm fine. The bleeding has nearly stopped." Michael sighed and rested his head against the back of the seat.

"Michael, are you sure?" Sophie lifted her jacket and looked at the wound.

"Yes, keep going." Then Michael looked at Sophie's face. "Besides, *Divina*, you worked in the hospitals, correct?"

"Yes, but I've never dealt with something like this on my own."

"Do not worry. If it gets worse, you can look at it. I trust you. You told me the truth about the gold. You urged me to listen. You were right; why did I think it would all be there?"

"How long will it take to get back to the air base, where the others are?" Sophie asked.

"Who?" Walt glanced over from the road for the briefest moment.

"Cesar is there . . . with Philip." She turned to Michael.

"Philip is there, right? You promised me."

"It'll take an hour. The plane is there, waiting for us." There was a tremor in Michael's voice. "And, yes, Philip is there. Just follow this road. Drive faster."

"Can you make it one hour? Will your leg be okay?" Sophie asked.

"I have no choice, do I?" Michael winced. "And if you want to get this shipment out of Nationalist territory, Walt, I think you had better start praying I make it."

"I'm not a praying man." Walt glanced over, and his eyes met Michael's.

Michael closed his eyes. "Then you depend on me more than you know."

"Don't worry," Sophie butted in. "I'll pray." She reached over and patted both Michael's and Walt's hands. "I'll pray for all of us."

Sophie noticed the light from a lone window in the aircraft hangar welcoming them as they pulled up to the airfield. As expected, a large cargo plane waited for them, prepared to carry Michael and the gold to France. Walt parked the truck in the middle of a half-dozen others, then climbed from the truck. He hurried toward the building, as if looking for a means of escape. Before he reached the door, a dozen armed soldiers were upon him.

"Hands where I can see them!" one man called in Spanish.

"What is he doing?" Sophie murmured. "Is he trying to get himself killed?"

She jumped from the truck and took two slow steps toward the building, wondering what she could possibly say or do to help. She also questioned where they held Philip. She hadn't seen him since he was taken away in the black sedan outside her hotel room window five days ago. Yet Michael had told her Philip would be here. He'd promised Philip's safe return in exchange for everything she knew about Walt.

She turned back to Michael, and he lifted his eyebrow as if waiting for her request.

"Help me. Take me to Philip. And you have to help Walt."

Sophie had no choice but to hope that the caring man she'd fallen in love with was still somewhere inside Michael. She had to trust he would follow through as he'd promised.

She helped him from the truck, and he wrapped his arm around her shoulders.

"What's going to happen now?" she asked as they limped toward the soldiers. When they were within ten feet, Sophie paused. Six men stood with guns pointed at Walt's chest.

Michael squeezed her shoulder. "Don't worry. I won't let any harm come to you."

"I'm not worried about me. What about my friends, Walt and Philip?"

"Is Philip simply a friend, Sophie? I have the feeling it is so much more." He looked away. "Both men have committed crimes against Franco," he continued in Spanish. "I'll have to leave that up to the general to decide."

Hearing those words, one soldier approached, grabbing Walt's upraised arms and yanking them behind his back, then quickly snapping handcuffs onto his wrist.

Sophie gasped and shrugged away from Michael's side. "But you promised we'd be safe . . . if I helped you."

"I told you I would keep the treasure safe. I also told you I'd reunite you with Philip. See . . ." Michael nodded his chin toward the hangar. Inside she could see Philip tied to a chair. Cesar waited by his side.

Sophie pulled back from Michael's touch. "What are you going to do to him?"

"That's not for me to decide."

"Can I go to him?"

"Depends." Michael took a step back, favoring his injured leg. "On whether you want to travel with me to France or offer yourself to the mercy of Franco's courts."

Michael motioned to the soldiers. All of them except the one who held Walt at gunpoint moved to the truck with the gold.

With two men to a box, they transferred the boxes to the aircraft. When the last box of gold was loaded, they shut the cargo door.

Sophie sucked in a breath. "But I showed you the truth of what happened to it. Half of it is already gone, sold by Franco."

"I know, and that is a shame. But I promise you the rest will go to a more deserving buyer. The gold will be protected. I give you my word."

She crossed her arms over her chest, staring at him through the dimness of the night. "Just as you promised you'd take care of Philip? As you promised you wouldn't hurt Walt?"

"I did take care of them. I dare you to find a scratch on either man." Michael jutted out his chin. "You choose, Sophie. Do you want to go with me to France, or stay? It's up to you."

She turned to gaze at Walt. "The gold . . . it's going to be lost now. I'm so sorry."

"It's out of your hands now, Sophie. Don't trust this man. . . ."

"Silence!" Michael shouted, hobbling over to Walt. Then he turned to Sophie, softening his voice. "Don't listen to him." He spoke just above a whisper. "It is all I ever wanted, *Divina*. To take care of you. To make sure you are safe. We have a house in France I purchased for us, remember? Finally you can be safe there."

"Walt's right. . . . I can't trust you. The gold is yours now, and nothing I can say or do will change that . . . or make you use it for a better cause. I'm staying."

She took a step closer to Walt, then turned to look in the window of the hangar. Philip's eyes were blindfolded, and she wished she could run to him, apologize for getting him mixed up in this mess, explain that what he had seen at the train station was simply an act. Instead she stood in silence at Walt's side, watching the men transfer the remainder of the gold to the aircraft.

When they finished loading, the small group of soldiers approached.

"You two"—Michael pointed to two soldiers—"relieve Cesar and tell him we are leaving. The rest of you, take care of our prisoners. Tie them up. In just a few hours someone from the police station will arrive to pick them up. I made the arrangements last night before we left for the tunnel. Of course," he added,

"Walt—or whatever his real name is—is a bonus. I told them to expect only two."

"So you planned to turn in Philip and me from the beginning?"

Michael shrugged. "I hoped you'd get some sense. But I'm not surprised. You have always chosen poorly . . . choosing to stand for what you believe is just without understanding the whole picture."

Sophie could see heartache in his gaze. He truly believed in Franco's cause.

With one slow step Michael approached her, placing a firm kiss on her lips. Sophie jerked her head away.

"Good-bye, *Divina*," he whispered.

Sophie refused to respond as she watched Cesar help Michael to the cargo plane. Tears came, but they were not for Michael. What had her actions brought on Walt and Philip?

In silence they watched as the aircraft prepared for takeoff, then disappeared into the night sky.

Sophie's knees trembled as she wondered what would happen next. It was easy to talk brave—harder to accept where those words led.

Without a word, the soldiers led Sophie and Walt inside the building. One soldier, who appeared to be in charge, approached the men guarding Philip. "Untie him. And hurry."

"What's going on? Don't hurt him," she called out.

"Sophie?" Philip's head lifted and he turned his face to her voice.

A soldier removed the blindfold from his eyes.

Philip blinked a few times, then focused on her face. "What's happening? Where are we?" Then his blue eyes widened. "Who was that man you were with? Was it Michael? Is your fiancé alive?"

Even though they were held at gunpoint by soldiers, Sophie realized this was the question that burned in Philip's mind.

"It *was* my fiancé. And, yes, he lives. He staged his death, along with other lies. He's gone now . . . out of my life for good."

Sophie waited for the soldiers to silence them, but instead they continued to untie Philip. When he was free, the soldier in charge motioned for Philip to stand.

She took a step toward him. "Are you all right?"

He shrugged. "If you call being held by enemy soldiers for a week, continually reliving that moment I saw you with . . . with *him* in my mind 'all right,' then I guess I'm dandy." He glanced at the others, as if waiting for what would happen next.

Even Walt stood silent, waiting.

"Michael lied to me," she explained. "He said if I helped him you'd go free."

"And you believed him?" Philip shook his head. "And you managed to get mixed up in the middle of this?"

Sophie nodded. "Yes, I did—to both questions." She could read more in his gaze, and knew what he really wanted to ask.

Instead Philip turned to Walt. "And the gold . . . did you find it?"

"How did you know about the gold?"

"I overheard the men talking."

"We found some, but not all of it," Sophie answered for him.

"They sold it . . . to fund Franco's work?"

"Yes. Most likely they sold it for weapons at a fraction of its value. But there are a few things that are more important right now. Like our lives . . ." She looked at the soldier in charge.

Walt cleared his throat. "Can you hurry this up? I'm waiting for you to kiss and make up." With a wave of his hand he motioned to the soldiers. Without a word, they left the room.

Sophie turned to him and opened her mouth to speak, but no words came out.

Walt shrugged. "I knew the shipment was set to leave Spain. And there was only one airport planning to transport *heavy* cargo to France. Once I found the right tunnel, with your help, I knew this had to be the right place. Then it was just a matter of calling my contacts to make sure the soldiers would work to my best interest . . . without Michael finding out, of course."

"Those thugs work for you?" Philip rubbed the red marks on his arms left by the ropes.

"Yes, though we don't have much time to chat." He shrugged. "I didn't know about the police. They aren't on my payroll. We need to go immediately." Walt turned to leave.

"But the gold." Sophie grasped Walt's arm. "You let him fly away with it. After all that?"

Walt readjusted his fedora. "Now, does that sound like something I'd do?" He motioned to the door. "Follow me."

Philip took Sophie's hand, rubbing his fingers over the back of it as they hurried to the trucks parked outside. Walt moved to the third one in line and opened the canvas. Sophie gasped as she saw it was filled with white ammunition boxes. Walt lifted the lid on one, and Sophie saw that it was filled with gold.

Philip picked up a handful of gold coins. "I don't understand. How did you do it?"

"I saw them . . . the soldiers." Sophie peered closer in disbelief. "I watched them load the boxes into the plane."

"Yes, they loaded boxes. But not these." He pointed to a second truck parked right beside the one they drove from the tunnel. Walt patted her shoulder. "You, my dear, made a wonderful distraction. I'm sorry to use you like that, but with his attention on you, Michael didn't even notice they unloaded the wrong truck."

"You counted on that . . . that confrontation?"

"I hoped." Walt smiled. "And you did not disappoint. I wish I could see Michael's face when his gold is unloaded in France. Won't his buyers be surprised, too?"

A shiver ran down Sophie's spine. "How come I have a feeling that isn't the last we'll see of Michael?" She clung tighter to Philip's hand and took a step toward him, pressing her cheek against his jacket.

Walt motioned to the cab of the truck. "I have no doubt that we will. But for now, he isn't our greatest concern."

Sophie hurried to the cab and climbed in. Philip slid in beside her.

Walt started the truck, then turned to her. "Any ideas for getting out of Nationalist territory with three Republican sympathizers and a truckload of priceless gold? If so, I'd love to hear them." Then he drove the truck toward the gates. Two soldiers motioned him through with a wave. Walt turned to the right onto a main road.

"Are you serious?" Philip's eyes widened. "You don't have a plan?"

"What about your contacts?" Sophie asked. "You have a hand in everything when it comes to Spain."

Philip blew out another breath as he looked out the window. Sophie followed his gaze and noticed in the distance the smallest line of pink sunlight brightening the horizon. "And just think. I came to Spain to help a friend run a race. . . ."

"That's it." Walt snapped his fingers in the air. Then he glanced to Philip. "I might just have an idea."

"Why am I not surprised?" Sophie commented. She turned to Philip. "I'm sorry to get you into the middle of all this."

Philip shook his head. "I don't know . . . it's as if you planned it." He took her hand again. "For some reason we've all been called to Spain to help in ways we've never expected. Called by Someone with a greater plan than our own."

Epilogue

$\mathcal{W}$eeks after the other exhibits of the World's Fair had opened, Father Manuel heard that the Spanish Pavilion was being unveiled. Even though it wasn't on the map, he had no problem finding it—he'd walked by it on numerous occasions during the previous week, watching its construction. Though it seemed a long shot, he hoped that he'd see someone familiar. It felt strange for him to think only of himself, care for only himself, in such a large city.

He sucked in a breath as he noticed the Nazi Germany Pavilion standing erect next to the Spanish one. Numerous flags waved in the breeze, and the image of the black swastika caused anger to boil inside his chest. He balled his fists, remembering those very symbols on the wings of the bombers as they had swept down over his town. Never had such intense hatred filled his soul, and Father Manuel didn't know how to face it. God asked that he forgive, but how could he? How could anyone after such atrocities?

The Nazi Germany Pavilion rose like a tall tower into the air. A large eagle rested on the top. Its magnificent presence seemed to dare anyone who attempted to bring down its glory. Crowds milled around the entrance, and Father Manuel thought of the idols worshiped by the Israelites numerous times during their history. History repeated itself, he supposed. Idols rising into the sky. Symbols of the evil schemes of men's hearts. A shudder traveled down his spine just thinking about it.

He moved through the crowd to the Spanish Pavilion. The building was small compared to the monumental buildings of the Soviet Union and Germany.

A crowd lingered, appreciating the sculpture next to the entrance, and Father Manuel moved forward to read the plaque. "The Spanish people have a path, it leads to a star," it read.

Near the door a poster was displayed, but the words were in French. Father Manuel turned to a man standing at the entrance. "Excuse me, *señor*, can you read that?"

The man peered up through his glasses and cleared his throat. "More than half a million Spaniards are standing ready with their bayonets in the trenches; they will not be walked over. The words come from President Azana." The man clicked his tongue. "Poor *amigos*," the man commented. "I left Spain as a young boy, but my heart is still with her. I've been waiting for weeks to see Picasso's work *Guernica*."

"Excuse me," Father Manuel asked. "What did you say?"

"*Guernica*. That is the title of his painting, named after the atrocious bombing. Picasso himself has painted her destruction. It is the main attraction."

Father Manuel pushed ahead without commenting. Entering, he noted people walking around a small fountain. They moved toward a huge canvas that filled the back wall. With eager steps he neared as close as the crowd allowed.

Tears filled his eyes as he noted the faces of the people, the animals, caught in the horror. The disemboweled screaming horse in the centerpiece. The dead woman fallen beneath it. The anguished hands and faces lifted skyward. There were no planes, but the reality of their presence was clear. Though Picasso had painted them in his familiar abstract, cubist style, the horror of the people could not be denied.

"So I see you've stayed, after all?"

Father Manuel didn't need to turn his head. He recognized the voice of the young man who had first helped him when he'd arrived in France—Berto, the one who'd taken him to Picasso's loft.

"I had no choice."

Berto didn't respond, but simply placed a hand on Father Manuel's shoulder. Despite himself, the priest shivered at the touch. It was one of compassion and authority, a strange combination, if he said so himself.

"Are you ready to return to Spain?"

"Yes, I believe I am. But . . ." Father Manuel finally turned, meeting the young man's gaze. "Do you think they will listen? I mean these people—" He swept his arm around the pavilion. "They view, but do they truly see? Do they know? Or have they only come because the name Picasso causes a stir?"

"That is a good question. One I cannot answer." Berto readjusted the red scarf with the Spanish national flag he had tied around his neck. "We do what we can to show them, to tell them, but in the end each person must make his own decision."

Father Manuel let out a low sigh. It was the same thing he felt God speaking to his soul. He was not responsible for the response of the people, only for his own actions. And the more he thought about it, the more he realized that had always been the case. Even with Christ himself. Christ had offered His body as a sacrifice in obedience to His Father's will, but He didn't force any man to listen, to see, to follow. Each man made his own decision. And if Christ obeyed, knowing this, how could a priest do any less?

"Yes, I will share my story the best I can. When do you need me?"

"Tomorrow is fine. I have some work to complete today. My cousin has just arrived in town. But tomorrow I will meet you. I will tell you about the plan for traveling back. We can meet here around this same time, if that suits you?"

Berto made the sign of this cross, then looked toward the back of the building where someone had obviously caught his attention.

Father Manuel looked and saw two men standing there. He wondered if one of them was Berto's cousin. "Yes, of course. See you then. God be with you."

With quick steps the young man was gone. Yet even though Father Manuel promised to speak, he still could not shake the nagging feeling that more would be asked of him.

He stood there, feet planted, watching those who moved around him. A man with a camera—an eager tourist—stood a few feet away snapping photographs, excited to see Picasso's latest.

As Father Manuel watched, an ache filled his chest. More than anything, he wished he could cry out. To force the people to really see and understand. To make them aware that it was more than art—it was life. And death.

But he was a priest, not a madman. So, not knowing what else to do, Father Manuel turned and left the pavilion. He didn't glance back to see the painting from the distance. The painting, he knew, was already emblazoned on his heart—as were the events, colors, and shapes it represented.

And the images that voiced the people's cries.